THE TRIAL OF INDIE CALOO

THE TRIAL OF
INDIE CALOO

MATTHEW NIES

RESOURCE *Publications* · Eugene, Oregon

THE TRIAL OF INDIE CALOO

Resource Publications
An Imprint of Wipf and Stock Publishers
199 W. 8th Ave., Suite 3
Eugene, OR 97401

www.wipfandstock.com

PAPERBACK ISBN: 979-8-3852-2315-2
HARDCOVER ISBN: 979-8-3852-2316-9
EBOOK ISBN: 979-8-3852-2317-6

07/24/24

For Larry Woiwode.

CONTENTS

PART I
DEATH

CHAPTER 1

THE NOTORIOUS OUTLAW INDIE CALOO was dead. Bullet wounds marked his head and heart. His graying limbs had paused breathless and rigid, and a fist was clenched. Corpse tremors had ended, and he had begun to freeze into a position of decomposition.

All around, the great expanse of southeastern Colorado Territory lived wild and breathed cold autumn morning air. Winter was arriving early. Jubilation tempered, but the fog of war—exuberance and extinction—jostled in the breath of every waking and sleeping beast. It was pure, sanctified, quiet, and holy, a glimpse of the original sixth day of Creation. God was there, one just had to look. No one was looking.

And then he breathed! The body cavity filled. Indie's wounded chest and skull sparkled with warming blood. He moved. He groaned. He was guttural gathering to rise and turn over his battered body, covered in undergarments, onto his side. He shivered.

Why is it so cold?

Indie moaned through motions and sitting up. He eyed unrealized dreams of cowards who have forgotten how big the world is, how fantastic and huge and overwhelming, and he shook his clenched fist at the clear sky and rising sun.

There are desperate cries that punctuate pain and loss too clearly for presentation. They are cries of hopeless self-pity, of vulnerable humiliation, and embarrassed debasement. Yet these wails cast necessary sanity like a net against consuming wrath and darkness. There are many who are not brave enough to utter such shouts. But Indie cried out. And his voice died as it left him.

Walls of rock cut by earth, air, and fire surrounded him. Dry dirt and sand sat cold beneath. He was small compared to it all. This land was a bridge between great mountains to the west and great plains to the east. He cursed at the magnificence. He rose, spit, and stumbled through forgotten hours.

Duncan hid a fur. I saw him hide it. There was something in it, too. Boots? Indie shook and rubbed his head. *Why he did—but I'm glad he did. Maybe he knew they'd only allow me one more day to show them where the gold's hidden.* He smiled. *At least I denied them that. But I've got to get back to the camp if I'm to have any hope. I won't last long out here this time of year in these few clothes. It's so cold.*

He worked slow and double-backed more than once, but by afternoon, he rediscovered his deserted party's camp from the previous night. He searched behind rocks. And he did find a fur. He unrolled it to boots inside.

"Thank you," Indie said in a breath.

He covered himself and turned to the ashes of a fire that had kept him and his companions warm. He relit it, and then he lay down on his back near the dancing flames and in the sun's full shine. It was late afternoon. He unclenched his fist which revealed a gold pocket watch. He rubbed it with his fingers.

"Why they didn't take this . . ." he sighed. "Yet, I'm glad they didn't." He enveloped the watch again in his fist and then turned on his side. He rubbed his head and chest, wincing each time, and looked at the blood his hands brought back. He shook his head and looked around. He ripped strips from his undergarments and grabbed sprigs of yarrow plants.

Indie sat down by the fire and stared at it for a long time. He built his breath. Then he grabbed a stick and bit it. He pressed his fingers into his wounds, first his chest and then his belly, face turning red and pain erupting from his clenched jaws. He found lead in each, and threw the lead to the ground shaking and sweating.

When his breath slowed, Indie cauterized himself with coals which renewed his mania, though the burning was quicker than the retrieving, which reflected in his recovery. He chewed the herbs he had gathered, wincing, then applied the paste to his wounds, wincing again. He secured it with his bandages. He sighed and fell asleep curled up in his fur.

He woke up the next morning and was walking. His head and chest had healed considerably. He followed his eyes and the ground through twists and ruts of jutting rocks and back to his death spot.

"Give me strength," he said, looking into the sky, "just enough to kill each of them."

He mumbled and stumbled out of the rocks and onto a slow hill that terminated into a small river. He maintained a bead on a meandering path through the midst of falling dirt and summer-long tough grass, tall with its glory, though hollow and holding against dust—dying green strokes to a brown canvas dotted with sagebrush and rising and falling indecision. He brushed past cattails and forded the stream, holding his hide above the shallow water. He re-warmed himself on the other side, and stopped long enough to take a drink and regain his trail. It was not difficult to find.

Those devils think they've killed me. Look how careless they lead the horses. And here, now they've mounted and ridden away. Lord, have mercy on their souls. I'm bringing them to you.

No doubt Duncan's being pulled against his will. Surely, he must've reserved some faith; the fur and boots are proof. He believed. What good it is believing in a dead man! I'll save him if I can. It's the other four—Fanny, Chaps, Slim, and especially Roberts—they've got to die. Didn't they have their chance to kill me? Yet here I am. I don't understand it; certainly, they know how to kill a man, especially Roberts, and when a man's dead. And it was Roberts who pulled the trigger! All else besides, an eye for an eye. They had their chance to kill me. I won't squander mine.

I see Roberts behind it all. He's been bit chomping since I put a hold on activity four months ago. They all have, except maybe Duncan; though he was squirrely, too. They couldn't stand inactivity. It's hard to live civil when you've lived wild. This whole plot has Roberts' evil in it. He's given the boys impetus for mutiny. He must've followed me or seen the map I put together.

But if he'd done either, would he have needed me to show him where the gold was? It's like him to scent and send others to flush a matter out. He's lazy. Thank goodness, he's lazy. If I could only kill one, it'd be Roberts.

Indie touched his shoulder and head again and winced. He struck out of the hidden hills and onto a little path.

It'll be no small feat catching them, unless I can find a horse to ride, too. But where I'll find a horse in these parts, it'd be as manna from heaven.

Indie turned as a wagon rode up on him. Its leading mule snorted; the driver called. He surveyed the buckboard wagon, mule and driver and a tethered Morgan horse behind, bay and tall. Boxes and blankets and burlap sacks filled the small bed of the back of the wagon.

"What's your business out here on foot?" the driver said. "I'll just say it; it strikes me odd to see you out here footing it, especially with naught but fur and boots. You look like you've been shot or gashed or poked or—I'll just say it—you look like hell.

"I'm a Star Route messenger," he continued. "I carry messages and the mail with 'celerity, certainty, and security.'" The messenger rose and held himself before spitting an exhale. "You look more dead than alive. Can I help you? But as I'm looking at you—I'll just say it—you look familiar. Have we met?"

The messenger mused and grabbed a canteen to take a draft after his line of rambling. Then he squeaked and put the liquid aside to grab a folded paper from his pocket.

"This is a bill, a notice. I remembered it just now drinking and looking at you. I thought, 'no,' but why not check?" And the messenger checked. Then he blanched. His lips trembled. He shook his head. "Him?"

The messenger showed the bulletin. The fresh weathered paper read "REWARD" across its top. Smaller type detailed a reward of $5,000 for the apprehension of "the notorious outlaw INDIE CALOO and his CALOO GANG." A crude sketch accompanied, and it was an image of the resurrected man: broad-shouldered with a muscular and bony face, slight eyes squinting.

"That's me. I'm Indie Caloo. I haven't seen $5,000 before. Must be a new offering?"

The messenger nodded. "It's a new bulletin. Please, don't kill me."

"Breaking firearms laws, stealing horses, robbing banks, murdering— same old grievances. And it's true." Indie waived his arm. "I'm done with that. I've four men to put six feet under, and I'm done with it all. I'm not going to kill you."

Indie looked at the Morgan tied to the back of the wagon. He spoke low. "No, I've no quarrel with you. Yet I can't catch my quarry on foot. And that's a fine Morgan you've got there. I've seen it before. Where'd you get it?"

"I bought it off a man yesterday. He was leading a group and said they didn't need the horse no more. He offered it to me for $10. It seems a fine horse for $10."

"My Strawberry Roan's finer. You know I'm Indie Caloo. And I'll bet you ascertain looking at me that those might have been my men who sold you the horse. They were. The man who sold it to you had a cherry eye and a twisted mouth?"

The messenger flinched and reached for a shotgun beneath his seat. Indie caught his quickness and pulled him by his leg, screaming from the bench. The messenger banged his head on the toe board. Indie grabbed his shirt and tossed him by it and his breeches away from the wagon. Then Indie grabbed the shotgun, checked it, and shook his head. He replaced it back underneath the wagon bench.

"I'm taking the horse," Indie said. He drank from a canteen behind the messenger's seat. He ate flour and old cakes. "I'm taking clothes, too." He found what he needed—pants, shirt, and a coat—as the reclining messenger looked on.

"I'll just say it, your head and chest look bad."

Indie winced as he slipped on a shirt. "Hurts worse."

After dressing, Indie searched the wagon further. He gave the messenger a long look when he found a strong box. He clicked his tongue and let it be. He un-roped the Morgan. "I'll leave $10 cash or more likely this animal at the stables in Stanchion or Racida or Cannonball Springs for you."

"I'm supposed to take your word for it? I'll just say it, I don't trust you. You're an outlaw."

"I'm an honest thief." Indie smiled. "I only keep guns I intend to use."

The messenger blanched. "A guy can't expect to cross paths with killers."

"Killers surround us. You've met five, now six, in two days. Ah, but the beauty of this land is its balance of life and death, cradle and coffin. The chains of humanity, our societal salves, carry little weight here. They cannot save us. Living's our business."

"You look like you're about dead."

Indie nodded. "I think I was." He mounted the Morgan. It was saddleless, but Indie had found reins which he used to control the animal. "Were you thinking you'd bring me in under a threat of violence with your shotgun? Clearly, I'd already tasted some. Maybe you thought I could hardly resist a fresh effort." He twisted his jaw.

"My mother gave me the gun," the messenger said. "It belonged to my grandfather. It's old. I don't have need of it, but I can't part with it. And it still has its uses from time to time."

"To each their own. I've found shotguns to be poor traveling companions without ammunition. Remembering *that* is how I've kept ahead of the law."

"That's coming to an end," the messenger said.

Indie dropped his smile. "Yes, and I said so. I told you that I'm almost done; just four of those five men you saw, dead, and I'll be done." He thanked the messenger, then clicked and rode away as the afternoon light began to fade into evening.

The air was cooling fast. A roadrunner ran out of cover and seemed to scare itself in seeing wagon, mule, and man. The messenger cursed at it and shivered. He surveyed the pillage of his load.

"I'll just say it," the messenger said to his mule, after starting the wagon again, "I've never been so close to realizing $5,000. I couldn't have gotten his gang, but I could've gotten him, if I'd kept the shotgun loaded. But he *was* on me faster than I could grab it to bear any way. He's a dangerous man, alright. I'm glad he's heading in a different direction than our road. Where is he heading?" The messenger cursed again and looked around. "I'll be, he's disappeared.

He clicked and the mule sped its walk.

"This is big news. The Caloo Gang hasn't been seen or heard of for three, four months. And now I run into them and then their leader, Indie Caloo himself, who's out walking on the steppe in nothing but a hide and boots. What a story!"

Chapter 2

Bang!

Lead capped an explosive end to a hurried getaway. It was magnificent. It was the sound of a soul untethering from its earthly dominion. It was flash and fury, and a young man awkwardly slumping off his saddle onto and over a cliff of red and reddening dirt, and then sliding down and to near the bottom.

Canyon walls echoed the terrible report, bouncing it off fractured stone and clay. The gully was called "Dead Man's Run" from a story Arapaho told of a warrior who fell off the nearly vertical cliff-side. Narrow, snaking paths cut down the cliff's face. The other side had a much shallower climb and was not as high. A fast brook cut at the canyon's roots. The water's drought-starved gurgle disappeared under the gunpowder crash. The canyon channeled sound well. It roared with the doom warning, sounding peace undone.

Coyotes listened—a gunshot can be a dinner bell—and turned in its direction. Birds stirred and re-alighted to their goodnight perches. A bear grunted at the news of close men.

The echoes faded. A light breeze whistled as it wound around the twisting walls and then died as an exhale into the expanse. The air at the bottom of the canyon again purled with the rhythm of the rill. Soundless as the climb, clear night descended on the gulch and empty lands around, in stark contrast to the brilliant stars and full moon revealing in the sky.

Two well-accustomed Sorrels, a Palomino, and an Appaloosa had bridled at the shocking shot but had kept their places near the stream bank. A fifth horse, a Strawberry Roan, ran back up the path it had descended not long before. It would have been hard riding to catch it, especially in the dark, especially as it was running terrified.

Bang!

A rifle shot tore through the air and missed the roan.

Bang! Bang!

Two more shots exploded near the animal's hooves and head. The twilight, distance, and speed would have been a challenge for any marksman. The shooter lowered his rifle. He stood with three other men on the other side of the quick stream, eyes widening. In lieu of discussion, one of them swore. Another affirmed with an oath.

The two complementary speakers were brothers and went by "Fanny" and "Chaps." Fanny was older but most would say Chaps was more mature. Fanny bore a scratch on his left brow that he said he got in a bar fight; Chaps said a horse kicked him. Chaps bore a raised-skin scar on the back of his right hand that he said he got from spilling hot bacon grease on himself; Fanny said he had poured the grease on a sleeping Chaps just to hear him howl. They were the wide-shouldered sons of German immigrants. They provided muscle for jobs, which Fanny especially enjoyed, and were loyal under a gun barrel. Fanny's green eyes gleamed at violence and mischief. Some said he was a sadist; he smiled at that. Chaps's gray eyes looked past you. Some said the only person he cared about in the whole world was his brother; he smiled at that. There are good men; there are bad men; and there are men who act on their behalf.

The third of the four murderers was called "Slim." He looked taller than he was. His bug-eyed demeanor gave an impression of perpetual surprise, a supposition he did not alleviate with his nervous way of talking and erratic fidgeting. He was very superstitious, which he was both proud and ashamed of. His voice had a bass quality that came and went, and when it went, it was shrill. Some said Slim's voice shrilled when he was scared. He had been educated somewhere. Depending on his sobriety—he was at his most convivial when inebriated and his most despondent when dried out— he would say he graduated from Princeton, Harvard, or Yale, or that he did not give a damn about education altogether. There are good men; there are bad men; and there are men who seek and follow direction.

Roberts, the shooter and last of the group, was a bad man. To those who did not know him, he was quiet and ingratiating; but to those that did know him or crossed him, Roberts was knotted rage, which he heaped on victims—person, animal, or object—with an explosive stage voice. Some said *it* was bigger than he was, as he was short and otherwise unremarkable. The most unremarkable often accomplish the most remarkable, and Roberts' determination captivated. Fanny, Chaps, and Slim watched their words around him, though Slim could forget propriety for worry. A few of Roberts' words still carried a Southern pitch, and a few of his stories, told dead sober, highlighted his and his homeland's lost cause in the war between the states.

His strong gut belied strong appetites. Sharp smile and eyes, he was beautiful like a loaded gun.

Chaps re-crossed to verify that the young man, Duncan, was dead. He was. His body was heaped as it had fallen. His mangled head still sported one of its two pale blue eyes.

We each possess what is unique and only manifest that which we choose, except through our eyes, glowing embers not entirely our own. Some say they are gateways to our souls, an indication of burning fire and our only physical feature unrestricted by willful domination. Duncan's eyes had once brightened with dreaming. Now, one was blown out and the other was flecked with dirt and glossed as if it were iced shut. His body lay to be scavenged, probably by coyotes. Rarely is anything like a dead body found undisturbed in the wild even shortly after its disposition. Seldom is anything wasted.

Chaps rejoined the other outlaws. They mounted their horses, which moaned less than their cold leather saddles. The riders clicked but did not need to spur the Sorrels, Appaloosa, or Palomino to move; the climb ahead was easy and the canyon was cold. The *clip-clop* of the horses' hooves faded quickly as they walked.

Up the opposite, steep side of the canyon, the roan had finished its rush on the narrow path; it sped over the open ground. The horse's saddle, old and polished, flexed on its bearer's hips. On one side, a Spencer repeating rifle shivered in a holder. A Greek key pattern decorated the cantle. The roan's muscular flanks wrapped around thick bones like railroad ties that narrowed to sharp, ironed hooves. Thickening and well-groomed gray and copper-spotted hair terminated nearly white on the rump and darkened into amber down the legs. Its muscles shook at each shocking hoof strike. Its mane was shorn short. It primed its ears forward. Its mouth foamed from the pace. Men and beasts unnerve at death. To survive is instinct. It knew purpose beyond reason for its dead run: seconds, minutes, hours.

The horse, synonymous with the west, is a relative newcomer. Spanish soldier explorers first brought the animals from Europe. How many escaped into the wild is not known, but they quickly multiplied and spawned a new era for the New World.

Man has always searched for increased ability to travel swiftly. Productivity has no greater ally than rapid transportation, a key also unlocking improved economy, personal well-being, and military and political advantage. There is no substitute for covering vast distances and covering them with speed. Imagine the Indian first discovering equine strength. The quick adoption and re-domestication of this animal hitherto unknown in the Americas speaks to its transformative superiority to walking. Native

Americans ascended to perhaps unrivaled horsemanship and cultivated new breeds. Their hunts and warfare were never the same.

Man and beast in ordered transport juxtapose to the chaos of the untamed. There is no more familiar western scene, which might have never been, than a dependent husbandry dyad riding across vast lands. They are both in need of each other—the rider depending on his horse for swift conduct through vast expanses, the broken horse trained to rely on its rider for food and direction. Separate them and each is less likely to survive.

While the roan ran one way, the Sorrels, Appaloosa, and Palomino carried their murderous riders the opposite. They struck sharp against the bright night sky and dull against the dark canyon as they ascended the last stones and climb of its shallower side. The men's hats concealed their heads from the bright moon by casting a shadow. They wore thick ponchos. Snow cracked under the horses' hooves striking the hard ground. The riders talked low.

"I wish it could've been quiet," Slim said. His voice sounded shrill.

"What could've we done different, you suppose?" Chaps said. "Got nothing quieter."

"Sure as hell do," Fanny said. "We should've just bashed his brains in—should've just smashed his face. We'd the horses—just trample him." He swore and looked at Roberts. With no reply, Fanny continued. "We could've cut his throat." He swore again. "Lots of ways to kill a man, especially on a cold night like this when a body would freeze."

"What's it matter, Slim?" Roberts said. "No one can hear our shot out here. And if they could, they wouldn't think it anything other than an attempt to scare off or kill a wild animal."

Slim shuddered. "I don't want to wake up the place! Don't wake—we don't want to stir up—"

"If you talk about spirits again—if you talk about Indian ghosts—I'll gut you. I'll *gut* you, like we should've gutted the kid. We should've gutted the kid. I've got knives." Fanny swore.

"Don't swear so much, no need." Chaps said.

Fanny eyed his brother. He eyed Slim and smiled. "Gutting would've been quiet."

There was a pause as the horses' hooves rasped the snow. Roberts ground his teeth and Fanny smiled.

"Slim's just tight," Chaps said. "You're too tight, Slim."

"I wish it wouldn't have been so loud. It was too loud."

Roberts gasped and surged his Palomino forward to cut Slim off. And as he stopped the Appaloosa, Roberts slapped Slim. The loud report of flesh on flesh popped off the vestiges of the canyon, catching itself before disappearing under the roar of Roberts' voice.

"Is that quiet enough for you?" Roberts swore. He laughed and swore with a yell that cut through the night. He turned his horse and jumped it forward before swirling to Fanny, Chaps, and Slim. "You've hardly got backbones. Why should we care about our actions being known if they can't be stopped or requited?

"I wouldn't have stopped any of you from riding after Duncan to slit his throat, bash his head in, whatever you would've fancied. You could've burned him alive or stuck him through with a stick. I'm not opposed to industry. I am against stupidity and inaction. While you guffawed, that roan was carrying Duncan beyond our reach. I shot him because it killed him. I shot him because it saved me from wading back through the water. And I shot him to avoid a wild chase. I don't take the joy in it like you do, Fanny; I welcome death, not its visitation. Let's be done with it. Shooting Duncan was quick, and it was a mercy to him, as much as death can be a mercy.

"And Slim, you can be a real pain. What could we wake up out here? There's nothing. The Indians are spooks. They terrify themselves with stories of spirits and look under any stone for a vision. You can't see the future when you're looking anywhere but the horizon. Wake up? There is—"

Roberts gathered himself. He spit, shook his head and turned his horse to gallop away. Then he turned back to Slim. "Duncan didn't have to run. I gave him a fair shake opportunity same as the rest of you. He chose himself over the gang, and at risk to the gang. I won't be prevented from looking out for us and doing what needs doing."

Roberts turned his Palomino again and struck it hard. It dug at the cold dirt, kicking a clump skyward. The horse ran away and disappeared with Roberts.

"Stuck through with a stick?" Fanny grinned and spit chewing tobacco when the party of three had started again. "That's one way to kill someone I ain't thought of before. Nothing wrong with a knife neither—maybe just use fists and boots. We could've beaten him to death."

"He's not the least bit—it's called 'Dead Man's Run'—and you're not the least bit wary, not the least bit scared, not the least—"

"Bunch of hooey. Those Indians—" Fanny swore. "Give me a handful of them and they'll all be wasted on fire water. They sure as hell didn't spook a man with any sense off a damn canyon wall." He laughed. Fanny laughed at his own jokes; no one else did. It was difficult to tell when he was joking. "There's nothing in them stories just as there's nothing in their brains. They're savages through and through. More likely they'd eat a man . . ." Fanny did not finish his thought. He never explained what he meant about Indians eating men. He used the phrase whenever he said Indians were savages.

"Like Roberts said, ain't likely anyone heard the gunshot," Chaps said. Slim shushed.

"Ain't worth shushing us, Slim. If there's things to wake up out here, they'd be awake." Fanny gave a wild yell. He laughed. "We should've done the exact thing to Indie and Duncan as we did to those savages we ran into a week ago." He licked his lips. "We should've done the exact same thing."

"You're a haunted man," Slim said. "You'll be haunted the more for your unbelief."

"I'll die one way or the other. Savage ghosts don't scare me."

"'The fear of the Lord is the beginning of wisdom.'"

"Lord?" Fanny swore. "Since when did you become a preacher, Slim? And anyway, haunts aren't the Lord Almighty. I'll take my chances with them."

"We should observe the dead. We should respect the departed! You never know what mischief will bring. I wish it wouldn't have been so loud."

CHAPTER 3

TUMBLEWEEDS BLEW DOWN RACIDA'S MAIN street, as they did in late summer and early fall when rain retreated and foliage dried in the wind. Snow dusted buildings were covered in dirt seasonally dried by trampling and kicked up by wind, horses, wagons, and people scurrying. Though winter provided the populace respite from dusty coughs and intermittent cycles of thick mud, it could snow feet, creating its own troubles. It was not yet the winter months, but winter was arriving early.

The street hosted a dozen or so buildings, most of the town being built away from Racida's main, dusty thoroughfare. The jail, well-built and often empty, was adjacent to the saloon, which was poorly built and often full. Folks said Racida well water was bad, more in jest than in earnest, which accounted for the saloon's occupancy. The jail's lack of tenants was unaccounted for, because Racida's citizens did not lack enthusiasm to see it full.

"It's too cold for this time of year," Sheriff Brick said. His real name was Solomon Bragg, and he was a young black man from Mississippi. Townsfolk called him "Brick" because he was built solid. He had been "elected" and named Racida's constable, then named its honorary sheriff due to his impeccable crimefighting and safeguarding.

Before coming west, Sheriff Brick had been a member of the 51st U.S. Colored Infantry Regiment during the war between the states. He told that to nearly everyone he met. Before soldiering, he had been a slave on a small plantation near the Yazoo River north of Vicksburg. He told that to hardly anyone he knew.

Sheriff Brick stood on his solemn weather pronouncement, shivered, and walked to his gun cabinet. He grabbed a Henry Repeating Rifle and returned to his seat by the jail stove. He had developed into an accurate shot with the rifle. He was diligent in maintaining it.

Matilda Schroeder, who was known as Mattie, sat across from Sheriff Brick in the otherwise empty jail. "The town is covered in snow," she said. "It's too early for it to stick for long. Nights are cold enough now but it's too warm in the day for the snow to stick around."

She smiled. "Don't get so out of sorts, Solomon." Mattie preferred to call Sheriff Brick by his real name. "It's just a dusting—quite beautiful in the sun—just a dusting."

"Maybe you forget I'm from Mississippi. We don't have such *beauty.*" He paused on the last word, "beauty," and wriggled his jaw like he was chewing gristle.

"You'll have to get used to the cold and snow."

"I didn't go too far north because I didn't want to have to get used to the cold. I don't think I ever could get accustomed to being cold. I can tolerate a heap, but I don't embrace it. There weren't a lot of things I appreciated about Mississippi; mild winters were one thing. I didn't know it then." He paused and smirked. "Funny how you don't appreciate something right in front of you, not good things you really should appreciate."

"That's true."

Mattie's mouth hovered open. Sheriff Brick looked up from his gun. She blushed and closed her lips. Some folks, and especially bachelors, considered Mattie the most beautiful woman in the world. It was unanimously agreed that she was the prettiest person in Racida, Stanchion, Cannonball Springs, or any place within at least 70 miles of those rural outposts of western civilization. She had dark brown hair that edged in curls and a bright and ready smile. She could use her amber eyes to great effect and had a calming voice. Women said she had the voice of a temptress, some even going so far as to call her "Matt-usa" in reference to the snake-haired Gorgon of Greek mythology whose look turned men to stone.

A congregation's ire can steam from jealousy, and jealousy stirred ire towards Mattie. But she had also cultivated congregational wrath through her rebelliousness, nearly costing her father, widowed Preacher Schroeder, his Lutheran pulpit. A rumor that she had an outlaw lover was the talk of the town. Preacher Schroeder was not one to engage in such talk. Mattie was content with letting "people believe what they'll believe."

Sheriff Brick had put a kettle of water on top of the stove. It started steaming strong and spitting.

"I wasn't expecting—I've got just the one cup and it can get mighty hot," Sheriff Brick said as he attended to the water. "But you're welcome to it. I think a warm drink would feel good on a cold night like this."

Mattie lifted her eyebrow. "What do you have to drink with the water?"

"I've coffee."

"Everyone has coffee."

"I've tea, too."

"Tea?"

Tea was not a common drink in Racida; folks drank coffee, water (despite the wells), and a lot of alcohol. The only Racida resident who drank tea often was Mattie. Any parsonage visitor knew of or soon discovered her tea habit, especially for chamomile tea— "too much," older women congregants would say to Preacher Schroeder. He never passed along such concerns to Mattie, though they found their way around town and to Mattie nonetheless.

"Chamomile."

Mattie whistled and laughed. "You have chamomile tea!"

"Ichabod Irving, the teacher, he gave me some leaves."

Mattie rolled her eyes.

"He said it was disappointing," Sheriff Brick said. "I'm not much of a tea person myself."

"Not the tea, *me*!" Mattie shook her head. "Despite what you may have heard, I *am* a lady. And ladies like tea." She waved her hand and laughed. "Yet no woman would take tea if it meant forfeiting her liberty. Ichabod wasn't disappointed in the tea. I disappointed him in not drinking it with him. He bought tea and asked me to drink it with him and I refused. He claims English ancestry. I don't care enough for the English to care for him."

"Are you insulting the English or Ichabod or his tea?" Sheriff Brick's eyes gleamed.

She laughed again. "Never the tea. It was difficult to refuse him because I like tea very much."

"I didn't know that."

"You're probably lying because everyone knows that. You even have my favorite tea."

"But I didn't know you liked tea. I didn't have to; Ichabod Irving had all the knowing I needed when he furnished me the leaves."

"That's true. Well, I'll take the tea if you're offering it. How's that?"

Sheriff Brick smiled and went to get the tea. "What do you know about the Caloo Gang?" He was looking at a bulletin on the table where he poured water into a mug with tea leaves. He brought the steaming cup to Mattie and held the bulletin in his other hand.

Sheriff Brick studied the weathered paper. It was an older version of the bulletin that the messenger had consulted on meeting its principal subject, Indie Caloo. Sheriff Brick snickered while he read it.

"Four thousand five hundred dollars." He whistled. "I only received $13 a month fighting in the war. Striking, isn't it, how much more profitable catching outlaws can be than fighting for your country?"

Mattie raised her eyebrows and continued cooling her tea. "I thought colored troops were paid $10 a month, $3 deducted for clothing."

"You keep abreast of affairs, even out here. Yes, that's what I heard, too, $10 a month. But I became free and then enlisted after Congress evened pay for all troops."

Mattie nodded. "Why do you ask about the Caloo Gang?"

"This notice predates me here in Racida," Sheriff Brick said. "I haven't received an update. I've asked around; folks say they've disbanded. I hope that's true, or that they're gone at any rate. Folks say the gang terrorized this area."

"They're notorious," Mattie said. "They may have disbanded, though they haven't been caught as far as I know. We would've heard if Indie Caloo and his Caloo Gang had been apprehended."

"I haven't met someone who believes they've been apprehended. But there's been nothing in the way of new criminal activity by the Caloo Gang. It was a quiet summer in these parts. Gangs move in the summer, not? It gets too cold in the winter."

"Yes, colder than tonight." Mattie's eyes lit up. Once, the fire in Mattie's eyes had convinced a young farm boy in her Sunday School to ask Preacher Schroeder for Mattie's hand. Her eyes had driven many a man and boy to mad love.

Sheriff Brick shook his head. "Queer thing a gang, men choosing to live contrary to the law and other men, choosing to live isolated and at war with society. Why would anyone choose that life? There's no ultimate end except destruction. They are selfish pariahs."

"At least an outlaw's an honest man." Mattie was looking up from her teacup. "The outlaw sees the land in all its beauty, that the west is an untamed world, and lives communing with God and his creation. He lives honestly with the land. His spirit is drawn to the harshness of living by strength and wits and luck. Is his life not devoted to tearing away fetters with which we have shackled the earth? The outlaw lives the rocks and timbers, we our false facades."

Mattie's voice had risen during her diatribe. Sheriff Brick listened. When she finished, he rose and returned the bulletin to the table.

He turned to Mattie, eyes red. "'What profit is it to a man if he gains the whole world'—all the rocks and timbers, what profit— 'and is himself destroyed?' Outlaws rage against society for their own gain. They are men at war with the guiding force that makes us men, feasting on the hard work of others like parasites." He spit.

Mattie shuffled in her seat. She gathered her cup and drank the hot liquid. "I must be going." Mattie handed Brick back his cup. "It's best we don't stoke rumors or town ire more than we have."

"A white woman and a black man, I expect it. For what it's worth, Wiley Pecker's the only outspoken dissident I've encountered. His kin fought and died at Bull Run and Antietam for the Confederacy in the war between the states, so I'm not surprised he objects to our nighttime discussions. He was scolding me last week when he slipped on manure in the street. His left foot scooted forward and his right planted so that his legs split apart, and his pants followed. 'Ain't got nothing to be ashamed of,' he said." Sheriff Brick laughed.

Mattie smiled and tried not to smile.

"Constable-ship carries a steady salary, though insufficient. I supplement with taking a fair portion of reasonable taxes, charging modest license fees, and ensuring businesses' doors are locked at night. I need to do a nightly tour. If you must leave for home now, let me escort you."

"And if I say 'no?'" Mattie said as the two left the jail.

"What may I have *heard*?" Sheriff Brick asked as he and Mattie reached the first business. "Before I got you tea, you said 'despite what you may have heard,' that you are a lady. I'd like to know what I might be spiting."

"Clever, and you were a slave?"

Sheriff Brick stiffened. "You could assume that any man with dark skin like mine was. And I was, yes. But slavery of the body isn't slavery of the mind. My mother was a mulatto, educated with a master's children until sold off to pay off a debt. That's how she came to where we grew up. My father was sold before I knew him. She endeavored to teach me and my older sisters as best she could, taught us to read, which was irregular for a slave."

"I didn't intend—she sounds remarkable, your mother."

"She was. And in an unfortunate way, she was beautiful, too."

"How can beauty be unfortunate?"

"I think you're aware that beauty can stir jealousy, and in evil men, lust. But my mother was a lady, despite not being treated so. That's why I determine character by action and intention, in addition to reputation."

Sheriff Brick checked then locked another business' door. He would do the same several more times. "I have heard talk that you worried your father and maybe compromised yourself. Your actions do not support these rumors. I think you are a lady because you act like a lady, though your reputation perplexes me.

"And yet, I think of myself. I am called 'sheriff' due to my reputation for locking up criminals and keeping the town safe. What have I done to earn it? I have locked up three drunks overnight who started fights, and a cattle thief who I then sent to Judge Fickle in Cannonball Springs for trial. I believe big reputations can stem from little actions. No one says you aren't a lady, just that you don't always act like one. If you say the rumors aren't true, I'll believe you."

"Me over the whole town?" Mattie's eyes and smile grew big as if she were about to laugh. "We've known each other for three, four months. You rode in and boarded at widow Bedford's house and she insisted on campaigning to have you fill Racida's vacant constabulary. '"Brick" Bragg for constable'—she even made a sign."

Sheriff Brick turned red. He had said "no" to widow Bedford. She had insisted, and no one had objected even to a black man becoming constable because no one wanted to be constable, even though folks said Racida needed one. The widow insisted on an election but Racida named Brick its constable with a tense gentleman's handshake at the saloon followed with approving shots of "coffin varnish," or whiskey. After Brick broke up a third drunken fight, the town patriarchy held another handshake at the saloon and vowed to call Brick "Sheriff." The title stuck.

"I appreciated your father's eulogy. I'm struck by the weight of her death when I only knew her for a few months."

"She was a friend. How many friends do you have here, Solomon?"

"Racida's a friendly town." Sheriff Brick smiled. "Certainly not Wiley Pecker."

He and Mattie laughed.

"I won't refute what you've heard. I don't think I could. Where would I begin? I'll tell you the truth because you're my friend. People have come west searching for opportunity, freedom, the wild land. And all share the common hope to be reborn, for change and new life. 'Old things have passed away; behold, all things have become new.' It's mostly men who come, men seeking new life and bringing their wives and families.

"Are they looking for support, for the societies they've left behind? How many ranchers and farmers work sunup to sundown in isolation, and do so happily? But all men desire a home to return to, a family to greet them. Racida is a small town, a small effort to re-create the world everyone here knew once and abandoned. We are profiteers of pioneers. We espouse the west and desire rebirth, but we seed again the world we left behind. We are colonizers of the wild, dishonest adventurers domesticating what has drawn us here to explore. Instead of learning from the Indian, we have bullied and removed him because he would not join us in reshaping the land into our image."

"You speak as if all we've brought with us is bad," Sheriff Brick said. "There is life where once only the desert winds blew and wild creatures roamed. If your quarrel is that Americans should foster less ambition, then you argue against our national pursuit to realize opportunity and personal happiness, unencumbered though instructed by previous generations. If your quarrel is that these adventurers should slip into the wild they encounter, then you argue against human need for companionship. The Indian, too, is a plurality."

"I don't contend with national identity or natural desire," Mattie said. "I'm dissatisfied with clinging to unsatisfactory traditions and conditions, circumstances we forsook for this land. Are we afraid of forsaking the nurturing blanket of society because it protects us from the elements? If we have come to live in the west, let us live in the west!

"My rebellion stemmed from such desire, and to explore and embrace the savage tranquility of earth so juxtaposed that it can compel men to their best and worst. I took father's horse to fill in my own maps and discover how the coyote eats in winter, where the pronghorns duel and give birth, the glimmer of a first sunrise above the plain and its setting under distant mountains. I sought the poetry and practicality of our surroundings."

"We still need laws and the marks of civilization that differentiate us from the animals," Sheriff Brick said. "'Righteousness exalteth a nation: but sin is a reproach to any people.' Racida is growing again, bigger than Stanchion and maybe even bigger than Cannonball Springs. It's because we have recognized law and order."

"Can you explain why Stanchion hasn't grown even though it has a constable?" Mattie said. "And Cannonball Springs has a sheriff and hypocritical Judge Blanche Fickle. Yet it has hardly grown since Judge Fickle declared the town to be the bastion seat of justice for the entire Purgatory River Valley." She hissed. "Folks say he's arranged more 'necktie parties' in Cannonball Springs than anywhere west of the Mississippi River—probably east of it, too—with a possible exception of Bannack in Montana Territory."

Sheriff Brick waved his arms. "Ah, Bannack, exactly! You've heard of the story then: self-entitled Montana Vigilantes hanged more than twenty men suspected of robbery and murder, including U.S. Deputy Marshal and Bannack's own sheriff Henry Plummer and his deputies Buck Stinson and Ned Ray. Is there no better example for why we need society than Bannack?" Sheriff Brick nodded his head. "This isn't Bannack, and I don't intend for it to become Bannack.

"A man of the law can be trusted because the law can be trusted. No judge upholds it without making enemies. But while friendless, law is good, and Judge Fickle applies it, and so he is good at least in his service."

Mattie smirked and shook her head. "You're naive. You must not have met the judge yet. He's a self-proclaimed 'anti-carpetbagging' lawyer from

New Orleans. He's a drunkard and cruelly disposed to kill men for show, beyond what any law demands. I'm convinced that Judge Fickle's audacity and sweet talk were the only reasons Territorial Governor McCook appointed him judge of the justice-of-the-peace court that serves Cannonball Springs, Racida, and Stanchion. I'm not the only one who thinks that."

Sheriff Brick and Mattie stopped in front of her home, the Lutheran parsonage. The house was a modest shack compared to the not-so-modest Lutheran church next door. Racida also had a Catholic church but its fewer congregants could not afford the Lutherans' opulence.

"I never answered your inquiry about my actions," Mattie said. "I want you to know my side of things, at least. I left to find the countryside. I discovered beauty I'll always cherish even if I never see it again. Before I left, I left notes for my father saying generally where I was going and when I'd return. I didn't think it'd worry him. I found out later that on every occasion of my leaving, he marched into Racida's packed saloon and worked up a posse to attack Indians and search for me. My father never goes into the saloon.

"Only once did a posse find Indians, and they escaped unharmed. After four roundups and disappointing searches, no one would help my father. When I would return, my father would ask what I was doing. I would tell him I was seeing the country. He would ask me why. I would say I needed to know. He would say I reminded him of my mother, and then he would walk away.

"I wasn't entirely forthcoming with my father, though I'm sure he guessed as much. I crossed paths with a young man. I'm sorry now to say I fell in love with him. He was wild and smart and handsome and kind. But he carried a deep sadness and guilt with him. He said it drove him to forsake me, which he did the last time I was out exploring.

"And now it doesn't appeal to me anymore. I don't see how it could ever show luster again, not like it did. Summiting a mountaintop is beautiful and spectacular, perhaps no more than the first time. A first breath-taking is unlike any other."

"Are you speaking of love or exploration?" Sheriff Brick said.

Mattie smiled. "I can only represent myself. And I've told you more about my impromptu travels than anyone except Agnes Guilfoyle. She's the only woman whose suspected reputation rivals mine, and that on account of her and her husband's wealth and spendthrift habits. What am I to be ashamed of? And yet, I am."

Mattie said goodnight and left Sheriff Brick standing in front of the parsonage's low wooden front porch. He inhaled the cool evening air and exhaled visible breath that swirled beyond his nose and lips and disappeared. He glanced at the stars and then turned to head back to the jail.

CHAPTER 4

"You suppose Roberts headed for the dead grove?" Chaps said.

"He's not likely to go anywhere else," Fanny said. "It's where we usually camp when we're in this area."

"It wouldn't be right to stay so near, kill a man and sleep by. Spirits are everywhere. You're," Slim quieted, almost whispering, "you're damn right I believe in them. At least I believe in something. I knew an old man who said there was too much blood, that's why the Indians never lived down here, too much blood. That's why the dirt's all red."

Fanny swore.

"Dirt's red lots of places," Chaps said.

"Not like here," Slim said. "This place, that canyon, is full of spirits. Duncan's spirit adds to Indie's which adds to the redskins'."

Chaps spoke. "I suppose there's spirits and all, but I don't think they do nothing. Red men make them up when they're smoking their pipes, like Roberts said. It's a superstition of church-pew-sitting-ninnies, told to keep little ones in line."

"If you say one more thing about a spirit, Slim, I'm going to gut you like we should've gutted the kid." Fanny spit tobacco. The horses' feet struck a rhythm. "We should've slit his throat. We're the muscle. We've always been the muscle. There's power comes with killing. But shooting's never sat right with me. Roberts has gone soft since he took over. He shot Indie; he shot Duncan. He should've scalped them."

Chaps laughed. "You scared as the Devil of him. When has he ever used anything but guns to kill? I suppose he's most comfortable with guns. He'd probably blow your head off right now if he heard you say he'd gone soft. He'd shoot you straight away. He'd shoot us all."

Fanny shifted in his seat and glared unseen in the dark at his brother. Slim whimpered and hunched his back, drawing himself closer to his Appaloosa's crest. The trio rode along.

"My question now though is, with Indie and Duncan dead, how will we find the gold? Roberts said he doesn't know where it is. And do you really think there ever was any gold?"

"You questioning Roberts?"

"I'm scared as the Devil of him."

"Sounds like disbelief."

"Just take the facts, we take our summer break. Indie leaves, then Roberts. We don't see them for four months. Roberts writes us to meet him in Santa Fe. He's raging when we do meet him and swears that Indie's been hiding gold from us. He produces Spanish gold and coins that he says he saw Indie giving to the poor. We write to Indie; we rendezvous. Roberts demands the location of the gold. Indie doesn't acknowledge that gold exists. Roberts shoots him and says Indie didn't hold the best interest of the gang."

"We didn't need stories of hidden gold, Indie was ripe for mutiny as far as I'm concerned," Fanny said. "He played fancy with robberies, like leaving loot in Racida, and imposed a summer hiatus so we could 'lie low.' I didn't need Roberts' gold story to convince me we needed to get rid of Indie."

"I suppose the story doesn't hurt any," Chaps said. "It's a little suspicious that Indie denied the gold under a gun-threat. Damn, if Roberts isn't patient when he's got a gun."

"The probability of it all is improbable," Slim said. "I don't see how there could be treasure; it's Roberts' story and a few coins. We're fools looking for fool's gold."

"I don't quite see it your way, Slim," Chaps said. "Roberts is a spit, but he's smart. And he's honest. Why would he make up a story about gold?" Chaps pulled a coin out of his pants pocket. He handed it to Slim. "Indie gave me that after Punto de Los Brazos. It was before he stole the roan. If you remember, he had an Appaloosa like yours. That horse got shot out from under him. I was riding behind and stopped to let him onto my Sorrel. A bullet grazed my shoulder. That's a Spanish piece of eight. It's very old, too; at least, that's what Indie told me when he gave it to me. I asked him where he got it and he said he'd found a few. He wouldn't say where. He smiled like he would when he had an idea about something, or a secret."

"I remember the Punto heist," Fanny said. "It was the only job Roberts planned, and it damn near got Indie and you killed."

Slim waved off Chaps. "Coins are coins. Roberts said it was a treasure trove. He had reason to make up a story: another straw on the scales of rebellion. Are we following Indie now or Roberts?"

The brothers were quiet in the face of Slim's grinning deductions. The men rode without another word for a long time. The night was heavy and clouds rolled in to obscure the brilliant heavens. They crested a low incline and saw the small orange light of a fire dancing in the shadows of lifeless trees. Roberts had made camp.

"He's bold, casting a light like that," Slim said.

"He don't care about ghost stories or spirits that could eat a man," Fanny said. He laughed by himself.

"Watch Roberts. I think he's not cutting us in on the whole picture. His gold gambit doesn't make sense. This isn't a country men come to to get lost in, mark my words. There's no gold or silver. We're short of the mountains. The land's no good."

"It'll produce if you work it," Chaps said. "But you've got to work it."

Fanny smiled. "You still fixing to set up a place?"

"Somewhere, I suppose. Here's hard. And we've got reputation following us."

Fanny spit tobacco and swore. "No one knows it's us been riding around. We haven't even been riding around for months! And in all that time, the towns we've been to and people we've rubbed shoulders with—no one suspected us! The law only knows Indie."

"And now he's dead." Chaps spit tobacco. "I'll concede that Indie was principally known. But folks know it's more than him, sure, just not who. And when we start robbing again and there's no Indie to take the spotlight, what happens in the quiet between the heists? It'd take just one slip-up and we'd be done."

"One might as well worry about falling off that canyon, unless you're fixing to turn yourself in. If a guy's not keen on living, who can stop him from self-destruction?"

"I'm terrified that we will never let it go, and so betray ourselves," Chaps said. "We haven't been at this for more than what, two years, two-and-a-half total? It's not like it was, folks moving west, setting up. Folks are settled now, and there's lawmen. I even hear that Racida has a negro lawman! And he's damned good if you can believe it."

"Where'd you hear that?" Fanny said. "I can't imagine such a man being good, especially damned good, at anything. Are you going to confess to him? I don't see how you figure on betraying yourself, unless you're keen on confession."

Chaps waved his brother off. "My point is that folks haven't forgotten the Caloo Gang. They're apt to investigate new mischief. I don't want to wait like a bridled horse hoping that no one tugs on my reins. And that's why when I settle down, I'm going to settle down somewhere else than here.

Besides, the land's not much good around here. I'd set up where the land is better and raise hogs like we used to have—fried bacon sizzling over a fire on a cold morning and the smell of salt and smoke just hanging in the kitchen air; baked beans and sugar." Chaps smacked his lips.

"I bet you'd have a little barn and corral, too, with your fanciful cabin?" Fanny said.

"Of course, with a cow or two for milking, a coop where chickens lay fresh brown eggs, young horses grazing in a corral and waiting to be broke. And the yard surrounded by fields, brown spelts and barley, and wheat ripening sweet until harvest." Chaps smiled. "Maybe even a Misses."

Fanny laughed. "You haven't the fixings."

"I do. *I* do. I'm not—" Chaps motioned with his head in Slim's direction.

The brothers laughed. Fanny spit tobacco.

"Imbeciles," Slim said.

Chaps cackled. Fanny spit tobacco again.

"I think a hundred acres would do," Chaps said. "I'd raise wheat and corn. And I'd have a big garden with beets and parsnips and potatoes and plenty of carrots to last the winter. I'd plant trees around the house. It's not going to be a cabin, roughshod. It'll be an elegant house with a large great room and a big hearth. It'll face south so the sun can warm it."

"You talk louder than a herd of buffalo," Roberts said.

Fanny, Chaps, and Slim were near enough for him to talk to them without yelling too loud. They dismounted.

"We supposed with the firelight, you didn't care so much about being noticed," Chaps said.

Roberts' face turned red. "Pull watch! A careless man might as well be coyote food. We're not on a joy ride through the wilderness. We've got to rest and rest the horses for tomorrow's trip." He spread himself out. The others kept their eyes on Roberts. "Indie was a fool. Among other missteps, he left our loot in Racida. Of course we escaped; we would've escaped even saddlebags and pockets loaded. Speed—" and Roberts scoffed. "We're recovering first what's ours. Racida in the morning. I've heard they've got a negro lawman, too. If there's time, we can teach him how the law stands here."

CHAPTER 5

SHERIFF BRICK WAS A TEMPERATE man. His resolutions had not made a whit of difference to Racida's saloon-goers, that is to say, the citizens of Racida.

"We've got to get Brick to drink," they had vowed.

They wore on him day and night, even threatening, until the young sheriff began to slip regular visits "next door" from the jail to the adjacent saloon. Dammed force is greater than unhindered capability. Most men start off slow. But when Sheriff Brick took drink, he drank lots of alcohol, even more than regulars. He had yet to pass out, and he was admired for it. Some even said they envied his fortitude. With the sheriff's admittance to the saloon's regular patronage, Preacher Schroeder was again the only Racida man of age who did not drink, which he held as a matter of pride, as did Mattie.

Thick yellow saloon light lit up Sheriff Brick's dark face as he opened the door and walked in. "I'll have a whiskey," he said to the bartender, who had one good eye and was often busy hand-drying glasses with a discolored towel.

The bartender grunted. He had not used to pour good whiskey for this new regular. But he grabbed good whiskey now, a black bottle from the top shelf. He poured a full glass for the sheriff.

With spirits in hand, Sheriff Brick squeezed into a tight table of men shoulder-to-shoulder and talking low. More stood surrounding the circle. They were faces he knew except one, a spectacled man, bald and fat-cheeked with whiskers covering his lips.

"I hope you've received a proper welcome," Sheriff Brick said.

"None better in these parts," the man said. And he smiled." At least as well as I could hope with the business I'm on."

"Business!" someone said. The men roared with laughter.

"Cut 'em up now!"

"Dance on their graves!"

"Good riddance, the whole lot!"

"Thieving ties, the noose!"

"Blight on society!"

"Nine thousand dollars stolen, Nine thousand dollars!"

"Blackguards!"

"Thieves!"

"Scalp them like savages!" This last cry drew hearty refrain, and those who had glasses drank from them.

"Sheriff, you'll be wondering the meaning of this, I'm sure!" the spectacled man said, smiling broader. "I've heard great commendations on your record, too, a fine job you've been doing protecting this town. But there's men even you can't catch, men too dangerous for any local law enforcement. Harmless snakes you can do away with, but broods of vipers, wicked men, that requires expert handling!"

Applause and approving grunts rose.

"We make do with what we have," Sheriff Brick said as the tumult quieted. "There hasn't been anything I couldn't handle since I took the job."

"No, so I gather. You've been doing a fine job, a fine job! Like I said. And I'm not here to interfere."

"What're you here for?"

"Brood of vipers! Like I said. I'm up from Mexico looking for outlaws. And I've heard tell of a notorious gang running around these parts, at least used to—the Caloo Gang! You've heard of them; yes, I'd think most people in these parts have, doubtless every badge man. And being sheriff of *this* town, you're especially aware as the Caloo Gang," he spoke low, "robbed the bank."

The mob hissed. Some uttered oaths.

"I've heard the gang's taken a leave of absence," Sheriff Brick said. "Which is to say I haven't heard anything of them since I assumed my post four months ago. Folks say that the gang's hightailed it with their ill-gotten gains. They'd be wise to have done so. They'll go to the jail and judge if they ever step foot into this town again, I can assure you."

The men murmured. "Ol' Sheriff, got his dander up."

"Careful, boy."

"Dead if they ever come here again."

"My gun's always loaded."

"Thieves."

"Brood of vipers."

The spectacled man laughed. "I've heard the same rumors. Curious, so I came back here from Mexico to find out. I once tracked Indie and the gang, back before you were Racida's lawman. Close is no reward and I needed to eat. There's easy money in Mexico so I left to stock.

"But an itch can go away harder than riding an unbroken mule. I thought I'd have Indie to chase whenever I pleased, like a promise of home, of sorts, because heaven knows no one has caught him, not even me, and I'm the best. I was sure he'd be here when I returned. Then I heard rumors he was gone or dead, and I couldn't believe it. I had to come back to see.

"Like I said, I'm not here to interfere with your business. You're right, if they're smart, the Caloo Gang has skittered with their ill-gotten gains. I think they're still here though, and I mean to find out. Cash and gold beckon, and I think, too, notoriety. That Indie's too smart to be unaware of his reputation, with any funds he'll need, to boot. He's not gone, just laying low, maybe hoping your kind will forget about him and his gang. You need to smoke out men like that, go to where they are. Sheriff, I'm a smoker."

"Am I to understand you're here for bounty, or blood?"

The man laughed. "Both, I suppose, if I can find it! There's money in both, what with the reward and all." He swore. "A man's got to eat. I understand the good people of this region desire revenge and are willing to pay for it even above a U.S. Marshal reward, seeing as how Marshals never come to this part of the country. Why should they? Well, my purpose is as a Marshal, of sorts. We're all moved by the Lord. And I'm his instrument in this to find and visit the iniquities of the suffering onto the causers of that suffering."

"And you mean to get rich, too," Sheriff Brick said. "Four thousand five hundred dollars is a lot of money, and it's what they're offering for the capture of Indie Caloo and his gang."

"Five thousand!"

The saloon turned to glare at the sudden outburst. It was the messenger. He held up the notice that he had held up the previous morning in identifying Indie.

"The reward is $5,000 now. And I can tell you, he's alive! Indie Caloo is alive!"

He nearly fainted. A drink and attentive ears revived him. The messenger told his story from the morning, changing details to present his nobility and courage. Patrons bought him more drinks.

Sheriff Brick listened with a serious eye. The messenger revived even more and told the captive audience about his encounter with Indie Caloo. He told the story again with more flair and mentioned the gang and buying the Morgan from them. The crowd hooted and hollered.

Sheriff Brick yawned after listening to the messenger's story for the third time, which had become sloppier and more fantastic with inebriation. Sheriff Brick rose to leave and the spectacled man, the bounty hunter, walked after him. He grabbed the sheriff by the arm and asked what he thought of the news that Indie and his gang were alive.

"I won't allow vigilante killing in my jurisdiction," Sheriff Brick said. "No matter the justifications they imagine, men are behooved to answer to the law. You're a bounty hunter, no doubt."

The bounty hunter smiled. "A hunter, yes."

"You're welcome to stay. I can't stop you. Hunt Indie and his gang. I'll laud you. But there'll be no blood in this town unanswered for, not in Racida. Don't bring fire on our heads. These men, as any man, will answer to the law if they fall into my hands. And if they come back, they'll fall into my hands." Sheriff Brick left the saloon. The entire saloon watched him leave.

CHAPTER 6

VIBRANT STARS COLORED THE CELESTIAL veil more blue than black as morning approached. Snow reflected sky light. Indie, wrapped in the thick coat he had taken from the messenger the day before, breathed clouds as he advanced the Morgan. They had ridden through day and night. He saw a black lump a hundred yards away. It revealed as a scene of equestrian destruction: the Strawberry Roan, so recently magnificent, had died running and lay as freezing flesh and bone. Indie reined his mount a few feet away to stop. He slipped from its back.

"A fine horse," he said as he looked at the roan. He kneeled, touched the muzzle, and reached into the mouth.

Not too frozen, recently dead, maybe a few hours. Its eyes were horrible and opened wide. *Duncan, Slim, Fanny, Chaps, and Roberts must be close. But this bodes ill for Duncan.* Indie shivered a sick feeling, which he tried to stomp into the ground.

He looked at the horse. *What terror and excitement when I stole him! I thought breaking would be the death of us both. He was magnificent in gallop and dangerous in walk. I never thought I'd see the day—hoped I wouldn't. I wouldn't have shot him if it'd come to that. I'd have nursed him, splinted whatever bone. Would shooting have been a better end than this? It would've been a mercy.*

Indie ran his hand over the roan's poll, crest, and withers to the horn of the saddle. He rubbed his hand over the shined, hard leather. He traced the Greek key pattern with his fingers. He looked up; he wanted to yell but did not. He clicked his tongue.

At least the saddle's still in fine shape. What a shame. Did they take the rifle? Indie looked at the saddle's rifle holder which still held the Spencer repeating rifle. He laughed. *Just my luck! Those idiots hardly know what's valuable—watch, rifle.* He took the rifle and examined it. He worked the

31

lever under the trigger and a bullet popped out, then again and again but no more bullets. He shook his head.

"Taken the eggs and left the hen; one bullet in the chamber," he said to the Morgan.

Indie pocketed the bullet and set the rifle to the side. He pulled a pencil and a leather-bound book from his jacket. He knelt on the dead horse to write for several minutes. "I might write one for you if it ever comes to it," he said to the Morgan. "But I'll try to get you back to that fella. He did buy you." The horse shivered.

Indie finished writing and replaced his book and pencil. "It's cold alright, best if we get up a fire." He looked at the lightening horizon.

It's morning. We've what, another day ahead of us? But we've ridden hard. The Morgan might have it in it; I don't have it in me. A little farther and then we'll rest. I fear the worst for Duncan. The roan came from the canyon. We're too close for them not to have gone the way of Dead Man's Run. It'll be warmer down there out of the wind. If we find Duncan there or on the way, it'll be his corpse. I hope we don't find him and he's alive.

Indie worked to remove the saddle from the dead horse, tying the roan's reins to the Morgan to use its power in repositioning the roan. It pulled hard. The saddle cleared its cinches and billet.

"That'll be better for both of us," Indie said to the Morgan as he put the saddle on its back. "There's only so much bareback riding I can take. I imagine you feel it, too. There's not a finer saddle than this in all the territory."

Indie petted the horse. He mounted and urged it to the canyon without hesitating to track for guidance.

When they reached the canyon, Indie reined his Morgan down the narrow, crisscrossing ledges in the dim morning light. His head was full of emotion, piqued by exhaustion. Small stones gave way at cuts where the horse's hooves got too close to the edge. The rocks fell and exploded on impact farther down.

The trail was slow. Indie knew its curves and twists and slopes. The Morgan did not, and only continued with prodding. Finally, he dismounted and led the horse. His foot slipped and he turned in one motion while falling to grab the rounded path edge. His fingers dug into the dirt but scraped away free as he slipped backwards onto stone and grit. A gush of breath escaped him, and Indie gasped the moments of pain until the Morgan paralleled him after guiding itself to his landing. Indie moaned and rose. He rested before resuming a more careful descent.

At the bottom of the twisting path, the stream spread as a silver belt tightened against a waist of red rock. It widened, and jutting rocks and stones evinced shallowness: a ford, the only good one for a long stretch.

Water is life in a desert, and a stream engenders hope. But Indie paused when he saw Duncan. He moaned and dropped the reins, then sauntered to the dead young man.

Rolling waves do not find their voice until considerable building, and we find them lapping not only at our feet but our ankles and knees. The grief building in Indie did not mark itself until he was heaving and sputtering in convulsive cries. His lonely wail competed above the brook's din for Duncan's song. He held his head low, channeling his grief to the ground as tears warmed his red cheeks.

The Morgan drank water from the stream. It walked into the vigil and snorted for attention. It was cold.

Indie picked up Duncan's perfect left arm and kissed the hand. "I'm sorry."

Returning to his horse, he grabbed two blankets from his saddle and unfurled them: one to sleep on to get his body off the ground and the other to cover himself with. The Morgan stayed near and ate the fresh grass.

It'll be sunup before we know it. We'll not have to ride hard to catch them. How far could they be? I think they're close. I only have the one bullet. Slim's probably got Fanny and Chaps on edge, at least Chaps, at least a little bit. Slim hated this place because he thought there were spirits haunting the rocks. Roberts is always on edge.

If there are spirits, Duncan's has joined the heavenly host and we've got nothing to worry about. If I had the bullets, I'd catch Roberts, Fanny, Chaps, and Slim. I've got to bury Duncan. I'm too tired to bury him now. But I can't leave his body here. Oh Duncan!

PART II
ROBBERY

CHAPTER 7

"GET UP, SLIM!" ROBERTS SAID. He was looking back from his lead in the morning ride.

"Where do you suppose you're going?" Chaps said.

Fanny spit tobacco. "You're lucky we don't tie you up and lead you around like a damned savage."

"I suppose you fell asleep again?" Chaps said.

"You can shut the hell up," Roberts said as he walked his Palomino back to the other outlaws. He glared at Chaps and then stared at Slim as though he were trying to break him with his eyes. Roberts' muscular frame flexed under his coat.

"I don't tolerate lying!" Roberts shouted. And he put his face in Slim's. "I *don't* tolerate lying."

"You've got him peeved." Fanny laughed and swore. "You know how he is when his dander's up."

"You can shut up, too. I swear," and Roberts swore. "And if you weren't good with a gun, I'd blow your face off, right here. I'd smash your teeth out with my pistol and break your nose. And then I'd shoot. I'd . . ." he trailed off.

"I was thinking," Slim said.

"About them spirits?" Chaps laughed.

Fanny swore. "Either I'm going to kill you or your damned superstitions will."

"You're stupidly superstitious," Roberts said. "Spirits, I'll . . ." Roberts shook his head and did not finish saying what he was saying. He spit and shook his head again. "Indie's dead and so is Duncan, as it should be. There'll be no spiritual retribution for it.

"If you're wanting to pin their deaths and spirits on me, I'll take it. You're a coward, Slim. I don't care a bit about killing you, how's that? None of you." Roberts glared at Slim, Chaps, and Fanny. "Don't slow us up." His words silenced the men.

The cold morning air was quiet except for the horses' rustle as they walked. The pall that Roberts had cast lingered over the party as he led them nearer and through outcroppings and jutting red rocks. They halted and watered their horses. Roberts walked to an edge of earth that revealed the open land below and beyond.

Whether by the Santa Fe or some other trail—or as many have done haplessly—the road west through Kansas, Indian Territory, and Texas trespasses drainage basins of rivers like the Smoky Hill, Walnut, Arkansas, Ninnescah, Cimarron, Purgatoire, and Canadian. The Red River forms the southern border of these drying plains, the Platte the northern. The corridor begins fruitful in the east. It then waxes westward into its great arid expanse, inviting and repelling, and host to indigenous masters, relocated Indians, and hopeful agriculturists often disappointed by spring and summer rains or the lack thereof. The land grows wilder westward, too, with shallow arroyos that can run deep into canyons. Then tough trees open vigil upon these canyons, and forests fence boundless land that finally rises to the sky.

So Roberts surveyed the foothills of the Sangre de Cristo Mountains: a red land of rocks, forests, shrubs, and dry grass, dotted with early snow. Racida's jagged buildings, small and tucked into a shallow valley, broke the blinding view. The distant mountains were white and brilliant catching the morning sun.

"When God created man," Roberts said, "he gave him dominion over the beasts of the earth, to subdue the whole damn thing. We've been subduing for a while now. There isn't a lawman with any sense who'd cross us, not without Marshal support. And there aren't any Marshals out here because there aren't enough white folks to give a damn about. And those are the only people Marshals give a damn about."

"Savages will eat a man," Fanny said, and laughed.

Roberts breathed deeply and turned to the gang. "We worked hard for our money in Racida. There's no fool Indie standing in our way now. No one knows it's there. It'll be an easy job to go and get it. The colored lawman won't stop us."

"Why're we going to Racida now?" Slim said. Roberts, Chaps, and Fanny turned to Slim.

"If you'd any more holes in your head, you'd leak when you drank," Roberts said. "Didn't you hear a damn—" he yelled and swore and trailed off. "Didn't you hear a damn . . ." when Roberts was angry, he did not finish sentences.

"Let me scalp him," Fanny said. He smiled and grabbed his knife.

Slim pressed on. "Why're we going back to Racida—"

Fanny ran to punch Slim. Slim saw the attack and ducked into his assailant's body. Fanny dived over Slim and grabbed him. His inertia carried the two of them into the ground, knocking the wind out of Slim. Fanny scraped his jaw. He channeled his fury into a quick recovery and kicks to Slim's face.

Chaps intervened. He pulled off his brother, who was laughing like a coyote on a hunt. Lather spilled from Fanny's lips. He eyed Slim like the Devil, and he sauntered to the horses. Blood covered Slim's face. He covered it with his arm bent at the elbow.

"Your nose looks broken," Chaps said, and spit in the dirt.

Slim stumbled to his feet. Chaps brought him his canteen to wash his face. Roberts had calmed watching the tussle. He walked to his horse.

"Of all the towns, Racida," Roberts said. "You think it had anything to do with that woman? You're damn right it did. It's ridiculous that we have to go back. It's no different staging a robbery than committing one. We should've taken the money from the start, plain and simple, and shot anyone who got in our way. We shot the clerk, not? Racida didn't even have a lawman. But no! And now we've got to clean up this . . ." he trailed off. Then he swore. "You're going to camp at the usual spot and wait until dark." Roberts pointed to a small bluff miles away. "Then sneak into town and finish the job tonight. We'll rendezvous in Cannonball Springs on Friday."

"You're not coming with?" Chaps said.

"You don't need me. It's a simple job. The money's under the floor behind the teller counter."

Slim cleaned himself up. His nose was not broken though it bled. When the horses were ready, the four men mounted to resume their journey. Roberts rode ahead. Slim gave a telling look to the brothers and urged his Appaloosa forward.

"Remember that paint you tried to break?" Chaps said to Fanny.

"You talking about the one that bucked me off and busted my lip?" Fanny said.

"And then drove you hard and over the corral fence."

"That spit was mean. I cut him up, though."

"I suppose you were even more violent then than now. But that horse would've killed you if you'd have kept at it."

"No."

"Yes! If Pa hadn't got you to come off that fence and out of the corral, if you'd gotten back at it, that horse would have knocked you down and stomped you dead."

"That's what you think? I was done having it out, that's all."

"You needed patience is all, and some common sense. That's how I got him tamed. It took time, but I got him tamed. You can't fight fire with fire."

Fanny swore. He stared like a hungry coyote at the back of Slim's hat. Blood still stained Slim's face. He slowed his horse and turned to the brothers, who slowed their horses, too.

"There's two things I'm trying to make sense of. What's Roberts up to? He's up to something."

"What's the second thing?" Chaps said.

"Don't you see it queer that we staged a robbery and left the money in Racida? Roberts almost killed Indie when he told us we were leaving the money, stow it in the floor to make a clean getaway, and then sneak back to get it later. It was odd then as it is now. What if Indie knew Roberts was going to kill him all along? He must've suspected. Did hiding the money hold Roberts off? But then Roberts knew where the money was the whole time, which is why It doesn't make sense. Indie knew we'd have to ride back into Racida. He wanted us to ride back there. Why?"

"Maybe so his spirit could haunt us?" Chaps laughed.

Fanny remained still and stared at Slim. "I wonder what you taste like." He rasped his tongue between his teeth. "I'm no damned savage." He smiled. "You can be thankful I'm not a savage."

"I'm not getting at spirits," Slim said.

"But I suppose you're thinking it, Slim?" Chaps said. "You're always thinking of spirits. I haven't met a holy man yet who thought more about spirits than you.

"I'll grant Roberts has been acting queer, running off when we were on hiatus, coming back with a grand plan, death marching Indie for treasure, shooting Duncan." Chaps shook his head.

"He's too much of a schemer to not be scheming, certainly," Slim said. "I'd like to know what he's got up his sleeve. Maybe it's not terrible. Maybe it is!"

"It's not terrible if he's not up to anything," Chaps said.

"You see haunts at every turn," Fanny said.

Slim paused, then flexed the corner of his mouth to his eye, like a grimace smile on the side of his face. "That horse that busted your lip, Fanny, it took patience to draw him out?"

The brothers stared. Chaps hesitated a nod.

"Do you think Roberts is a pure soul? He's up to mischief. Whatever he's up to, the reason he's abandoning us, there's something of personal gain in it, mark me. He's set on cutting us out of whatever it is. He'll set his plan in motion and leave us with no part. Roberts is loyal only to himself; let Indie and Duncan's blood bear witness. We all once committed ourselves to each other and the gang. Roberts killed them."

"We only need two to load out the gold," Chaps said. "One of us could keep an eye on Roberts. I don't suppose we need Slim in Racida. Dark, spooky, who knows if the bank building's been used since our heist. He'd be a wreck about it, what with his mind full of haunts and spirits."

Fanny's smile faded. He grimaced and gnashed his teeth.

Roberts turned ahead and spurred his horse back to the three outlaws. He tore through the calm conspiracy with profanity.

"Damn . . ." Roberts said. His voice trailed off. He bit his lips and dismounted all at once.

Slim shook. He turned. His Appaloosa stopped and flinched away from Roberts, who pressed near the horse. He grabbed Slim by the coat and dragged him to the ground. He pressed on top of him and drew a LeMat pistol, cocked it, *click,* and with his hand on the trigger, pressed the barrel into Slim's face.

It happened so fast—the dismantlement of Slim's surety—that Fanny and Chaps did not flinch from Roberts' life-threatening rush. They stared silent at the madness.

"You keep slowing us down," Roberts said. "Tell me why you keep slowing us down. I've a mind to fill your face with lead."

Slim shook under Roberts's heavy hand. "Indie wanted us to go back to, to Racida, to get the money. I was thinking it over." He apologized.

Roberts drew deep breaths that slowed. Then he let go of Slim and returned to his horse. Slim coughed. Fanny chuckled. Chaps pursed his lips.

"Sometimes it's hard for me to believe you're not stupider than Fanny," Roberts said. "There's not a lawman, negro or otherwise, who'd cross us in these parts. I'd like to teach that negro sheriff in Racida a lesson. We should teach him . . ." He mounted his horse. "I'll shoot the next bastard who slows . . ." he did not finish saying what he was saying and his face flushed. Roberts shook his head, turned his horse, and resumed the trail.

Chapter 8

INDIE AWOKE STIFF AND COLD from a short sleep. He looked older than he was, a face like weathered leather, patched and rippled, though not yet dried out. Many said Indie's features were representative of his personality and that you could tell his entire disposition with one look at his face. He denied this.

Hard tack breakfast goes down hard. And there was a body to bury.

Oh Duncan!

Indie sighed and thought about the dead young man. He ate little. Duncan had been a big breakfast eater: bacon, hotcakes with molasses or sorghum syrup, biscuits, salted meat. Duncan was fire and smoke except in the quiet of a morning, gathered around a fire with a pan and food steaming alongside coffee in a blackened pot. Mornings were cold and stiff; Duncan was their antithesis in rapture.

Indie shirked his disinterest for the awful task that caught his throat and knotted his belly: burial. He tore a piece of paper from his notebook, folded it, and placed it under the dead boy's crossed hands over his chest.

Indie dug and dug with a crude tool until he hollowed out a shallow hole. It did not swallow Duncan's body, and he finished his work by piling stones over the corpse. There was little doubt this would serve as a temporary grave until birds and beasts ate the remains. Thus, Duncan would pass without ceremony into bellies and gizzards. But Indie would remember. He cried and mounted his horse.

The stream bubbled over itself, fed by fresh snow. More would melt and feed its furor. Minerals veined the red rock canyon wall by which Indie and the Morgan had descended hours before. Duncan, too, had ridden down its snaking path on the heels of doom; his body lay at its base.

Indie clicked and the Morgan marched through the cold water. It grunted. Indie did not turn back. A small bird alighted onto the monument he had built.

He grimaced as he rode. He pushed his horse to a trot. Indie picked his way along the outlaws' trail and passed through their previous night's camp in the dead grove.

I could've taken them by surprise last night if I'd more than one bullet. This place is more exposed than I remember. Yet, Duncan.

The trail muddied as it led from the camp. Two branches, then three—animals had also noticed the outlaws' camp. Indie stopped and looked at the diverging paths, then took the one that disappeared in the brush. He rode slow, studying the ground.

There's game here, a bear and coyotes. It's not common to see a bear out this far. There's not a lot for him to eat out here, not like in the mountains. Here's a far trek for a bear. He must be pretty big. But this isn't his trail, not entirely. The boys traveled this way. No animal tries to cover its tracks. They're instinctual. Men are practical.

The brush thinned after a few hundred yards and the trail left by the outlaws resumed, single file at first, then abreast and thus easy to see that more than one horse and rider had traversed the terrain. Indie looked at the tracks, then ahead, and he squinted in the light of the morning sun.

They're making for the fork to Racida or Cannonball Springs. The tracks show it plain. That makes the most sense, too. We don't need to slowly navigate by these. I know a fast way to the crossroads. Maybe we can head them off.

He clicked and the Morgan ran.

Waning summer days stretch long like those that have passed. Rhythm punctuates time and travel, especially horse travel, and whispers a spell of bewilderment. Without help, who can measure exactly a day's passage except in the exchange of rugged terrain for rugged terrain and the gradual rise and fall of the sun? Indie was accustomed to such riding and held fast against rocking off to sleep, tired as he was. He checked his pocket watch against freshening tracks. He was gaining on the outlaws.

There's an hour or two of riding that separates us. We'll ride the path a half hour more. Then there's a path I doubt they know, and it'll close the gap. It'll be close, but we'll just catch them. That old Arapaho warrior said a patient hunter never goes hungry.

Hours later, Indie waited at a crossroads as his mutinous gang came into view. He watched from a quarter mile through a crack between two enormous red boulders. Roberts, Fanny, Chaps, and Slim stopped at the diverging trails. One led northeast to Racida, the other west to Cannonball Springs. Indie held his Spencer repeater rifle and rubbed it. He strained to hear but the distance was too great to hear anything besides echoing laughs from Fanny.

The outlaws did not stop long. Slim, Fanny, and Chaps took the path to Racida. Roberts took the path to Cannonball Springs. Indie watched them disappear behind the terrain.

Strange they're splitting up. There's mischief in it. Roberts has his reasons. He's the real trouble. I could deal with Slim, Chaps, and Fanny later.

There'll be mischief down in Racida though, no doubt. They're going after the money. Fanny's a madman. He's a killer. What'll they do? I promised Mattie I'd never again set foot in Racida. She said she'd kill me if she ever saw me again. But what'll they do?

Indie saw Matilda Schroeder and her wild eyes. His temples shivered through his spine for the beauty and fury of a memory he tried to forget. He was ashamed of the words he had uttered, words that had turned her forever away. He loved her. He had not understood her love. In a twist of reason, he had risen to a vague but clear call of benevolent separation. She had slipped into a depression for which he had not found salve.

He stared into the steel covering his rifle's breechblock; the gun could never be more than an object in his hands, a tool to manipulate or cast aside at will. His heart weighed as a twisted rope. He saw himself as a fool and he regretted choosing outlawing and the life he knew—*his legend*—over Mattie.

Slim rode back to the crossroads and Indie stopped musing. He watched Slim slow his horse, stop, shake his head, then start for the Cannonball Springs trail after Roberts.

Slim's following Roberts? He suspects him of indiscretion. I hope for Slim's sake he's improved his discretion; else it'll be one less body to kill. Roberts is the real danger. And what's Slim suspect him of? I'll warrant Chaps and Fanny entertain some notion, too.

Then Indie thought of misdeeds: a bar fight in Kansas, violent interactions with Indians, animal torture, lighting crops ablaze. Roberts had drawn him and the gang into the retributive and daring. Indie had rewarded Roberts and the gang with clever robberies and anonymity. Indie remembered Mattie again and an image of her stark features turning back to him against the lanterns of Racida and the more brilliant lights overhead of a wild night. A man can talk of hair and skin and a woman's being, but Indie picked at the hope of desire. She was inspiration and energy, beautiful even in a half-shade, perhaps more. Maybe she was forgiveness, too. And so, Indie mounted the Morgan and walked through the requirements for an unnoticed ride to Racida.

The forking trails provided the only immediate, passable routes to Cannonball Springs and Racida, with steep cliffs walling off detours. Yet farther along, the Raicda road opened up, allowing another difficult short-cut that Indie could use to beat Fanny and Chaps to Racida, as he had done to beat the outlaws to the crossroads.

We'll wait forty minutes to make sure to not ride up on them. When the road opens up, we'll take the shortcut they don't know about. They don't know this land like I do, just the expected. Roberts takes time to see beyond the trails and settlements in between. But even he doesn't see like I do. We'll have to fol-low in their tracks for about a mile. There's no way around it. Then we'll take my shortcut and beat them to Racida.

Chapter 9

THE ROBBERY OF RACIDA'S PIONEER Bank was a catalyst for law enforcement recruitment, the effort for which was nevertheless fruitless until Sheriff
Brick arrived in town because no one else wanted the job. "Tall" Jim Payne
and his great uncle Elbe had established the old Pioneer Bank in 1867 using
capital, rumor said, from generous federal government contracts during the
war between the states. Elbe was confined to his bed; Tall Jim was diligent
but bad with numbers. Folks said the business would have faltered if not for
Jim's care for people, though Racida had need of a bank and only one. Folks
for miles around deposited their money and other valuables in the Pioneer
Bank. Some had taken loans, too. Tall Jim's goodwill and Beaumont-Adams
revolver assuaged fears that the bank vault was open too often, one of a
handful of security improprieties identified with hindsight.

"Who would rob Tall Jim and his uncle Elbe?" folks used to say. "He
has his gun—beautiful, English, must be rich—and he's so nice."

The Pioneer Bank was robbed on a windy Thursday afternoon. A bad
barn fire at Theodore Tuck's farm captured the attention of do-gooders
and curious folks, which happened to be a considerable portion of Racida's
population, so the town was almost empty. The few and differing accounts
of the robbery agree that a group of six men came riding into Racida like
lightning. It had been particularly dry, and the swirling dust had transformed the figures into apparitions, "like shadows behind a veil," the town's
telegrapher said.

The robbers fired into the air which stirred confusion. Three men entered the bank: one by diving through a front window, the other two by
walking through the open door. Tall Jim was in the bank and his uncle Elbe
was upstairs. The three robbers who stayed outside the bank turned on its
low porch toward the street, brandished their rifles, and vowed to shoot

anyone who got too close. They even fired at the telegrapher who did get too close.

Then, almost as soon as they whirled in, a gunshot erupted from within the bank and the robbers hurried out. All six found their horses and galloped hard out of town. One of them discharged a pistol and the bullet lodged in a blacksmith's sign down the street.

The few witnessing town people rushed into the Pioneer Bank. The iron gate that separated the waiting room from the working area and vault was open. The vault was open, too, and it was empty. Tall Jim had been shot in the chest and he was slumped over the counter with his head pressed against the iron bars of the teller window. "Caloo Gang" was scrawled on a piece of paper next to him on the counter. A responder tore upstairs to awaken Uncle Elbe.

Word was sent to Theodore Tuck's. Many angry people returned. After considerable squabble, they formed a posse to apprehend the perpetrators. The mob rode in the wrong direction out of town, though not far, and routed back through to pick up the run-away-trail. An old mountain man had been chosen to lead the group because of his tracking experience. But he was too drunk to ride more than a hundred yards in the correct direction without falling off his horse. So they tied him to the horn of his saddle. But he slipped the knot and fell off again. The posse left him in Racida.

After a long, fruitless ride, the posse turned back. Wiley Pecker had mistaken a Norwegian farmer and fellow vigilante for an outlaw and shot him in the leg. The farmer was taken to Dr. Bludegats who wanted to amputate. Mrs. Bludegats said the bullet had entered the side of the calf and passed through. She washed the injured farmer's leg, gave him a tonic, and sent him home with instructions to keep it clean. The farmer said later that the tonic made his hair fall out.

The robbery lowered the spirit of Racida's citizenry. It was rumored that a rancher committed suicide. It was not known for certain how much money had been stolen, because Tall Jim had been bad with numbers and had kept an incomplete recording. But folks settled on nine thousand dollars and that number stuck in people's minds.

The only person who benefitted from the whole affair seemed to be Reverend Schroeder who had a full congregation the next few Sundays. He had not lost money, preferring to keep his worldly possessions out of the bank.

Uncle Elbe died not long after the whole affair. Men said it was old age. Women said it was heartbreak. Dr. Bludegats said it was nothing a good bleeding couldn't have cured. Elbe died in a fit of hysteria before the good doctor could implement his cure. The peculiarity of death—no known cause, Elbe's mania, and its suddenness—bred rumors that Uncle Elbe's spirit haunted the old bank.

Tall Jim's cousin Alfred, a successful banker out east who also had an office in London, rode in on a stagecoach about two weeks after Uncle Elbe's death. "I'll set this aright and then, back home," he said. He liked to talk with his hands. He had Jim and Elbe's bodies exhumed and buried at the other, sunnier end of the Lutheran cemetery. People said it was right he did that.

They asked Alfred if he intended to re-open the Pioneer bank. "I'll set it aright and then, back home," he said. But instead of using the old Pioneer Bank building, Alfred built another on the other side of town. People said it was right he did that.

Alfred met Mattie and began attending the Lutheran church. He talked to Mattie every Sunday. He began talking less of setting his "western affairs aright" and began to mention setting his "eastern affairs aright." He opened the new Pioneer Bank and ran it on his own. He was better with numbers than his cousin Tall Jim, to say the least, and he worked hard enough so the money could make itself. He was bad with people and he had no firearm, but Alfred's lack of goodwill and common sense was overlooked for his short-order success.

He asked Mattie to marry him. She declined. He asked a homely woman to marry him—the daughter of a respectable but not respected rancher—and she said "yes." Their wedding was approaching, and Mattie discussed it with Sheriff Brick who did not say much about it.

"Can you imagine being married to Alfred Payne?" Mattie said.

Sheriff Brick rocked on the jail's porch, a polished Henry rifle across his lap. He wore his winter jacket. It was another cold night, though no snow. He grunted.

"I can't imagine it at all!" Mattie said. "I'd dislike it, certainly. And I can't imagine something I'd dislike, not something like marriage."

"You can't imagine marrying Mr. Payne?" Sheriff Brick said.

"No. It would be," Mattie paused and smiled, "it'd be dreadful, how's that?"

"Sitting outside on a cold night is dreadful."

"It's fortifying."

Sheriff Brick ducked his eyes at Mattie and shivered a smile. "I suppose one could say the same about marriage."

"Marriage shouldn't be dreadful. It should be wonderful! I wouldn't imagine it otherwise."

"That's sentimental, very romantic."

"Yes, certainly. And why shouldn't it be?" Mattie twisted her body around her shoulder. "If we can't be sentimental or romantic about marriage, the ultimate consequence of love, what else could we be sentimental or romantic about? Marriage defines and is defined by those words."

"What would you say to —."

"Of course, one's choices do not hold for another. I would say 'congratulations.' I intend to say 'congratulations.' You know father's performing the ceremony?"

"She's not Catholic?"

"No, and neither is Mr. Payne. Did you hear he's Jewish? He doesn't look it. But he is a banker."

"Does that make him Jewish?"

"It's indicative."

"Was his cousin—what was his name—was he Jewish?"

"Tall Jim? I don't believe so. He attended our church, so I don't think he was Jewish. Mr. Payne doesn't attend church, not regularly, not, at least, for church's sake."

"I hear he began attending on your account."

"Did he? I don't remember. If it was on my account, then he was wasting his time."

"An odd thing for a preacher's daughter to say: 'wasting his time' going to church."

"That's not what I meant."

"It's what you said."

Mattie perched her brow. Folks said she perched her brow when she was readying for a fight. "I didn't realize this was an argument. You probably heard, you allude as much, that Mr. Payne asked me to marry him. That was a waste of the breath he put into the words. Any attempt of his to capture my attentions . . ." Mattie slid back in her chair and waved off her thoughts.

"I'm not going to argue," Sheriff Brick said. "Heaven knows it'd be a waste of time to argue with you. I've not known you long, but you're the most persistent arguer I've met. You're very good at it. A man should know better than to argue with you. It's indicative."

"Indicative? Indicative of what?" Mattie's cheeks crimsoned.

Sheriff Brick smiled. "You're the one and only Matilda Schroeder."

"I want to speak about something else." There was a pause and then Mattie said "do you ever think about unsavory possibilities, how life may have been different had not Providence intervened?" She spoke with airs that deepened her voice, as perhaps a proud duchess would speak to a layman.

Sheriff Brick sighed. "Providence either kept me in my chains or set me free from them. I might never have been here had not Providence intervened. Being a slave is living a master's bidding. While there may be life in spite of a forced resignation of will and personhood, slavery is evil and irredeemable.

"We lived west of Yazoo City, north of Vicksburg, near Panther Swamp and the Yazoo River. Loess Manor, it was called." Sheriff Brick looked far away. "We dreamed of freedom. I'd have run away if my," he waved his arm, "if only I would have faced consequences, I'd have run away. At any attempt, the master paid suffering and even death on those left behind. I didn't care about me, but my mother and sisters would've suffered if I'd fled. What's it matter if a man loses his own soul? The cost for others is too much to bear.

"We heard bits and pieces of the war. We prayed and hoped. Then the master and his thugs were gone. We didn't know where they went. Troops in blue uniforms marched up the walk and told us we were all free by order of the Emancipation Proclamation. Naturally, we were ecstatic. I wanted to do whatever I could to secure my freedom. That's why I enlisted in the Army. I didn't love the Army, I didn't know what it was, not really—and how can you love something you don't know about really? But I'd have done anything to secure freedom for all men like me.

"Then I became Providence for others as those soldiers had been for me. Yes, in answer to your question, I often think about the drudgery of my bondage, and I thank God I'm free. Could he not have loosed me sooner? I'm free now, which is more than others before me could say. How wickedness could be legal, condoned and perpetuated by our government, is beyond me. I can only believe that all men might be evil if you give them the chance. Providence has breathed a new breath on this nation. I aim to carry that banner forth. It's not lost on me that I uphold law and that, given other circumstances, law is what kept me in my chains. Does dressed-up injustice invalidate true justice? We cannot ensure truth without pledging our skins to its proclamation."

Mattie's face flushed while Sheriff Brick talked. His face had flushed, too, magnificent, reflecting a lamp's flickering light and another brilliant night sky beyond the jail porch and Racida and Colorado Territory.

"Unsavory possibilities brought me west. I want to fight against complacent brutality and see it never takes root because it is a seed of destruction. There are fulcrum moments when one man's voice and actions can carry us to good or evil. If I can stand and assert for the good, I will count myself a successful man, lawman or otherwise. I couldn't act before to really sway. I'll never forget the capture and murder of an innocent man accused of being a runaway slave—"

Bang!

Mattie and Sheriff Brick stiffened as a gun fired in the distance. They turned to each other, focused, and listened to the dying echoes. They rose and sounded alarm.

CHAPTER 10

RACIDA'S MAIN STREET BENT SLIGHTLY, with the saloon at its crux, so that the road at one end of town was not visible from the other. It was not known why there was a bend; there was no need for one. One end of the street featured dilapidated buildings, including the old Pioneer Bank. That part of town was called "Old Town."

Though it had not been long since its robbery and abandonment, the old Pioneer Bank had fallen into significant disrepair. The smashed window by the front door had been boarded up. Wood strips had been nailed onto the heavy oak front door. The building's white paint had begun to fleck, exposing the wood underneath, which grayed uncoated.

Adjacent to the bank was an often-empty accountant's shop and an abandoned general store. Across the street stood a seldom-used lumber yard, which was little more than a pole barn.

Chaps and Fanny rode in darkness into the half-empty barn to secure their Sorrels. Only Indie, hidden in shadows, saw them. He sat with his Spencer rifle and watched them dismount. Chaps had a long rope looped around his shoulder. The rope had an iron hook affixed at one end.

After the outlaws slipped out of the open warehouse to the rear of the old bank, Indie approached the hitched horses and hummed low so they would know it was a man and not a wild animal. They had heard his whistle before. He grabbed their saddle cinches and unhooked them. He listened and heard a dull noise from across the street.

They must be anchoring that rope Chaps wore to the upper window on the back side of the building. They'll climb in, no doubt, saving watch and noise by entering through the fortified front.

Indie walked to the front of the pole barn to survey the empty street and the quiet old Pioneer Bank. He walked into the illuminating moonlight. He wore moccasins and ran to the building's rear. There, a glassless window looked out from the upper living quarters. He reached out, feeling along the building's shiplap siding, and found the hook-secured rope that Chaps and Fanny had used to climb and enter the bank through the top floor.

He secured his rifle and pulled the rope taut. He rose slowly, elbows bending, and planted his moccasins on the wall. He slipped. He stopped. He held his breath. He had not made much noise, but it had been noise. He counted on his lips and resumed. He reached the second-floor window and climbed inside.

Physical feats are complicated by accomplishing them slowly and quietly. The smoothness with which Indie executed his maneuvers manifested excellent capability of body. He was even muscular underneath his too-big clothes.

The weather-worn, dirty apartment was bare except for an old bed topped by a straw mattress. Furniture in this part of the world seldom went unclaimed because every finished item had to be shipped in or laboriously created. Yet no one had risked using a haunted bed. Uncle Elbe had died in it.

Indie listened to knocking crowbars that pried boards from their nailed supports on the ground floor below. And he heard Fanny and Chaps whispering harshly to each other.

"Only a bag?" Chaps said.

"There was much more before." Fanny said. "We put much more than a bag—" he slammed his fist into the floor.

"We're looking in the right spot?"

Indie smiled. He drew his watch from his pocket and rubbed it between his right thumb and fingers. Outside, the moonlit night drew its star-spangled curtain across the sky. He picked up the rope and held its terminating hook out of the window. The brothers talked muffled about the lack of expected bounty. Indie listened and shook his head, drawing the rope back in. He wedged it against the sill where it had been wedged. He walked to the stairs and stared to their black bottom. He drew his rifle and rubbed its steel with his thumb. He looked at the bed then walked to it and slammed it on its side.

The outlaws paused their hushed work.

"Did you hear that?" Chaps said.

Fanny spit tobacco and swore.

"I suppose one of us should investigate."

"You volunteering?" Fanny said. "I think you'd be a perfect volunteer."

Chaps cocked his Remington-Beals revolver, he and Fanny both had one, and walked around the counter to the stairs. Each step creaked under his weight. The night was cold, but he sweated. He leaned over the landing and looked into the apartment. Window light outlined itself on the floor but obscured the rest of the dark room. Chaps held his breath and trained his eyes.

Bang!

Indie fired—the same shot that startled Sheriff Brick and Mattie and eventually the entire town. Chaps fell backwards and collapsed.

Fanny startled at the report and ducked behind the counter. He exhaled, rose, and seeing nothing, crossed the room to the stairs. "Chaps." His voice quivered. Chaps answered with a groan. Fanny walked up the stairs, and then peered around the wall into the upper room. He shook. He stopped and gasped. Indie stared back at him, gun drawn.

"Hello, Fanny." He cocked the repeater's lever, ejecting the spent bullet.

Fanny screamed. He fell backward down the stairs with a head-leading summersault. Whether fueled by adrenaline or madness, he picked up his distorted and bruised limbs and ran at the front door. It crashed opened, nailed-up door boards condemning what half-hearted craftsmanship had put them there because few trespass where no one wants to be. Fanny fell forward and rolled onto the porch. He stood and ran to the warehouse and his horse.

Uncinched, Fanny fell off with his saddle. But his Sorrel was steadier than he was. He re-mounted bareback and rode out of town. He could see the lantern lights of a gathering mob not yet close enough to illuminate him. He rode away hunched on his horse and covered by thick night.

Indie walked over to Chaps and knelt beside him. Chaps was breathing a sort of moan. His eyes were closed; he was unconscious.

In me dwelleth no good thing. It should've been Fanny here. You've that farm you talk about whenever you've the opportunity. There's hope in that you don't realize. Will you go there?

Indie drew a letter from his shirt and tucked it into Chaps' pocket.

"Give yourself up," a voice said from the bottom of the stairs. It was the bounty hunter. He had stolen into the old bank after Fanny's flight.

"Sheriff?" Indie said.

"No. But I might as well be. I'm your reckoning."

"There can be only one."

"A guy's got to be horror itself to send a fellow out of here like a madman."

Indie turned slowly to address the bounty hunter below. "You must be a Marshal or a bounty hunter. And since you haven't identified yourself, other than as my reckoning, I'd say you're a bounty hunter. Besides, I've never met a Marshal in this part of the country. And your voice, I *know* you."

"Perceptive. I *know* you, too. I've been looking for you. There's quite a bounty on your head."

Indie smiled in the darkness. "Dead or alive? Yes, I think you've been looking for me for quite some time."

The bounty hunter drew his Colt Dragoon revolver. Sheriff Brick and Mattie burst into the bank. Indie bolted away from Chaps and the top of the stairs as the bounty hunter fired up at him. The hunter rushed for the stairs after the explosions, but Sheriff Brick shoved him into the wall and stepped in his way. The sheriff was a big man, much bigger than the bounty hunter. The hunter had a wild look in his eyes visible even in the darkness, but he could not run over the sheriff.

"No one takes the law into their own hands in my town," Sheriff Brick said. "Justice will be done. And I am justice here."

The bounty hunter stared at the sheriff. Sheriff Brick turned and looked at the dark stairs. Gathering lanterns outside brightened the bank.

"Hold them," Sheriff Brick shouted to his deputy, Clovis. The mob met the deputy's instructions with murmured, drunken disapproval.

"What good's a mob?" Sheriff Brick said to Mattie.

"Good men can be an overwhelming force against evil," Mattie said.

"Can be." Sheriff Brick snorted. He turned and raised his voice, filling the bank. "Who's there?"

He grabbed his Colt Army revolver from his holster. He ascended the stairs followed by Mattie and the bounty hunter. Sheriff Brick overstepped the unconscious Chaps and glided into the upstairs apartment. He scanned the room. He walked to the tipped-over bed Indie had used for cover. He kicked it over and rushed behind: nothing. The room was empty. At the open door, the bounty hunter cursed.

"He's still alive," Mattie said. She held Chaps' arm to check his pulse. "He needs a doctor."

"Is Bludegats home?" Sheriff Brick said. He returned to the pair.

The bounty hunter allowed the sheriff to pass, then he also surveyed the empty apartment. He spit and pushed past Mattie and Sheriff Brick who had huddled over Chaps on the crowded landing. He stormed down the stairs and outside.

Clovis could not hold back the citizenry which rushed into the bank as the bounty hunter exited. Men filtered up the stairs. Sheriff Brick enlisted volunteers to take Chaps to the home of Dr. Bludegats. Mattie was one of several who hoisted him away.

A cheer rose from the main room below. The mob had found the bag that Fanny and Chaps had earlier pulled from a hole in the floor. Some shouted to open it. A thick throng slowed Sheriff Brick in joining the downstairs assembly. He directed Clovis to grab the bag, still unopened, so he could assess it.

"Hole!"

"There's a hole?"

"The rug's been peeled back."

"The floor's been peeled back."

"It's sure nifty."

"A hole in the floor!"

"Well-disguised."

"Is the hole big enough for a man?" Sheriff Brick asked amid the filtering exclamations. Men squeezed thick between him and the floor hole. He tried to look into it over the gaggle.

Someone said "no, couldn't fit a man," and Sheriff Brick grunted. He procured a lantern and returned to the upper room to search it with a handful of curious revelers. They watched his methodical observation. He found nothing.

"Sheriff, Matilda found this on the fellow," a sheepish young man said. He produced the letter which Indie had shoved into Chaps' shirt pocket. "She said to give it to you."

"He was searched?"

"Yes, before they carried him to Bludegats'."

The paper was folded over a silver coin. Sheriff Brick held it up in the light then tossed it to an onlooker before examining the letter.

"Do you need someone to read for you, sheriff?" the rancher Wiley Pecker said, and he smiled.

"*Silver*. What're these markings?" the onlooker said, scrutinizing the coin.

"Spanish, I believe," Sheriff Brick said. "It's a piece of eight. You haven't seen one before? They're not uncommon, though they're not used for currency anymore. My old—well, I've seen them. Still, this one is older than any I've ever seen."

Sheriff Brick turned back to the letter. "This is a eulogy. It's unsigned." He put the paper in his pocket and grabbed the coin. He marched downstairs and asked about the bounty hunter.

"He stomped out of here like a cat in cold water," Clovis said. "Mattie's gone, too, to Bludegats'."

"I didn't ask about Mattie," Sheriff Brick said.

"You didn't need to." Clovis winked.

Sheriff Brick slapped Clovis and sent him to Dr. Bludegats'. Then he asked onlookers if the hole in the floor was big enough for a man to scurry into or hide in. They said it was. Sheriff Brick still clutched the money bag that had been drawn from the floor and the eulogy letter and coin from Indie. He turned to the room and relayed what he had seen, raising his precious props in demonstration.

"Unless you can get hold of that bounty hunter to see what he knows, I believe any productive work here is done for the evening. Tear apart this place if you will; no more is to be ascertained." Then he left the bank.

Chapter 11

After escorting Chaps to Dr. Bludegats' home, Mattie slipped into the night and the empty street. She glanced around and walked to the parsonage, which was dark and thus indicative that her heavy-sleeping father slept. She opened the door to the root cellar at the back of the house.

"I keep an extra candle down there," Mattie said, in a muffled voice. "If you're down there, can you light it?"

A snap of a match flickered a faint light, and then a glow warmed the cold. Mattie shivered. She ducked inside and closed the door over her.

Indie held the candle. His hard features cast shadows and his eyes gleamed. "You figure on coming down here in the dark by having this extra candle handy?"

"I told you I'd kill you if you ever came back to Racida," Mattie said. "Didn't you think I meant it?"

Indie nodded. "It wasn't up to me. Fanny and Chaps came back for the money in the old bank. I didn't want things to get out of hand, even if that meant dying by your hand."

"Money? You're talking about the robbery you masterminded!" Mattie shook her head. "We never caught your gang or recovered the money. You know that."

"I never told you. But the money never left town."

Mattie gaped. She curled her lips and pursed her jaw. "You'd better explain yourself, Indie Caloo."

"Didn't you miss me?"

Mattie gasped. Then she slapped Indie. She slapped him hard and over the small flame which danced on the wick. "Miss disappointment, betrayal, lies? You still don't know how to talk to a woman. I loved you for it once: pert and brash foolishness; I see it now." She caught her lip in her teeth.

"Are you going to tell me why Fanny and Chaps brought you here, about the money?"

"It never left. The old banker had a hiding place under the floor, hidden under a rug. We took the cash and gold and stowed it there, to hold for more unhurried removal. This ensured a quick getaway."

"The robbery was confusion and shooting. You're telling me it was a ruse?"

Indie nodded and chuckled. "You've got a strong arm. I liked that about you. You've got a strong brain, too, and you use it. Yes, it was a ruse, for the town and, more importantly, for the gang. I needed insurance.

"But I've stashed the money in a secret place now, where there's real treasure. I made a map to it, too, because what good's a treasure if no one is likely to find it? I'll not be alive forever, and probably shouldn't be alive now.

"I put the gang on hiatus so I could come back to Racida to get the money to put away for safekeeping. I came back and hid the money. Then I found you looking for me, and you told me to never come back to Racida. And I've been true to my word from then until now."

"I told you a lot of things. Not coming back to Racida is hardly what I remember as the most significant. As far as I can see, you're standing in your own lies, no matter how you sweet talk it. What did the people of Racida do to you? It's their money. You had no claim on it."

"I'm no different than a banker who shuts his doors and disappears everything inside. He does his work little by little. I just do my work more dramatically."

"Where's the honor in theft?"

"You didn't object to the other robberies."

"I was in love with you!" Mattie's eye dripped a tear. She fell back at her own outburst. She caught herself. "Yes, love, and how blinding it can be." She straightened her back. "There's no honor in theft, in outlawing. And yet, you returned for the money. 'A dog returns to its own vomit.'"

"It was more than the money. I was planning to return it. The money was insurance against the worst, against what has happened. Haven't you wondered about me since we last saw each other?"

Mattie shook her head. "No. When I walked away from you, I expected I'd never see you again. I'd hoped . . ." she paused. She smiled when she caught Indie leaning into her words. "I'd hoped you'd listen to me and never bother me or the people of Racida again. Didn't you tell me the same when you said we could never be together? I sought you out to chastise you for the callous brute you've become. You think I say 'I loved you' lightly? It burns my throat like vinegar to think that I ever said that. The best I could offer, all of me, you threw away like a rotten apple. No, I'm not done. You're evil."

"I'm not evil, Mattie," Indie interrupted. "You're right that I've done evil things. I'll not deny the truth in that. What man is without stain? But I am a new man now! I am God's man, on His mission.

"The gang mutinied. Roberts turned Fanny, Chaps, Slim, and even Duncan against me. I don't know how I'm alive. Divine resurrection, I think. But, oh, Duncan," Indie pushed the words out one at a time, "he is dead. They shot him, too."

Indie worked through Mattie's gasp. His jaw quivered. He waved his arm. "The matter at hand—the bank was empty tonight of its money. But the money's out there. I left a bag in the floor. I think I made out that Fanny and Chaps found it. In the bag are rocks and a riddle like I used to write. Follow the riddle to the map. Then follow the map to the money."

"You're giving me a treasure?"

"A map."

"Why not take me there now and we'll settle it?"

"There's more at work than that money. You need to *find* it."

Indie blew the candle out and darted past Mattie. She shuffled to block him but he brushed her aside. He opened the root cellar door and dropped it back against its frame. A heavy thud followed and shook dirt from the door onto Mattie.

Mattie gathered herself and lunged at the door. It moaned. Several lunges shook free the source of the thud: a rock that Indie had quickly slid on top before fleeing. She rushed out. He was gone.

Mattie grunted and walked to the jail, where candlelight crept beneath a shade. The mob was dispersing from the old Pioneer Bank and Mattie watched Clovis and a group of ten men file into the saloon. She composed herself and pulled at her hair before entering the jail. Sheriff Brick had brewed coffee. He sat at his desk examining the evidence of the letter and bag.

"What're your conclusions?" she said.

He started and spilled some of the hot liquid. "I thought I'd locked the door." Sheriff Brick wiped the coffee off of himself. "It's late. How's the prisoner?"

"Prisoner?"

"Yes! He's under my care, officially, until he's cleared, and that makes him a prisoner."

"He's about the same as when you last saw him. He might die from the wound. But Mrs. Bludegats will do all she can."

"You mean Dr. Bludegats."

Mattie smiled. "He'll probably do what he can, too."

"I think he wasn't at the old Pioneer Bank to be shot at," Sheriff Brick said. "That may be an obvious statement. But I have my theory and I want to talk it out with you since you're the only one here to talk it out with."

"A matter of convenience."

"I value your opinion, too, of course." Sheriff Brick smiled at Mattie. She raised an eyebrow and he dropped his smile. "I think that he was there to get something. We know that because the floor was open. We recovered this bag," Sheriff Brick highlighted the bag, "and the letter you recovered and sent back to me." Sheriff Brick held up the letter. "It seems that the prisoner's name is Chaps. And what's more, it sounds like he's a member of the notorious Caloo Gang! We found a saddle on the ground and a horse with an unhooked saddle on it at the lumber yard. So it seems there were three people at the bank before we got there."

Mattie blanched.

"This letter is interesting; it ends:

> The certainty of human nature is that there will always be high exploits and abhorrent decay. It is when these are paired together that societal plagues are unleashed. Chaps was just one member of a recent and noted plague, though his chief wrong was to not cut from himself the millstone hung around his neck. He was a good man, even if the law cannot see it that way. Perhaps that impartial stare is for the best, to warn other good men and keep them from going astray. Justice may be blind, but her executors' eyes are not closed. This is as far as anyone could plead for fair treatment for a guilty man.

"Guilty of what?" Sheriff Brick said. "I think there's more to this than robbery. And the bag we found? There's nothing in it but rocks and another note, a riddle, I suppose."

Sheriff Brick opened the bag recovered from the bank floor hole. He pulled out a note and handed it to Mattie.

"For the good people of Racida, if you find this:

> Just ask around
> For one, at least,
> Knows drinking ground
> Cache, and there will be the key
> To monetary re-discovery."

"What do you think it means?" Sheriff Brick asked Mattie when she looked up from reading the note.

Mattie played on her lip with her teeth. She had driven more than one man wild with such play. She said it was a habitual repose of contemplation, but older church women said it exemplified Mattie's poor manners, if not her unholy character.

"Chaps was shot," Sheriff Brick continued. "and he received a personal eulogy, so we know that Chaps and the shooter were acquainted. They knew each other. Do you think the man the bounty hunter saw was Indie Caloo? And suppose they knew each other, too, the bounty hunter and Caloo— then that means Indie Caloo, *the* Indie Caloo, was just in front of us tonight!

"The bounty hunter maybe knew what this was all about. There was someone at the top of the stairs for him to shoot. And Chaps and this letter prove it. That bounty hunter is reckless, not a maniac. But do you think I can find him? He's disappeared. This whole business is odd. You wouldn't know anything more?"

"Why do you ask me?"

Sheriff Brick reddened. "It's indelicate." He sipped his coffee and tried to speak again. "Rumors, you remember our conversation the other night?"

Mattie straightened herself and leaned into her answer. "If you're asking me to help you in this case, I'll help you. If you want to know the truth, I'll tell you. But I'm not an open book, Solomon."

Sheriff Brick thanked her for her kindness. He excused himself for any perceived insinuation and said he thought the bounty hunter would be the best source to answer for the night's business. Mattie said it was late and she left the jail. After she left, Sheriff Brick repeated the words "an open book" and sipped his coffee.

"Drinking ground cache," Mattie said to herself as she reached home. She let go of the front door handle and walked back to the main street, catching the shadows. She stole to the back of the saloon. Mattie listened to the revelry inside where Clovis commanded conversation which speculated the very worst and most ostentatious of the night's events. She groped the foundation until she found a loose rock, which she pulled out. She reached into its cavity and pulled out a paper. She replaced the rock and went home with her discovery.

PART III
AMBUSH

CHAPTER 12

THE CONSOLIDATED TELEGRAPH SYSTEM, ESSENTIALLY Western Union, transformed American communication because of its unsurpassed accuracy, reliability, and most importantly, speed of service. But the telegraph cannot physically transfer mail, goods, and people; and unlike in the eastern United States, trains only provide a limited patchwork for western travel and transportation, even still as the continent has been bridged. Besides the individual and horse, stagecoaches and wagons, often operated by small commercial operations, provide the intermediary infrastructure. Their racing teams pull Concord coaches and less comfortable wagons filled with necessities for rural towns, moving commerce with often remarkable consistency.

These four-wheeled contraptions are more like clockwork than anything else in the desert steppe except for the passing of the sun; and for that, they are unnatural to it. Wheeled dust billows and settles onto soft ridge lines of rolling hills and massive scenes; it obscures red canyon rock that lies under open-handed sky; it glides over and along rutted gullies and an occasional deep blue or brown snake of water. Wagons and coaches wrestle with these enemy obstacles that were befriended by the West's gentler civilizing predecessors, whose news and goods to bear were already there, in the wild lands: countries of their own.

Racida's bounty was enriched and plundered each day around 3:00 o'clock thanks to the industriousness of a Mr. Alfred Guilfoyle, who had brought west a sizable portion of his New York family's trapping riches to start a stagecoach and wagon business, the "Guilfoyle Line," as folks came to call it. Unique and stubborn, he bucked increasingly common contracting with Wells Fargo, which, along with its Overland Mail Company, had constructed an empire of movement. Guilfoyle liked to say he "would be damned to be a Wells Fargo man!" And though his operation was inefficient—many said there was no way it could be profitable—he nevertheless maintained regional supremacy for organized transportation.

Arriving wagon materials were often raw goods though sometimes included finer things like teacups and revolvers. Racida's dusty streets promptly baptized arriving coach passengers. In turn, materials like grain and produce were loaded onto wagons, and passengers—criminals were the most common—shuffled into coaches.

Besides Racida, the Guilfoyle network served Stanchion and Cannonball Springs in the next valley over, both a considerable distance from Racida but near enough to each other. Guilfoyle hired out a station house and outfitted four swing stations between Racida and her "sister cities," the only American civilizations for many miles. Each populace asserted independence in every way except that folks in Stanchion and Racida were happy to send criminals to Judge Fickle's court in Cannonball Springs.

"Dangerous man. Stop. Send by coach. Stop. Trial set. Stop."

Sheriff Brick read Judge Fickle's answer regarding Chaps. "He doesn't waste time."

"That's a telegraph from Cannonball Springs?" the telegrapher said.

Sheriff Brick raised his eyebrows. Some said he raised his eyebrows when he felt awkward. Others, the telegrapher being one, said Sheriff Brick raised his eyebrows when he didn't have anything to say.

"They certainly *don't* waste time up there," the telegrapher continued. "Yes, sir, he gets right down to it. The judge lines them up and sentences them and lines them up and hangs them." He giggled. "I heard tell they strung up four horse thieves two days ago, and they've got another six waiting, and but for the gallows needing repair, they'd be six feet under, too."

"'Let judgment run down like waters, and righteousness like a mighty stream,'" Sheriff Brick said.

"Damned efficient. And I say good, don't keep rascals around. You know what happens when rascals is kept around? Ask them in Santa Fe what happens when rascals is kept around. Did I ever tell you, sheriff, about the time I went to Santa Fe?"

Sheriff Brick did not reply.

"It was about fifteen years ago now, I reckon—my, how time flies!—and it was me and the missis there for a fortnight."

"Don't you tell him that blasted story about how you got pickpocketed in Santa Fe!" the telegrapher's wife called from the next room. "The money fell out of your pants and onto the ground because you had a hole in them. There weren't no pickpockets at all."

The telegrapher blushed and sucked in his lips and cheeks, which made him look like a fish beneath his wiry gray beard.

The sheriff relaxed his face, moved his hand across his forehead, and looked down again at the message.

"Send a reply," Sheriff Brick said. "Can you reply? Say, 'As soon as prisoner heals.' No, 'yes, when prisoner heals.' There, four words."

"Ten word message minimum rate, so it makes no difference—four, five words, up to ten words if you were inclined. Ten word message minimum rate. Bill the usual?"

Sheriff Brick nodded. "Much obliged." He turned to leave.

"You know, if you were looking to send that vagabond you've got, that prisoner, if you wanted to send him to Cannonball Springs today, the coach comes in at three o'clock promptly. It always comes at that time now."

"You know that Guilfoyle started that coach line when he first came? It's a mess, but before him, it was an even bigger mess, and to try to get something shipped out or in," the telegrapher whistled. "No regularity. Sometimes you'd get a coach or a wagon that'd come in the middle of the night and there'd be no one to meet it, so they'd just throw everyone or everything onto the ground and keep moving. I had a typewriter they did that to. And then it was too banged up to type. I had to buy a new one in Santa Fe.

"Now the coach service is prompt and punctual, always three o'clock. It's at least that. But it's not very profitable, they say. I'm no expert, but I think it's Guilfoyles's disposition to gamble and take drink, and especially take drink, that's causing him to falter. My cousin said he saw him—" another interruptive accosting by the telegrapher's wife rendered him red and fish-faced and silent.

Sheriff Brick nodded. "Much obliged." He walked out.

CHAPTER 13

FANNY HAD RIDDEN FROM RACIDA and the botched robbery of the old Pioneer Bank in a furious full gallop away from town, and then toward the first rising of a steep and impassable rocky ascent. A cloudy sky hid his advance. It would have been hard to track him, even if the law had been in pursuit. No one had pursued him.

It is dangerous—especially in vast, open land—to kill a horse by riding it too hard. Fanny had more than once said he was proud to be known for riding his mounts hard. He had shot lamed steeds or had run them dead, always after another one had been secured. As it was, he did not have a spare horse on which to rely, and the Sorrel tired. Fanny cursed and allowed the sweaty animal to slow. He pounded his fist into his hand.

Fanny sheltered behind boulders. It was a cold night but he did not light a fire. He slept on his saddle but not well. He was awake and shivering when dawn began to break. He saddled his horse.

"Damn, Chaps. But I've got to go for him. He'd go for me."

When Fanny reached Racida again, the sun had risen over a bright morning. The town, typically quiet in mornings, was abuzz with news of the previous night. All manner of folks crowded outside the jail. Preacher Schroeder and Mattie stood near the front lines, which improved the crowd's behavior almost as much as the two armed men that Sheriff Brick had asked to keep peace at the jail while Clovis guarded Chaps and he visited the telegraph office.

Fanny shuffled in behind some rough-looking fellows as Sheriff Brick reached the jail. Fanny leaned his head and spit at the ground; the black mucus struck the boots of an oblivious cowhand.

Sheriff Brick slowed as he reached the jail. He surveyed the crowd, from which emanated haphazard questions about re-discovered money.

Sheriff Brick took out the telegram paper he had received and showed it to the crowd.

"I received this this morning. It's a message from the honorable Judge Fickle in Cannonball Springs."

The crowd laughed. Sheriff Brick furrowed his brow and continued.

"It says the prisoner is dangerous. I replied that I mean to send him for trial when he is well and ready. Dr. Bludegats and his wife are seeing to the recovery."

Someone jeered. The crowd laughed. Sheriff Brick blushed and clenched his jaw.

"I bet you're not here for an update on the prisoner, though. Well, there's no money. It was a liar who said there was any, except this piece of eight that hardly serves any of us." He pulled out the piece of eight that had been folded in Chaps' eulogy, and he flicked it into the throng. Two men reached for it and it fell into a woman's hands.

All at once, the crowd hurled questions at Sheriff Brick. He walked into the jail and came out with the bag recovered from the floor of the old Pioneer Bank.

"This bag was all that was recovered last night. Inside," he dumped the bag out; and rocks fell, "there was a letter, too."

He read the riddle and then posted the letter on the jail wall where notices were nailed for display. The silent crowd watched him.

Fanny grinned as he walked away from the gathering, which began to crowd around the posted letter. He bought tobacco at the general store. The general store manager, with his right eyebrow raised, asked Fanny who he was. Fanny paid and left the store without answering.

The general store manager had developed a reputation for falsely raising alarm with townsfolk. He had mistaken persons as suspicious when they had only been guilty of not associating with him. After Fanny left, he discussed "that peculiar man" with a housewife who bought pickled beets and salt. She told him he should not cry wolf.

Fanny paused outside the telegraph office to scoop some tobacco into his lip. He overheard the operator talking to a dusty cowboy with hunched shoulders, crossed arms, and a hat too big for his head. It was impossible not to overhear the telegraph operator if you were close to his vicinity.

"That criminal won't be here too long. You know how efficient they are up in Cannonball Springs—Judge Fickle is marvelous. I'd vote for him for whatever he ran for, except maybe against Robert E. Lee for president, if the general ever ran for President. They all esteem General Grant, and why so? Military genius, magnanimous? No, there's no finer man than General Lee.

"Judge Fickle is the second finest man, I think—the finest man in these parts, surely, and the second finest man in all of America. His booming voice weakens my knees, and I'm not even a criminal. Have you ever been to one of his proceedings? Magnificent. Magnificent!

"And he sent a message to the sheriff just this morning to send the prisoner—that horrible man they dragged from the bank last night—the judge said to send him immediately. He's a dangerous man. From the way it sounds, talking to him earlier, Sheriff Brick means to send him when he's well, at least, that's what I suggested. He really should send him today. Whenever he does, I hope he doesn't send him alone, two guards minimum. The sheriff should go himself, if you want to know what I think. The sheriff should go!

"Those Guilfoyle coaches might be timely but they're not secure. I heard once they sent a horse thief from Stanchion to Cannonball Springs, only to have him sprung by his brother a couple of miles from town. What kind of security is that?" The telegrapher's wife yelled and he fell silent.

"That's it," Fanny said low.

And he walked away from the telegraph station. He bought a room at the hotel with a view of the jail. Over the next few days, he would make a careful pillage of the town: securing liquor and additional tobacco, stealing ammunition, and buying a new horse.

CHAPTER 14

CHAPS, RECOVERING AT DR. BLUDEGATS', had not drunk or eaten anything since his capture and bullet-removal surgery. Dr. Bludegats had mostly refused to see him.

"I don't doctor ruffians," he had said. "They're God's to take or make well. He'll make a recovery, or I'm no doctor. And who's going to pay me for it? Ay yai yai, medicine isn't cheap, it's no charity for me. And for what, so he can bank rob again? Ay yai yai."

"How's he doing?" Sheriff Brick asked Clovis who was posted outside of Chaps' room.

"Doctor says he'll live," Clovis said. "He seems to be in a good amount of pain though, so it's not all bad." He smiled. Everyone said Clovis was sadistic.

Sheriff Brick told Clovis to go cool off. He grabbed his hat, whistled, and walked outside. Clovis often cooled off in the saloon.

"To what can I ascribe this visit?" Mrs. Bludegats asked Sheriff Brick when he entered Chaps' room. Mrs. Bludegats, who many said made a better doctor than her husband, continued to attend Chaps despite her husband's reluctant objections.

"Recovering?" Sheriff Brick said. He gestured at Chaps.

She nodded. "He was this morning, too, remember? What time did you come in to look after him? He'll be back on his feet in a few days I'd say, though he'll have to take it easy even then."

"He doesn't have much to look forward to but a trial."

"You're fixing to send him to Judge Fickle?"

"Yes, the judge telegraphed this morning."

Mrs. Bludegats nodded to Chaps. "Then he's only to go from frying pan to fire. A hanging awaits."

"Justice awaits."

"Is it just to hang a man?"

"Judge Fickle will see to the matter."

"His hands are the only hands that can twist the hangman's noose into any trespass. The noose awaits this man. Judge Fickle's hanged men for much less than trying to rob a bank."

"I think you're wrong about that," Sheriff Brick said. "We must submit to authority and law, or what else are we?"

"Law and authority are no good in the hands of evil men. Maybe you don't see it for ideals and how things should be. *You're* a good lawman. Fickle isn't your equal."

Sheriff Brick shook his head. He watched Chaps breathe, now easy and rhythmic. "You've done a good job. I can see he's mending. Thank you for your work. I might be the only one to say so."

"As always, you're welcome, sheriff. Might I inquire when you plan on shipping him out? Judge Fickle isn't patient."

"Depends more on him than me. I'm hoping we'll be rid of him in a few days. But I won't send him along until he'll take the journey well. There's no reason to rush him to trial, especially as he's laid up."

"What'd the judge say?" the bounty hunter interjected. He had entered the doctor's house as Clovis had left, and had crept into the room, just catching Sheriff Brick and Mrs. Bludegats' conversation.

Sheriff Brick turned to face him.

"What'd the judge say?" the bounty hunter said again before Sheriff Brick could speak. "No lawman should think of himself more than he is and let his badge go to his head, least of all a lawman like you."

"Are you a lawman? I execute the law, not criminals. I'm sending him along for judgment, but it'd be execution to do so before he's able to endure the journey. It's a rough road to Cannonball Springs."

"It's all rough roads around here. What's it to you if he dies? He'll die anyway, the judge will see to that."

Sheriff Brick shook his head again. He turned to Mrs. Bludegats and excused himself and the bounty hunter. They walked outside and into a narrow, excluded alley running between the Bludegats' house and a livery.

"Perhaps you're unaware of how I work," Sheriff Brick said. "While I wear this badge, it doesn't matter much how I feel, I've got a duty to perform. I'm an instrument of the law, an apparatus. And as such," Sheriff Brick grabbed the bounty hunter and threw him against the livery wall, "I can't settle personal grievances." He pinned the bounty hunter against the wood siding with his left forearm against his chest and neck and his right hand dug into the bounty hunter's chest. "Tell me what you're up to and who you took aim against at the bank last night."

The bounty hunter looked stunned. He laughed, gagging, as Sheriff Brick's eyes flashed. "I've—heard—of—your—reputation." He gasped each word. Then *click*.

Sheriff Brick lowered his eyes. He relaxed his choke pin and allowed the bounty hunter to slide back to the ground. He backed away. The bounty hunter held a cocked Derringer pistol. He coughed and rubbed his neck.

"Intuitive, exacting, hard but fair—your reputation proceeds you, sheriff, every man's does. But you're a hell of a lot bigger and stronger than they say.

"I'm more of a drifter myself. We're in the same business, you and I; but I exact justice discriminately; I get paid more; and I can settle personal grievances, which I do. It doesn't matter how I get my man. It matters that I get him."

"And where's that line?"

The bounty hunter laughed. "Line, sheriff?"

"How we measure will be measured back to us."

"I ascribe to church jargon when I'm in church. You'll kindly stay out of my way." The bounty hunter swore. "You won't stop me again from getting my man. That's who I took aim against, and you'll not stop me from getting him." He un-cocked his pistol and put it away.

"Who were those men last night?"

The bounty hunter smiled. "There were three of them. One you have; two escaped, one an inconsequential maniac and the other," the bounty hunter smiled and rasped his voice, "the other one is mine." His eyes sparkled. "I've been following him for a while now."

"Indie Caloo?"

The bounty hunter's smile faded. "You've got to be careful of him. He could've easily killed us all. He should've killed that prisoner of yours. The only reason he didn't is because he didn't want to. And that's what's got me worried. You've got a town to worry about here. Why don't you let me worry about him?"

He turned and walked away. He shouted back, "Don't get in my way, sheriff. Don't get in my way."

Later, Sheriff Brick could not find the bounty hunter. No one had seen him since the morning; no one knew where he was.

CHAPTER 15

AFTER LEAVING THE GANG AT the crossroads, Roberts changed his route and began to head north instead of west and to Cannonball Springs. Though less heedless than Fanny of his mount's limits, he was in many ways a more ruthless horseman. It was all Slim could do to keep eyes on his boss and not be seen by him. He did his utmost to remain subtle. Roberts seemed hellbent on his intentions.

"It's open country he's heading to," Slim said low to his Appaloosa. "Who's he fixing to meet?"

Roberts met cowhands, a couple small groups a day. They flocked to him, then rode off after short or long conversations.

"This is Mormon Hyram's territory," Slim said. "And those are his pokes. What's their business with Roberts?"

Each day, the land opened up more, a large valley rimmed by rising rocks, and it was good for grazing cattle. Sage brush dotted the landscape of easy grass. Rain was the sparsest ingredient for green health; what little fell, fell from higher ground and found its way into the sod or snaking paths, which eventually gathered together and turned into arroyos. But everything was dry in fall.

Slim was not much of a tracker, yet he maintained Roberts' trail, catching prints from his horse in the dust of several dry creek beds. The path the outlaw king traced graced nearer to the western slopes of this undulating, thick prairie.

On the third day of his tracking, Slim had fallen far behind Roberts. Slim crested a bank and hill and stopped. He surveyed the expanse, empty except for a distant dark mass of cattle and the almost imperceptible figure of Roberts riding alone.

"This is the devil's land. And there he rides."

The ground stirred behind him like a rattlesnake. Slim shouted and spurred his horse. It ran until it was tired, but he spurred it again. His dash spurred a quick path to the west and near the rise of the land. He did not spur when the horse slowed again to a more reasonable pace. He was sweating more than the Appaloosa and breathing hard. He reined it short before a hill.

"Sure as hell there's spirits here! What did Indie used to say about the Pueblo? Or was it Comanche?" Slim swore, then muttered Roberts' name, and looked around. He saw nothing, no one. He eyed a summit high on a ridge which commanded a dominant view. Slim clicked and the Appaloosa began to climb. He rode until coming to the ledge he had spied. He dismounted as the sky began to purple with sunset.

He looked east and saw the cattle again. "There's a few hands on the outer edge to the southeast. I would've ridden up on them if I'd kept my trail earlier. Premonition, thank you, spirits.

"It's strange—such a large herd and so few riders. Mormon Hyram—if those are his cattle, which I think they are—he needs eight hands at least to control that many head. There must be at least three, four thousand. I certainly saw more than the few I see now with the cattle. Something isn't right."

A creek, similar to others he had ridden through that day, folded the land. He followed it with his eyes from the herd to where it met another, and then he saw a small dugout. Faint smoke rose from the chimney. Maybe a dozen horses, not quite individually distinguishable from that distance, were hitched or grazed in a makeshift corral. Light filtered from the dugout's windows.

Slim shivered. The sun had lowered. It was getting dark and cold. Who can tell what gives a man courage? Forgetting fear is a sure way, and whether too curious to be scared, a desire to be warm, or some other reason, Slim rode down and then sneaked to the dugout. He crouched below a window.

Cattle branding's roots delve as deep in time as the pyramids of ancient Egypt. There is no surer mark of ownership than an owner's brand burned indelibly into an animal's hide. Conquistadors brought branding to the Americas with their animals and husbandry traditions. No matter where the stock roams, an owner's brand is an essential distinguishing mark. A brand is as much of a guarantee a cattleman can secure. It ensures continuity throughout life and, most importantly, until death. Brands ensure who gets paid when herds are rounded up together to be driven east and transformed from bovine to beef, from investment to payoff.

The brands of Mexican ranchers mark their cattle with curlicues and adornments. Simpler American brands incorporate initials to improve owner recognition. Branding's widespread adoption highlights its cost-effective ease to effect and difficulty to alter. A successful rustler must alter brands well enough so their original design cannot be discerned.

And this was the thrust of the dugout conversation that escaped to Slim through the building's ill-fitting window. The indistinguishable speakers spoke loudly, even shouting.

"The 'H's' thick belt is a dead giveaway, a dead giveaway."

"Beehive's what does it. Hyram's the only big Mormon rancher in these parts."

"It's impossible to change the brand."

"We won't never trick an astute examination."

"Couldn't pull one over on the law."

"Any look at those cattle and they'd know they're Hyram's, square."

"He's too many head."

"Three thousand."

"No, four."

"Five at least."

"He's got two roundups a summer; seven thousand head or my name's not —."

"There's no veteran cattleman doesn't know Hyram's brand."

"Got to be another way."

"We'll get caught, sure."

"My neck ain't right for hanging."

"I'm not asking," a voice boomed. It was Roberts. Slim's eyes widened when he heard him

"We're taking. And if any man wants to leave because he's uncomfortable with getting his hands dirty or he's grown a damned conscience, I'm not standing in his way."

The room paused. Then a rider said they'd all be damned if they threw in their lot with Roberts, and then he opened the door to leave.

Bang! Bang! Bang!

Slim saw blood and flesh fly in the open-door beam of illuminated darkness. The body fell forward into the dirt.

"Anyone else?" Roberts said. Slim shook. He watched three riders emerge to carry the dead man off. Roberts began again inside the dugout.

Slim crawled from the building and skirted the light from the window. He stood and ran to a clump of reeds near the creek.

"What was that?" one of the body-carriers said, stopping. "We should check it out!"

Another body-carrier swore. "It's an animal, no doubt. Let's go. He's heavy."

"That wasn't no animal. If it was, it was running hard when it hit those reeds. And it's big, whatever it was. That had to be a man."

"Who'd be out here?" the third body-carrier said. "There's no one besides us"

"How the hell would I know?"

The men dropped their body, cocked their Remington pistols, and searched the reeds. There was not much to search. Slim crawled to the creek. A long, dry summer had taken its toll; only a little water remained and mud.

Then Slim ran. His boot sank and stuck, then his other boot. The men shouted at Slim but only one shot. Slim pulled his feet from his boots, leaving them in the mud, and splashed to the other bank and his horse.

He heard Roberts' voice cursing as he rode away. "We'll catch —!" Roberts did not finish what he tried to say. And it was the last thing Slim heard before his Appaloosa's hooves drowned out all other noise.

He awoke the next morning with cold feet. He looked at them, bare and muddy. He looked at his horse, which was lying down, saddled, next to him. The Appaloosa had a habit for lying down, earning it the nickname "Lazy." Slim refrained from using this moniker and shook his head at anyone who did. He defended Lazy by saying it was a trick horse from a traveling show. He also said he had bought the Appaloosa from cattle baron Charles Goodnight, or more spectacularly, that he had won the animal in a poker game with former Colorado Territory Governor William Gilpin, who was known, among other things, as a land speculator but not a gambler.

"Why you lie down, beats me." Slim moaned and grabbed his lower back as he sat up. "I'm stiff."

The Appaloosa jerked up on its belly, lurched, and rose, withers first then dock. It rocked its head and shivered.

"I wish I had your spirit. I feel terrible." He slid his hand over his face.

A voice startled Slim and Lazy: "Are you well?"

Slim screamed and dove forward into the dirt. His horse bolted a few feet, then turned to look at the speaker.

An Indian appeared from the sagebrush not ten yards from the prostrate outlaw. He laughed. "I might feel terrible, too, if I fell off my horse. Get up, I will not hurt you. I could have killed you. It was easy. But it is not why I am here. This should show you that I am peaceful?"

Slim rose. His dive had scraped him. But he did not bleed. "Who are you?"

The Indian extended his hand and smiled. "I am Inuna-Ina, that is, my people. *My* name, you would not remember." He smiled and waved his hand. "You call us Arapaho. I was a warrior. I fought white men like you once, though that was not our way. I am old, too old for fighting."

Slim rose and shook. The old Arapaho warrior laughed.

"What's your business with me?" Slim said.

"You rode furious. You stampeded near my camp. Then you fell off your horse. I want to ask you what your business is."

Slim rubbed his back and raised a brow. "Living."

The Indian raised a brow.

Slim continued, "I mean to say, my business is to not die. That's what I was about. I was riding for my life. Excuse me, but Roberts—it was his men trying to kill me—he hates Indians. He'd prefer to kill them all, to kill *you* all. And he about had me killed, his men anyway, and that's why I was riding hard.

"I must've fallen asleep." Slim swore. "My back is all kinds of sore. Did I land on something?"

"You said your killer, attempted killer, his name was Roberts?"

"Yes, mean cuss!"

"I knew a man named Roberts. He was in the militia, a captain. He was evil. I will kill him if I see *him* again."

Slim's eyes grew big. "I worked with Roberts a spell, several years as it now stands. But I never," Slim scratched his cheek and pursed his lips, "he never said anything about a militia, just the Confederacy. He was a rebel cavalryman, rode with Nathan Bedford Forrest. He didn't elaborate, just mentioned it a few times. But he never mentioned—was it the territory militia?"

The old Arapaho warrior nodded. "Maybe it is a different man. I knew a man named Roberts; he was a killer. You mentioned a man named Roberts; he is a killer. There are many white men, more than my people, and a lot of killers. I would venture, more than one Roberts, too."

"Yes, a lot."

The old Arapaho warrior laughed. He nodded, turned, and walked away.

"Where are you going?" Slim said.

The Indian did not answer. Slim cursed and grabbed Lazy. He followed the old Arapaho Warrior. Then he found himself in the Indian's camp. The warrior invited Slim to stay to recover himself.

CHAPTER 16

CHAPS HEALED AS PREDICTED, ENOUGH that, after a week, Sheriff Brick and Clovis transported him from the Bludegats' house to the jail. Chaps was still in rough shape, something Clovis noted as he left for the saloon. He cursed at several cowhands gathered outside the jail to study the letter and its riddle.

Mattie passed Clovis and walked into the jail. "I'm here to stop this," she said. "You can't send Chaps to Cannonball Springs! He's hardly well enough to stay in the jail, not to mention travel.

"It's unjust! He could easily die on the way. He probably will die on the way. And for what? There's no hurry. Let him recover his strength."

"I know he's not well," Sheriff Brick said. "But he's well enough."

"You're sheriff."

"I'm a man under authority. I'm not U.S. Grant, not even governor or a judge. I don't have the convenience to shirk responsibility. His fate is in Judge Fickle's hands. I think there's a good chance Chaps will make the journey to Cannonball Springs. It's only two days and a night."

"On rough roads! Where is your—you're a stronger man than this. Who's Judge Fickle?"

"This isn't a corruption of principles. Chaps is rightfully arrested, Mattie. Remember, we found him in the bank, caught him red-handed."

"He'll die, Solomon. He'll die and then," Mattie threw up her hands, "where's the justice in that?"

Sheriff Brick smiled. "No one calls me 'Solomon' except you."

"It's your name."

"It is. But no one else out here calls me by it."

Mattie leaned in. "Solomon, don't send Chaps to Cannonball Springs, not yet."

"He's a prisoner. He deserves due process, and I'll not hold that from him longer than is needed."

Mattie guffawed "And you'll send him to Judge Fickle! He's a criminal himself. How can a criminal try criminals? It's unbelievable to me that he hasn't been removed. It's not justice. You, of all people, how can you participate in this farce? You're no better than King Darius feeding men to lions. There's no shred of justice in Judge Fickle's court—our Nebuchadnezzar, our Nero, hanging men to satiate a mob and his own bloodlust!"

"The law has no heart," Sheriff Brick said. "It's black and white. Men will dash themselves to pieces on it. Judge Fickle is only an instrument of the law. God raises up men to lead us. It can take a thick stomach to do what the law requires. I don't ultimately determine guilt; I bring men to a higher authority, Judge Fickle, duly appointed."

"Complicity speaks even through barred teeth. *Ha!* Appointed? There should be a ballot."

"These things are out of our hands as it stands."

"And you're going to send the prisoner along as you've been told. You do as you're told."

Sheriff Brick screwed up his nose. "Your anger lies with the system."

"No, in the corruption of it! I've no qualms with law. But Judge Fickle is a corruption, a manipulating overseer of a would-be free land. I've done what I can, and I've not received welcome. If it were my father or any other man—but I'm a woman. Moreover, I am a gossiped-about woman. I've gained a poor reputation. Even you've accused me of collusion."

"I asked—"

"How would I know anything? My reputation invites suspicion. Even talking to you isn't proper. I know people talk about us talking."

Mattie swept her arm. "I hate it. There's not a family besides the Guilfoyles that'll take dinner with us. And without our visits, I'd be surprised if Mrs. Guilfoyle entertained any company, what with their reputation, especially her husband's—driving through their family's eastern fortune. She's eager to host someone.

"My father doesn't tell me the half of the talking. I'm not dense. I don't know if I'd care so much about the gossip if it were just talk. We aren't sole proprietors of our reputations. I have my place in life, fair or not, and I see it better than I did a year ago. What can I do?"

Sheriff Brick pointed to his ear. "I've a scar behind my ear. I got it for telling the truth. Before freedom, before the war, my master hunted down runaway slaves. I think he did it more for the pleasure of capturing men and women than for the extra income. He was wealthy enough.

"They once brought in a man—it'd been a hot day and the horses and men were wet—they said they'd chased him down near the Yazoo River. He said he was a free man. I knew he was a free man. He was our preacher and led church every Sunday, a magnificent singer, too. He was married to a free woman and they had four daughters and a baby boy. He resembled a drawing of a runaway, but he was not the man.

"I pointed out that the notice said the missing man had a scar on the back of his neck, and that this man, our preacher, had no scar. A brutal ruffian they called 'Roberts' smacked me across my head which left this scar. 'That's for learning how to read,' he said."

Sheriff Brick exhaled and seemed to look beyond the wall he was looking at. "I carry those words with me, just like my scar. It's a different world but not so different. Yes, I'm a free man. But I get news that black men, sheriffs even, have been put down—lynched, or worse. I know we might be west of the Mississippi, but men's prejudices know no boundaries."

Sheriff Brick cleared his throat and he looked at Mattie. "Any man is safer with a gun in his hand and the law on his side. I don't see how keeping a prisoner around will improve his condition. It's not summer; transporting him won't be as rough; it won't be so hot. And it's not so cold yet, either. Last week's snow has already melted. You say you see your place. Well, it's not here, not today, not for him."

Mattie turned to leave. The jail's front door shook and a man opened it. He was tall with broad shoulders, a gaunt chest, and generous stomach. His head was enveloped by a faded brown bucket hat that stopped just short of his gray eyebrows. His bushy, gray mustache covered the top half of his mouth. White bristle covered his chin, cheeks, and neck like sandpaper that has been used on soft wood.

"Constable?" he said. His voice was high, almost like a woman's, with a deep drawl. He looked at Mattie and Sheriff Brick, squinting at each in turn. Then he spit black mucus and tobacco. "You are dressed like one," he said, motioning with his chin to Sheriff Brick. "But I have not seen a lawman the like of *you*."

"I'm the lawman," Sheriff Brick said. He shifted his eyes to Mattie, then back to the entrant. "They call me Sheriff Brick. How can I help you?"

The man lifted up his left hand slowly, middle finger extended. "That your prisoner?"

"He is."

"I am here to get him."

Sheriff Brick eyed the man. "You'll excuse my asking, who are you?"

"Oh, I must have forgotten myself," the man said. He used his extended hand to grab his hat, which he brought to his chest and bowed. "I am Darwin Proachman."

He stood erect again and replaced his bucket hat. He made a tremendous rumbling in his mouth as he worked chew to its edge. He spit black mucus beyond his left shoulder.

"I am a U.S. Marshal." He flashed his badge. "And as a Marshal, as you are probably aware, it is my duty to courier folks like that one." He pointed to Chaps. "It is a duty. Judge Fickle asked me to come down as a personal favor. I was talking with a fellow at the telegraph office. He directed me here. I said that I was here to take that fellow," he pointed to Chaps, "off your hands."

Another man burst through the jail door. "Sheriff!" His eyes were as open as a horse in heat and sweat beaded on his forehead. "There's an emergency over at Pecker's!"

"What kind of emergency?" Sheriff Brick said

"It's an explosion. He said, that is, Pecker's boy Sonny said it was an explosion. He rode up fast as lightning to our place and said there was an explosion. He said the barn had been torn apart, fire everywhere!"

"Constable," Darwin said. "I do not have time to wait. I need to get back to Cannonball Springs with the prisoner. It is a priority for Judge Fickle."

Sheriff Brick raised his eyebrows.

"Go," Mattie said to Sheriff Brick. "You're needed there. I can't say I'm overly sorry to hear of the misfortune—"

The news messenger gasped.

"I'm not glad to say it, but no, I'm not sorry," Mattie continued. "Wiley's wife has always been good to me and his children are sweet. How they're his, I don't understand. But you've got to go help, and haste. I say it for their sake, not his."

"I don't—excuse me, sir," Sheriff Brick said to Darwin, "but I've never heard of a Marshal in these parts. Why wasn't I informed you were coming?"

Darwin stared at Sheriff Brick, one eyebrow perched higher than the other. A tense interlude of silence pervaded. Then Darwin pierced it with a laugh. "You were not informed?"

"I'm his nurse," Mattie said. She winked at Sheriff Brick. Darwin turned to face her. "This prisoner, he's my charge. I'll be coming with."

Darwin's eyes enlarged. "I do not—"

"You do have room. He was shot only a week ago, so horse travel is impossible. He'd fall off a mount. He'll have to go either by wagon or coach. And it should be coach. I trust the government has the money to hire one?"

Darwin stammered.

"Guilfoyle has a spare, I'm sure, and horses to go with it."

"A criminal coach is no place for a lady," Darwin said.

"A woman can face a dusty road as well as any man."

"But suppose you were to get shot—"

"In what kind of coach is one shot with a U.S. Marshal?"

"An explosion!" the messenger interjected. "At Pecker's!"

"There's no reason to wait," Mattie said to Sheriff Brick. "You need to go look at that explosion. Leave Chaps to me. I'll ensure he gets to Cannonball Springs."

"It is an awful ride," Darwin said. "It would be you, me, and the prisoner." He raised his hand and pointed at Chaps again.

"I've been through more than a bad carriage ride. I wasn't asking for permission. I'm going. I'm his nurse. Now if you'll excuse me, I'll go get my things and meet you at the station."

Mattie exited. Darwin took a deep breath and exhaled forcefully.

Then Clovis burst through the door. "Sheriff, explosion!" He hiccuped and nearly swooned.

Sheriff Brick took a deep breath. "You're certainly in fine shape." He spit. "Stay with the prisoner. This man, Marshal, he's going to take him to Cannonball Springs." He turned to Darwin. "You said Judge Fickle sent you, and then you're a Marshal. Please forgive my pause. Of course, the prisoner will be in good hands."

Sheriff Brick motioned at the messenger and they turned to leave together. Sheriff Brick stopped at the door and turned to Darwin. "Mattie's more than capable of taking care of herself. And she will. Even so, take care no harm comes to her."

Darwin assumed an attentive stance and nodded assent. Sheriff Brick wrinkled his nose and walked out with the messenger. They were greeted by foaming citizens. Sheriff Brick mounted his horse and led the group in galloping to Wiley Pecker's farm.

He glared as he rode. One man, in joining the sheriff's contingent, told his wife it was a "man's duty to help his neighbor." Another had told his wife that "duty must be done, even to help someone like goose neck Wiley Pecker."

The horses' furious galloping was deafening. The messenger was just a boy and an inexperienced rider. He almost fell off several times. Sheriff Brick told him to slow down to a manageable pace, and he fell behind.

The group, minus the messenger, arrived at the Pecker farm where dark orange fire and gray smoke enveloped the main barn, the farm's centerpiece. Folks had raised the barn, mostly in gratitude to Mrs. Pecker, a few years prior. Wiley was then too drunk to help but insisted on the most unusual subtleties for his barn, none of which were pertinent or correct to the build. The builders discarded his suggestions.

The building was not unusual in its construction, only its scale. Wiley had insisted on buying too much wood and too-large timbers. His wife, as usual, had not said anything, but Mrs. Pecker did not have to say anything for one to know what she thought. Wiley said he did not care what his wife thought.

A deep well supplied water to the farm, and the fire fighters had been pumping it hard. But the Peckers' pump was old and inefficient and leaked so much water that the pumpers were caked with mud.

Sheriff Brick dismounted and directed men to use heavy cloths, shovels, and blankets to suffocate the flames. Even though these new efforts beat back the flames, the building was too far gone to save.

CHAPTER 17

MATTIE MET DARWIN AT THE GUILFOYLE stagecoach station. He had secured a wagon and, with Clovis, loaded the stretcher-borne Chaps into it. Clovis passed by Mattie as she approached.

"He mumbled about a nap," Darwin said to Mattie's inquiring glance at Clovis who walked away. He spit tobacco into the dirt. She nodded.

An old Tennessee pacer and an old mule chewed hay. Both had ribs showing from under their liver-colored skins.

"They look ready," Mattie said. She raised the right corner of her mouth. Some folks said she raised her mouth when she meant sarcasm or mischief.

"It is a disgraceful team," Darwin said. He laughed. "It was all Guilfoyle had. He did not charge too much for their use. I would prefer to just take one or the other but Guilfoyle said they prefer each other's company. And he's holding my horse as collateral. What should I do? You can see these, old, maybe too old for the journey, so maybe we will lose one and still make it." He offered Mattie his hand.

Mattie scorned his offer and climbed into the wagon. Darwin untied the animals and packed up the hay, then followed Mattie in climbing up. He urged the horse and mule, and the heavy box squealed forward.

"Did you think I wouldn't recognize you?" Mattie said to Darwin after they had passed Racida's outskirts. "Where is he?"

"Good to see you again," Darwin said. "I think it has been—"

"Where is he?"

"Six months, a year?"

"You'd got your pinkie finger caught in your horse's bridle and nearly torn it off, that's what I remember. We dragged you into Borger's saloon in Patchpa and put you up on a table to sew it back on."

"Oh yes! Then it has been a year. Time flies."

"Is he meeting us?"

"He?"

"You're either denser than a rock, stupider than a turkey, or acting like a John Wilkes Booth. I know it was him at the bank last week. I spoke to him. So, if it's hot air you're blowing, blow."

Darwin laughed. "I have never heard a woman talk like that. I did not think I would ever hear a woman talk like that. What is all this? I think you know more about this business than I do. You said you talked to him. The two of you were close, if I remember correctly."

Mattie stared at Darwin. "He's up to something."

Darwin stared at Mattie. "You are a different kind of girl than I am used to."

"I shouldn't think you're used to any kind of girl."

Darwin paused. "I am not used to being sassed. I do not know if you are being rude or stubborn. It is not becoming."

"He sent you here to get *him*." Mattie motioned to Chaps. "I can only see two options—he's either going to kill him or you are."

"You two were close. And you talked to him. You would know better than me what he plans to do, not?" Darwin winked.

"You've no right—"

"Yes, he sent me here, and yes, he is meeting us on the road. I do not know how you got me to procure this ridiculous getup. We will be more conspicuous. And I am to return it to Racida for my horse. You would think a Marshal's word would be sufficient collateral. I think Guilfoyle odd.

"Whatever Indie has planned, it is for him to figure out, wagon or not. He is good at figuring stuff out. He called in a debt—the Patchpa pinkie affair actually—and I will have satisfied it when he meets us. Truth be told, I do not know what he intends to do after he has this fellow. He and I are not intimate acquaintances, like you. I fancy myself a good judge of character, that is why I joined the Marshals. But for as long as I have known Indie Caloo, I have never quite put my finger on him. And I have never seen him like this."

Mattie straightened herself. Darwin did not notice. He spoke in a rhythm like the hard wheels, dirt, and hooves of their animal bearers.

"He always had some evil in him," Darwin said. "Indie has an eye on the weaknesses of others. That is mostly what he used to talk about: how he was going to steal something or teach this or that lawman a lesson. There was never direction in it. He robbed and stole and—well, you know him better than I do. It always seemed to me he did those things to do those things, even if he said some foolish thing like being a true frontier man in the face of societal corruption. He had an itch he could not help but scratch.

"Now there is a marked change in him. He does not talk as much. But when he does, all he talks about is how he is changed, how he is a new man—dead, now alive—working for God.

"Apparently, his boys killed him." Darwin motioned his head toward Chaps. "He did not go into it, just that he was dead and now he is alive, and he was doing the Lord's work. It all sounded like something a preacher might say."

Darwin paused. The wagon rattled and clicked. "I heard—that deputy Clovis told me your father is a preacher?"

Mattie nodded.

"He also said he would be damned if you were a nurse. I have not seen enough womanly tenderness from you to disagree. Yet, preacher's daughter, so maybe you have an idea: how can a man die and come back to life? This is not the Holy Land. They must not have killed him, I figure. They must have thought they killed him. He thought they killed him, certainly, so they must have thought the same. That must be it."

"No. He *was* dead," Chaps said loud over the clamor.

Mattie and Darwin startled and turned to look at him. His face looked paler under the bonnet-filtered light. He had propped himself on his elbows. He manipulated his face as he spoke.

"He was dead. I suppose I would've sworn on my life on that. We tied Indie up and stripped him down to undergarments for easy pickings. I suppose you're well aware, it gets cold in the desert at night, especially this time of year. The cold alone can kill you. But Roberts killed him; he shot Indie twice. And Indie had nothing on. He couldn't have survived the cold even if he'd survived the bullets. Have you ever seen a man die?"

Mattie stared at Chaps. Darwin turned back to the horses. He gurgled and spit.

"He had a hole in his chest and a hole in his stomach. When he stopped wriggling, I walked over and checked him. He was dead."

Darwin laughed. "I am glad you are not a doctor. He is alive."

"I still can't believe he shot me."

CHAPTER 18

AFTERNOON HAD ADVANCED BY THE time work at the Pecker farm had reduced the disaster to small coals and smoldering timbers. Mrs. Pecker prepared food for the would-be barn rescuers; and surrounding farm wives and Racida citizens—who continued to arrive even after danger had passed—reinforced her insufficient victuals. It was a feast.

With so many people assembled, drink and games and music furnished themselves. Someone suggested a dance but was shushed to show empathy. Wiley drank a lot and said "If people want to dance, let them dance!" But even with this blessing, only a few young folks did dance.

Sheriff Brick was tight-lipped, as he had been all day at the farm except in directing fire extinction efforts. He investigated the cause of the fire and discovered a huge black powder blast mark on the ground. A number of cattle and sheep were unaccounted for, "blown to smithereens or incinerated, no doubt" Sheriff Brick said. His words were repeated; they supported Wiley Pecker's witness account of an explosion.

After his investigation, Sheriff Brick eyed then partook of the refreshments. "I suppose one more," he said as a cowhand offered him alcohol again. He had already drained two glasses. Many men and just three women surrounded Sheriff Brick, all in good spirits and all with glasses or bottles. They greeted his libation acceptance with bewildered jubilation.

"Sheriff," a one-eyed man said, "quite a week. First the bank, now the fire."

"Criminals and fires."

"We're lucky to have you."

"Very heroic."

"Even for a—"

"Man such as yourself."

Laughter followed, as it was not what the interrupted speaker had intended to say. But even Wiley Pecker was not disparaging. Sheriff Brick smiled.

Sheriff Brick looked in his glass; a clear, pungent liquid filled the bottom. "Turpentine?" He cocked his ears back and drank.

"This was a queer fire," an old farmer said. He had two yellow teeth and a raspy voice sounding like a dog that has barked through a lightning storm. "Pecker said it was an explosion—just like that," he snapped his fingers. "Out of thin air! I've only ever heard of such a thing in these parts once before."

The gathered hushed. Drinkers stopped drinking.

The old farmer continued. "Do you remember when the Pioneer Bank was robbed the first time? It was windy. You bet it was dusty, choke kicking up and spitting in your face. Businesses even closed on account of it. I was getting supplies at the general store and old Brewster closed up when I was done. But the bank was open. Tall Jim always had the bank open. I saw lamp lights through the haze as I loaded up my wagon. You all know the story about the robbery, so I won't repeat it."

"We're thankful you stopped last week's robbery!" filtered to Sheriff Brick.

"He didn't stop it!"

"It wasn't a robbery!"

"Who would've thought that after all, there was a hole and a bag with riddling and rocks."

"In the floor."

"Riddling?"

"A riddle!"

"Anyone got any idea what it means?"

"Riddling?"

"The riddle!"

Expletives and exclamations highlighted that the riddle was unsolved. A man cursed the Caloo Gang and threw his fists through the air. Sheriff Brick sipped the last of his pungent drink.

The old farmer continued his story. "No one remembers anything other than that original robbery; they don't remember the fire that proceeded it." He coughed and leaned forward. "But I do. And more than one of you was there to help me fight it, too.

"It was a queer fire, similar to this one—an explosion with collateral damage—Theodore Tuck's barn. He said the building just erupted in flames, a bang that blew the side and roof away. The blast-side of the building fell in on itself because there was nothing there that had been. It took three-and-a-half hours to tamp down the flames. Six sheep and two cows dead. And while we fought that fire, ruffians robbed the bank."

The farmer trailed off with expletives. Others joined in the swearing. More than one storyteller vied to finish the robbery yarn. Sheriff Brick finished his alcohol.

The farmer shushed the crowd and began again. "Most of us formed the posse when we found out about the bank robbery, and we chased, we followed the faint tracks as best we could. But they disappeared about two miles outside of town, near Berrier's Farm. All traces vanished. Berrier didn't know what was going on; he never does."

There was a laugh. Berrier did not laugh.

"You know how worked up he can get, and he was true to form. Then we heard a shot! And who should we find, but Jesse Hobbins crying with a dead chicken in his hands."

The group burst out laughing except for Jesse Hobbins. He did not laugh. "It scared me," he said.

"Almighty vengeance!" the old farmer said. "Both these fires were God's wrath! On my life, I know it."

"No doubt the Almighty could blow up a barn," Sheriff Brick said. "But I don't think he'd use black powder. I don't think God needs men's tools."

"Black powder?"

"Where'd it come from?"

"No one has black powder just laying around for barn firing."

"Outlaws!"

"Indians!"

"Government!" The suggestion drew praise.

"If it isn't the Almighty," the old farmer said, "then it seems to me, sheriff, that we've got a crazed arsonist on the loose. You need to find him."

A woman said that the arsonist could be a woman. The crowd laughed including Jessie Hobbins and Berrier. Some said it was ridiculous, just co-incidence. Others said Sheriff Brick had better things to do than chase wild suppositions. Talk turned to other stories. Folks dispersed and mingled in other groups.

Sheriff Brick pulled the old farmer aside. "Can you tell me more about that fire at Tuck's, about the day of the robbery?"

The old man screamed and ran away to his daughter who glared at Sheriff Brick. She kissed her father and they walked to their wagon. Sheriff Brick watched them and scratched his chin. Then he turned in the direction of the Pecker family outhouse.

The relaxed atmosphere of a latrine has stirred more than one good idea and offered many a man a chance to think through events. Sheriff Brick relaxed himself for relief in the acrid outhouse. He talked to himself with alcohol on his breath.

"An explosion and a fire—strange, just like the day the bank was robbed. Pecker's got no store of powder. You'd need a keg to blow up a barn like that, I can see that. So then, was it blown up on purpose? The motive to kill was ineffective. Unless, a distraction? There's hardly a reason to blow up a barn today."

His eyes enlarged. He wiped his ass, closed his pants, and ran outside. "I need to leave." He mounted his horse and rode for Racida.

CHAPTER 19

THE WAGON CARRYING MATTIE, DARWIN, and Chaps was overused. Dust had penetrated the old birch wood, completely graying it, thin and deep-ridged. A yellowed tarp covered the bonnet. The hub bands were rusty though the steel tires gleamed from frequent use. It squeaked and groaned whenever it was in motion.

They approached a rocky outcrop. A man walked out from behind a boulder, rifle in hand. It was a Spencer repeater. He wore black clothes covered by a black poncho. A sagging sombrero hung low from his head and obscured his eyes.

Darwin reined and slowed the horses to a stop.

"Good afternoon," the black-clothed man said in a forced voice.

Mattie blushed.

"Thank goodness," Darwin said. "I have had it with this squeaking. This wagon might be the worst I have ever driven." He swore.

"Indie?" Mattie said.

Indie had not seen Mattie at first glance from under the shadow of his sombrero. He looked with open eyes and saw her: beautiful, stern, sad, like all the grace in the world spurned and calling back regrets in sweetness. His stomach dropped and his head flashed into and out of swooning.

Like the day I met her, no, even more. How the bloom reaches beyond itself for new heights! If ever there was a subject of the poets, here she sits. What a fool I've been! And I have been a fool. She doesn't welcome me. Her eyes flash sadness and grief.

"Matilda." Indie stammered. He cleared his throat. "Darwin, I said bring Chaps. You were *only* supposed to bring Chaps."

Darwin grunted assent. "She is his nurse, see? I could have aroused the sheriff's suspicions and refused her subterfuge. But they were talking before I got to the jail, just the two of them, and I assumed they knew each other.

Maybe she really was his nurse? She helped you sew my finger back on. I know now that she is not a nurse, or else she is a terrible one. Beg pardon," he said aside to Mattie.

"What're you planning?" Mattie said to Indie.

"Do I need plans?" Indie said.

"Keep your plans out of my ears," Darwin said. "Whatever your machinations, it would be best if you did not tell me and thus make me an accomplice. I am a lawman, after all."

Indie winked and climbed into the wagon. "The greatest experiences of our lives are born out of accidents and circumstances beyond our control, not by plans. A river always has its twists, as life its detours. Plans?" Indie laughed. "Drive."

Darwin frowned and whistled at the horses. The wagon lurched and its huge wheels turned slowly quicker, humming then bouncing on the hard dirt road.

"What're you up to?" Mattie said to Indie. She motioned to Chaps. "He said you were dead. Then the bank. Now this interception."

Indie looked at Mattie for a long time. "Yes," he said. "I was dead; part of me still is." He smiled and clapped his hands "'Old things are passed away; behold, all things are become new.' That's what scripture says."

"I know what scripture says. I'm a preacher's daughter."

"I'm a new man, more alive than I've ever been! The old man has passed away. I'm glad of it. All things are new."

"The Apostle Paul was discussing reconciliation."

"I've been reconciled! I *am* reconciled. I don't understand how, but I know I was dead and now I'm alive. And with this new life, I have a new purpose, a plan to follow that's not my own. I don't know where it'll lead, but I need to follow it."

"Are you going to kill him?" Mattie indicated Chaps, who stared at Indie.

"Kill him out of my sight," Darwin said. "I am a lawman, and as such, you must respect, if not me, at least my badge. You are a wanted man. I will not suffer any more from you."

Indie spoke. "Did Chaps tell you Roberts shot me here and here?" He indicated his stomach and chest. "I remember the first bullet—a sudden pang, then darkness. I woke up after they'd left me, and in pain. I still hurt from the wounds."

Indie rubbed his chest. "All I could think about when I woke up was surviving. I don't know of any impulse stronger than the will to survive. The final stages of life are terrifying."

Indie exhaled. He told Mattie and Darwin and Chaps how he had found a fur and taken clothes from a messenger. Then he cried. "I found Duncan's body two days later. It was a little over a week ago now. Oh, Duncan!" he shouted. "You believed in the face of death. Did you believe when he called for you?"

Mattie shuddered and cried. "I know you loved him."

"What did you do about the bullets?" Darwin said. "As our nurse friend knows, a bullet will become infected unless it is removed. And you had two bullets in you?"

"I removed them."

Mattie winced. Darwin laughed.

"This fellow," Darwin motioned to Chaps, "says you shot him. That was one bullet. And he has only just pulled through. You are galavanting about. You were shot twice? And not long ago, and you had to remove the bullets yourself. Quite a recovery," and he whistled.

"I can't account for it, other than it being supernatural," Indie said. "I was touched by the Divine. I saw what I couldn't before: the gang, my legacy, the Caloo Gang, had to be destroyed. I've come to put an end to it."

Chaps squinted his eyes. He shook his head. He laughed hard. What a sound, ringing above the crush of the wagon! Then he coughed, winced, and stopped laughing.

"You are planning to kill this fellow?," Darwin said.

Indie smiled. "Yes."

"Where's the money?" Chaps said.

Indie laughed. "Convincing you all to leave it there wasn't easy."

"Did you take it—is there really gold?"

Indie winked. "How much of our lives, wasted, and at the expense of others! I might never get another opportunity, Mattie, so I'll tell you now, honestly. I am a changed man."

Darwin interrupted Indie's monologue. "Someone is following us." He pointed to a faint cloud of dust rising in the sky from the path they had been on.

"It's his brother," Indie said. "It's your brother, Chaps. It's Fanny!"

Chaps blinked his eyes. He tried to prop himself up on his elbows but he winced and rested back on his cot on the wagon floor.

"At least I hope it's Fanny. I've been planning this ambush since our encounter at the bank. Fanny's a lot of things; patient isn't one of them. He isn't particularly insightful or smart either, so I had to make sure he'd know you were to be taken to Cannonball Springs. Otherwise, he'd probably have tried days ago to spring you from the jail.

"The riskiest part of my plan was the sheriff. My friend in the Cannonball Springs telegraph office sent Racida a Judge Fickle message to persuade him to send Chaps along. Judge Fickle is eager for what he calls justice, but he's not well-informed or capable like me; sometimes I need to help him out a bit. I did think that Sheriff Brick would be suspicious of the request. I worried more he'd escort you.

"He's a devoted lawman and a good shot. The emergency fire at Pecker's, obviously he had to go. And the sudden appearance of a U.S. Marshal—there's never a Marshal in this part of the country, you know—well that all put him into a corner.

"And I'm glad he acted as I thought he would; that is, how he has acted by allowing Darwin to take Chaps, though I wasn't expecting you, too, Mattie."

Indie lowered his eyes. "I wonder if he recognizes how frequently you visit him, and even alone."

Mattie blushed. "Nonsense and nothing to do with anything."

"You're not ashamed? We were never ashamed."

"I was always ashamed! You had me parade into the desert like a hussy. You beckoned and I came forth. Where were you to shepherd me away?"

"I'm an outlaw."

Mattie swallowed in gathering herself. "I've never been ashamed to talk with Solomon."

Indie squinted. He and Mattie studied each other.

Darwin broke in. "He is gaining."

"Getting Fanny to follow us was easy," Indie said, looking through the back of the wagon bonnet at Fanny's distant, rising figure. "Just had to make sure he'd hear of your transfer and the story of a man who sprang his brother on a jail wagon from Stanchion to Cannonball Springs. The telegrapher hadn't, and I imagine neither had Fanny or anyone else." Indie winked again. "But once he did hear, I knew Fanny would be smart enough to wait for an ambush chance. Human nature can be very predictable."

"You wanted him to follow us?" Chaps said.

"We can't outride him with a wagon. Fanny rides like the devil. We'll have a shootout. One can't plan too much. You have to adapt. We're better positioned in that he can only use one gun at a time."

"You'd risk our lives?" Mattie said. "I see nothing has changed. But you used to be more of a gentleman. You never tried to risk my life."

"I never tried to be or do anything but what was honest. Fanny isn't exactly offering peace even were we to give it to him. He's more likely to kill us all than let any of us live, even if we gave up without a fight."

"You were dead," Chaps said. He was pale as he spoke. "I checked; you were dead."

"I'm glad you're not a doctor," Indie said to Chaps. He laughed. "I'm also glad you're not a nurse," he said to Mattie. "We might all die today—I think not, but we might—one day, absolutely."

Indie obtained Darwin's shotgun. "A shotgun gives a superior moving shot."

He crawled to the back of the wagon, curling back a fold of the bonnet curtain with Darwin's gun. He shot. The explosion filled the air as the hammer smashed into the cap which burst in a shock of light and smoke and the bb pellets shot out. The wagon horse and mule lurched forward in response. Darwin cursed.

"Missed, probably still too far away," Indie shouted. He crawled back to the front of the wagon. "Why would God bring me back to life except for some purpose, to undo what I've done? Yet, it's good to show mercy where we can and to those who deserve it. Chaps, I have a proposal for you.

"I had you the other night feet away with a loaded gun in my hand. It would've been easier to kill you than to keep you alive. But if I'd killed you, then what? Fanny would've gotten away. How long would it have taken me to track him down? That's why I needed you, Chaps, to get captured; and that's why I didn't kill you. I needed you in prison to keep Fanny close.

"But there's another reason, too. Of all in the gang, you're the one who most deserves a second chance. You're a good man with a bad brother. You live in his shadow and allow him to control your ultimate actions. I'm going to remove that shadow.

"You talk about a farm. Go to it, wherever you make it. Your brother's actions have come due. He's been weighed; he's been measured; and he's been found wanting. There's nothing you can do to change that. But you can change your future."

"He is on us," Darwin said.

They drove like mad and bounced over the rough terrain of a small canyon. The wheels cried for destruction but held. The road opened a little into wide, flat ground covered by sagebrush. Red rocks still rose high, but in easier climbs.

Fanny used the landscape to ride parallel with the wagon while keeping distance. Darwin turned with a pistol in hand and the outlaw dropped behind the wagon as Darwin fired several rounds. The driver's box was awkward and prevented him from following Fanny's movements. He swore at Indie to get to the back of the wagon and shoot at the outlaw. Indie laughed.

The horses ran at tremendous speed, enlivened by the gunfire. The squeaking wagon lurched in violent crashes. Chaps moaned. Mattie held fast and prayed. Darwin said it would be a miracle if they did not shake apart. Indie smiled. Then Fanny fired his pistol and a bullet ripped the wagon bonnet and sprayed bits of wood from the frame into the air and into Indie's face.

Indie, again at the wagon's back, fired another round at Fanny. The shot missed.

Fanny crouched into his sorrel's mane and ushered it forward with a click of his heels. He drew close to the wagon and fired.

Bang. Bang. Bang. Bang.

All missed flesh, though one ripped through Mattie's flailing hair. Indie reloaded and fired again and again. Dust flew up where the bullets struck the ground near Fanny's horse. The horse veered away from the close ricochets. Fanny worked to keep his saddle.

He pushed to the front of the wagon. Darwin scooted to the far side of the driver's box. Fanny drew his other pistol and fired several times at Darwin. None of the bullets found their mark.

"He is a terrible shot," Darwin said. "You all are."

Fanny reined his horse and the animal narrowly missed the wagon's large wheels. He hit the side of the wagon with the butt of his pistol.

Indie shoved the shotgun through the wagon cover canvas. Fanny had kept pace along the left side of the wagon. He was riding close, almost touching the wagon, when Indie pulled the trigger.

Moments of true madness happen just as all others. Yet the effect from such moments is methodical. The trigger pulled; the firing pin jutted into the cap; the cap exploded into the primer; the primer ignited gunpowder; gunpowder unleashed the small pieces of lead. And then with a flash, Fanny's sorrel whinnied and fell neck-first into the jagged terrain.

Fanny was thrown off the dead animal and into the front of the wagon. The huge wheels, front and back, ran over him and ground him into the earth. His extensive wounds and broken bones incapacitated him so that he bounced into the air limp after the back wheels crushed and flung him out.

Dust from the wagon whipped into the air as Darwin slowed the large contraption. The light blue sky, scattered with puffs of clouds, welcomed the flying substance as the desert plain's vastness swallowed up human catastrophe.

"It is a miracle the wheels did not shatter to pieces," Darwin said. He circled the wagon back to Fanny's mangled body.

"Stay here," Indie said to Mattie. He jumped down and ran to the writhing outlaw.

"You're alive?" Fanny muttered to Indie when he saw him.

"I am," Indie said.

"How?"

"I don't know. I was dead, or as nearly as one can be to being dead. It's something, being dead and now being alive, something that's changed me. Do you know why I've come?"

Fanny did not say anything. He was dead.

PART IV
BETRAYAL

CHAPTER 20

"HOW LONG IS THIS ROAD?" Sheriff Brick said, riding back to Racida. He paced his horse but rode with purpose and a rare look that folks said could kill a man. He had named his horse Dabney after Confederate general Dabney H. Maury, "Commander of the forces we fought at Fort Blakeley," Sheriff Brick would tell inquirers. He had told only Mattie more than that. "As a slave. I was ridden hard. I can ride hard, too. I don't want to forget how we whipped the rebels at Blakeley. Dabney's a good horse, but I whip him. And then I remember how we whipped them." Mattie had said she was not sure what to make of that statement.

A bay quarter horse with powerful flanks, Dabney lacked desirable height at the withers which some swore left him disproportionate. Folks in Stanchion had a saying about disproportionate horses; no one in Racida remembered how it went, yet they said Dabney would be a terrible ride. Sheriff Brick scolded scoffers at Dabney's sale and said a horse's look mattered only as much as his ability. He took great care of Dabney and transformed him into the fastest and strongest horse in Racida. Rumors said Sheriff Brick had gotten Dabney too cheap. Some envied.

"Sheriff!" Entreaty floated over the passing wind. "Sheriff, stop!"

Sheriff Brick turned his head and pulled on Dabney's reins. The horse slowed its frenetic pace and stopped. Sheriff Brick patted him and stroked Dabney's neck, working his way up poll and ears. A group of riders slowed and leveled with him.

"Why're you hauling back to town?" said one of the riders, a rancher who lived beyond Pecker's farm. He was an unsuccessful and sordid man.

"Why'd you ride after me?" Sheriff Brick said. "I didn't ask you to ride with me. Y'all will miss the festivities back at Pecker's. Or was it Pecker sent you?"

No answer.

Sheriff Brick shifted in his saddle and drew his gun. The men exclaimed; some drew their guns. "Easy, sheriff."

Sheriff Brick tucked his revolver, a powerful Colt Army model, across his lap. "What's your business?" he said. "I know two of you are former rebels, and the rest are like Pecker and old Confederate sympathizers. I've heard about your meetings, nights in Pecker's barn, the very one that burned down today. It must bother you that you've got a black sheriff, a good one, too; and a former Union soldier to boot."

"You were in the Union army?" a young man said. He was very skinny with buck teeth and hair that matted into triangles that stuck to his forehead. Someone slapped him; another cursed at him.

"Seems you know our business," the rancher said. "Burning down a barn is enough to hang a man, no matter if even he's sheriff." The rancher swore.

Sheriff Brick curled his mustache upward and unfurled a smile. He blinked hard and slow, as if he were beginning to nod to sleep, and kept his eyes on the rancher. "Say that again."

The rancher swore again. The young man looked surprised and stupid, and the other men gawked, laughed, or smirked.

Fury is an immediate itch. It shivers up and down the spine with tremendous speed and has no rational explanation. In some men, fury can be dangerous, spilling into wrath; in others, fury can be marvelous, reckoning righteousness. Uncultivated, fury is un-calculated destruction. But Sheriff Brick knew himself enough to loosen his grip on his revolver and speak instead.

"I always shudder when I hear —" Sheriff Brick said. "I'm sure you've suspected, but I was a slave once. An old oak tree, gnarled and scarred with a tremendous hollow, grew next to our house on the plantation. A gulf storm unlike any ever seen hurled up the Yazoo River and split that tree in half. One side fell safely clear, the other fell onto our house. It was the middle of the night and we were soaked in an instant—the roof splintered and the wind howled. Eight were instantly released from all bondage."

Sheriff Brick paused and fiddled with his canteen. He seemed to savor opening it, but when he did, he took a swig of water quicker than he took to open and close the canteen. The other men watched, unmoved. The horses swished their tails; Dabney bit at his front leg and twitched his skin.

"Two others were trapped; they later died from their injuries. It was horrible confusion: deafening thunder, trees like manic symbols in the swirl, complete darkness except for blinding lightning, everything wet. Someone ran for help. We huddled and sheltered. An old hand started praying;

mothers sang to quiet their little ones. And then the storm stopped all of a sudden. We heard it cutting away; we were safe then.

"The headmaster laughed when he heard that the tree had fallen and killed so many. He charged four slaves to cut up the tree, and he watched. He was evil. They flattened the big stump. From then on, that's where he'd whip slaves. He called it 'Slave-killer.' He'd call us terrible names and whip us. Whenever I hear what you just said, I think of being whipped. I feel it."

"Gee, I'm sorry, sheriff." The rancher leaned forward in his saddle and turned with a smile to the other riders. He laughed and swore again.

Though controlled, Sheriff Brick had a temper. He had once pointed a gun at Clovis, which amused the aimless deputy. He had slapped prisoners. In breaking up bar row, Sheriff Brick had knocked teeth out of the mouths of two drifters, three cowhands, and a rancher.

The men sat silent and waited for rebuttal. The horses twitched their skins. Flies buzzed and hummed. A cloud, one of a few in the forever stretching sky, drew across the sun and shadowed them.

Sheriff Brick returned his pistol to its holster. He grabbed Dabney's reins. "You're too cowardly to kill me for burning Pecker's barn. Men like you," he spoke to the rancher, "both deserve and don't deserve my bullet. But shootouts aren't the way of the law. I didn't have anything to do with the fire at Pecker's, and you know it. I'll not give you reason to kill me here; you'll have to do it without excuse." He told the riders not to follow him. Then he turned Dabney and spurred forRacida.

The rancher tried to speak but nothing coherent came out of his mouth. The young man fell off his horse. The other men swore almost in unison, though uniquely, and giggled.

"Get up!" the rancher said to the young man. Then the group turned and rode back to Pecker's farm.

Sheriff Brick arrived in Racida hot and sweaty. He picketed his horse to a hitching post and entered the jail. Clovis stood on his heels.

"Gone?" Sheriff Brick said.

"He went with that Marshal and Mattie," Clovis said.

Sheriff Brick screamed. "I had him! He was right under my nose and now he's gone."

"If you're talking about the prisoner, he's in the Marshal's care."

"I don't think that Marshal was on official Marshal business. The prisoner was one of the Caloo Gang. By 'he' I meant Indie Caloo. I see it now, the barn fire was a ruse, which means Indie Caloo cared about springing that prisoner, Chaps. If I'd only kept him, who knows but I'd have caught Caloo."

Sheriff Brick held his hat in his big hands. He ran his fingers over his wet brow and hair. Then he tossed his hat onto the desk and walked to the wall above the tea stand. He grabbed the bill about the Caloo Gang. He studied it and hummed "My Eyes Have Seen the Glory." Sheriff Brick said he hummed when he was thinking. People said he hummed when he was annoyed.

He walked to Clovis and gave him the paper. He spoke as Clovis glanced at the notice, which he and everyone in town had talked about since the Star Route mail messenger had brought it. "That notice offers the highest reward I've ever seen. The messenger who brought it said he'd seen Caloo."

"The barn fire's a ruse?" Clovis said. "Wasn't it on fire?"

"Yes, it was on fire. But it was a distraction. You've got to watch criminals, Clovis, they've patterns to how they do things. The Caloo gang robbed the Old Pioneer before I was sheriff. There was a fire then, too, that very day, and similarly explosive like at Pecker's. I found black powder residue on the ground. As likely as it might seem, I don't think Pecker would accidentally set his barn on fire. And he doesn't have explosives or the wherewithal to use them. That blaze was started, just like the day of the robbery."

"We both know Pecker, and you like him less than I do. But no one in these parts would blow up his barn. Why would anyone want to do that?"

Sheriff Brick exhaled through his nose, making a sound. "That's what I was thinking, too. 'Why?' Then I saw all the town gathered, myself included—Racida empty. Who couldn't come or go in the town as they pleased? It's ideal for an infamous character, like Caloo."

"But the Marshal, sheriff, it's not my place, but I'll remind you the Marshal took the criminal. I watched him and the preacher's daughter load him up and drive out of town. There was no sign of Indie Caloo."

Sheriff Brick snatched the paper out of Clovis' hand. "Has there ever been a Marshal in these parts before?"

CHAPTER 21

"HE'S DEAD," INDIE SAID. HE stood over Fanny's mangled corpse. Darwin and Mattie joined him.

"That was horrific," Darwin said. "I will say it again, it is a miracle the wagon wheels are not shattered to pieces."

Mattie gasped. She knelt beside Fanny. She closed his eyelids.

"I have never seen a man ride as reckless as him." Darwin clicked his tongue.

"Reckless?" Indie said. "It was hardened stupidity. I don't think he ever thought much when his dander was up. His dander was always up."

Mattie stood and spoke to Indie. "You're one to speak, behaving like a maniac. Were you planning to kill him?"

"I don't exactly know. He deserved to die; they all do." Indie paused. "We all do. 'All have sinned.'"

"'The Lord is not willing that any should perish,'" Mattie said. "You said you're about God's work. Is this his directing or is it revenge?"

Indie tucked his head and played in the dirt with his boot. "Doesn't have to be one or the other. It can be both."

"Since you seem suddenly fond of scripture, 'Beholdest thou the mote that is in thy brother's eye, but considerest not the beam that is in thine own?' You're as guilty as he was."

Indie laughed. "You're a preacher's daughter, alright. I'm merely an instrument of divine justice."

"He's dead?" Chaps said.

Mattie, Indie, and Darwin turned to look at him. Chaps was leaning over the front corner edge of the wagon. He shook. He was pale.

"See for yourself." Indie pointed at Fanny's mangled remains.

"I have never seen a man die like that," Darwin said. He shouted to Chaps. "You are a criminal. But I am sorry for your loss. I know he was your brother."

Mattie walked to the wagon and Chaps. "You shouldn't look," she said. "It's awful."

Chaps winced and hoisted himself up and over the wagon's side. He hit the ground hard but on his feet, then fell on his bottom to the ground. He hesitated, twitched, and gathered himself. Mattie moved so he could lean on her. The pair hobbled to Fanny's body. Chaps began to cry.

When it rains hard in the desert, especially after a drought, torrents converge to flood, decimating more completely than the sapping heat and sun. The smoothed rock and stripped vegetation they leave behind look alien to what was before. Only anchored elements remain. In the same way, torrential grief can overwhelm a man. What will be left when the waves of loss and pain sweep clean? If we could be certain of our post-grief states, if we were certain we could last through the pain, perhaps we would not fear it. But torrents sweep away whatever they encounter that is not rooted well, and we cannot know if grief will leave us bare.

Chaps knelt down against Fanny for a long time. The steady wind gusted stronger, kicking up and swirling dust. The wagon horse and mule swatted at flies. The makeshift funeral party sat in lengthening afternoon shadows cast by rising red rocks running parallel to the road. Sparse bushes dotted the landscape of old grass and red dirt.

"I suppose now's as good a time as any to be hanged," Chaps said. "I suppose now's as good a time as any."

"We all die," Darwin said. "It is not our time to choose when, only how, and sometimes not even that. Just look at—look at . . ." he did not finish his sentence, only pointed with his middle finger at Fanny's dead body before bringing his hand back down to his side.

Mattie looked at Darwin. "You're no comfort," she said. "We need to take him with us. A dead man out here is little more than carrion waiting to be plucked by buzzards."

Indie walked from the group over to Fanny's dead Sorrel. He turned around fast and ran back. "The horse!" he shouted as he passed Chaps, Mattie, and Darwin and jumped into the wagon. "It was shot hill-side. Wasn't my bullet, someone else shot and killed Fanny's horse!"

No sooner did Indie hide himself, than the bounty hunter with two animals—a mule he rode with Indie's Morgan tied to it—galloped into view. Mattie was the first to see them and she gasped. The bounty hunter reined his mule hard and the company stopped at the group.

"Afternoon, folks. What's all this?"

"Afternoon," Darwin said. "This is a prisoner transfer. This man," he pointed to Chaps, "is a criminal. I am taking him to Cannonball Springs. I am a U.S. Marshal." He flashed his badge. "She is his nurse. He," Darwin pointed to Fanny, "attacked us. Perhaps you heard the shooting. He was not discreet. As you can see, he is dead."

"What business are you about?" Mattie said.

The bounty hunter smiled. "I'm a hunter."

"Not much game where we stand."

"I hunt people." The bounty hunter dismounted. "I've been on the hunt for Indie Caloo for quite some time now. You've heard of him, no doubt; I'd say everyone has, especially every lawman and Marshal. I was close on his trail, him and his gang's—and you know they say no one knows what his gang looks like, just white men in bandanas. He's the only one who'd show his face during a job. There's brilliance in that; folks focus on what they know, if they know something, and don't bother finding out more.

"The gang's trail went cold. No activity. They changed their pattern of behavior. Well, I have to eat, so I went south to work along the border. But I couldn't stay away. I couldn't let the gang rest. I had to find Indie one way or another. That's how I found myself in Racida last week, the site of their last big job, to pick up the trail. Then, just my luck, they're back at it again. He was there, too. That boneheaded sheriff let him get away. I've been on his tail this last week. That's why I'm out here. And it's a good thing for you I was." He nodded toward Fanny's body.

"Did you see our confrontation?" Darwin said.

The bounty hunter nodded. "I shot his horse down, if I'm not mistaken."

"Then I do not need to tell you about it. We are much obliged. He was about on us. If he was not a terrible shot, he would have taken one or more of us with him."

"May I ask why he was chasing you?" The bounty hunter circled around Mattie, Darwin, and Chaps, putting himself between them and their wagon.

"He was kin to this criminal," Darwin said.

The bounty hunter nodded, and in one motion pulled out a knife and slit through the wagon's bonnet canvas. He peered inside. He jumped in and rummaged around the wooden boxes and supply trunks that Darwin and Mattie had packed.

"What are you doing?"

The bounty hunter snorted and jumped out of the wagon. He turned to Mattie, Darwin, and Chaps. "Indie Caloo is a dangerous man. You take care if you see him." He whistled. His mule and the Morgan ran up beside him. He jumped on the mule and rode away with it and the horse in tow.

Indie walked from behind a rock. "That horse is better than he is. Both the horse and the mule are better than he is." He hissed.

"Who was he?" Mattie said. "You didn't mention you were being chased."

"That bounty hunter has chased me for a long time. What's different about now? He thinks he's a good tracker. He's improved, I'll give him that. Yesterday, he came up on my horse grazing while I was pooping. I heard the whole thing. That's a Morgan, and a good horse, not like my Roan, but there isn't a horse like my roan. The Morgan's good and I let the bounty hunter have him. I didn't mind so much as I was going to run into you; though I'd have liked to have kept my saddle."

Indie snorted and spit for them to go. Mattie protested.

"You'd just leave the body?"

"I can't think of a more fitting burial for Fanny. Coyotes need food, too. The wind and dust will bury the rest. That sheriff of yours, Mattie, will be after us if he sees through my distraction at Pecker's farm, and I think he will. We must keep as much time as we can between us and him."

"We're not leaving his body. We need to dedicate his soul to God. The better man you say you've become would commit to that."

"I commit only to using the tools that the Lord has seen it good to equip us with. There is a time and a place for all things. The Lord has set aside here and now—beneath an open sky, towering stones and great plains—for Fanny's judgment. 'Vengeance is Mine,' says the Lord. We shouldn't stand opposed to God's will. Let him be avenged on Fanny."

"There is a verse in the Bible for pretty much everything," Darwin said.

"God's will is that all should turn to him," Mattie said. "And my will is to take the body. If spiritual sensibilities won't compel you, consider the bounty hunter. I bet he'll circle back. Would a U.S. Marshal leave a dead body? He'd take it with him for evidence or maybe bury it and mark the spot as proof. We have a wagon; I hardly think a Marshal would leave a body in such a circumstance. Leave Fanny's body and increase the bounty hunter's suspicions."

"She does present a compelling consideration," Darwin said. "I would of course typically take a body with me if I could, And with a wagon, I can."

Indie was mad. He thought about a thousand things to say.

Nothing can change her mind. She's a stalwart opponent, especially when in the right. Why Fanny's body? It stares as if we've unleashed horror. I did God's will. He deserved death. What could I say to change their minds and keep this evil away from me?

"I have his eulogy," Indie said. He pulled from his shirt the black, leather-bound book he had considered before. It was twice the size of his strong hands, in which his veins visibly pulsed as they ran over curving muscle and sharp tendons. "Perhaps if you know the man you're defending, you won't want to bring him with us."

Chaps, Mattie, and Darwin stared. Mattie dropped her chin, exposing brilliant teeth which women around Racida said were unnaturally white. Men raved about her teeth.

Indie opened his book and read: "The life of Benjamin Franklin Vestige, 'Fanny,' brother of Charles Pinckney Vestige, 'Chaps,' and a member of the Caloo Gang, is thus captured: 'the kingdom of heaven suffereth violence, and the violent take it by force.' This magnificent west—God's rugged kingdom on earth—has it not been tamed by violent men like Fanny? We shared a maniacal drive. In my worst outbursts, I could not compare to him. I was never comfortable with him around but I knew I had another gun at my side, which gave me a terrible hope in the face of despair. Blood begets blood."

Darwin laughed, first low, then building violent and full-bellied. "That is the worst eulogy I have ever heard. Blood begets blood? You should have been a poet." He laughed more guttural laughs. "Remind me to never ask you to write my eulogy."

Indie lowered his eyebrows. Mattie mirrored his pained look. Chaps did not change his expression of despondence. While Darwin wiped away his laughing tears, Indie tore out the book page bearing the just-read eulogy. He rolled it, took out a string, and tied it to Fanny's lifeless hand.

"Do you still stand to take him with us?"

Mattie and Darwin threw Fanny's body into the wagon. It hit hard with a thud that only corpses exclaim. The lifeless limbs were tied to its chest, hands pressing down Indie's eulogy. Mattie covered it with a blanket.

"What's my eulogy?" Chaps asked Indie when the wagon was moving again.

Indie's graying stubble matured his appearance, and his weathered face, deep set and evocative, did not look young.

"You're still alive," he said. "I can't give your eulogy while you're still alive. Though I'm glad you asked." Indie held aloft his black leather-bound book. "It's in here. Your eulogy was difficult to write. I wrote it intending to kill you; I intended to kill all in the gang. But I've had time to think. How often does a body get what he deserves? Roberts shot me. Did I deserve to die? I should've died out there in the desert. It's a mercy I didn't die; it's a grace I live now. Is this grace unique for me? I've been thinking about that a lot."

"Well?"

"I think it's for all folks, some just have to give it, and some have to receive it. Chaps, I want to extend you grace. Receive it. Go, start that farm you used to talk off our ears about. I think if Fanny didn't want it, he certainly wanted you to have a farm: bacon over a hot fire, kitchen smelling like salt and smoke, horses in a corral, cows to milk, chickens and fresh eggs, spelts waving in the breeze until harvest. You deserve that opportunity maybe more than I deserve life. Find a woman, Chaps, and settle down, have babies. 'My grace is sufficient for you.' You're free to go."

Chaps never left off watching Indie. His face flushed when Indie talked about the farm. Chaps shed tears.

Mattie and Darwin had caught Indie's words, too. She exclaimed.

"You cannot simply let this hardened criminal go," Darwin said. "What would we say when we got to Cannonball Springs?"

"They don't know he's coming," Indie said. "My man in the Cannonball Springs telegraph office intercepted Sheriff Brick's communications, at least I told him to. I replied back through him, and I was successful, based on the messages Sheriff Brick got back. In short, Judge Fickle knows nothing."

"Sheriff Brick does. Will he not make inquiries?"

Indie clapped his hands and pointed to Fanny's body. "There lies Chaps of the Caloo Gang."

He ordered Darwin to stop the wagon. The horse and mule slowed and the creaking totality ground to a halt. Indie unhitched the horse from the wagon and gave it to Chaps. "There's a lot of this land. It's hard to traverse it by foot."

"You're just going to take the horse?" Darwin said.

"You're assisting me."

"That is on account of a debt accrued before I became a U.S. Marshal. It would not be right for me to hide behind my badge and deny a natural justice, paying a debt for a debt. But mark me, when you have released me from my obligation, I will assume for you the standards I assume for every man, and that is as an instrument of the law. Man is not a law unto himself." Darwin spit tobacco into the dust.

"Chaps doesn't deserve to be hanged. You mentioned natural justice; there are natural laws, too, those of God and nature, inviolable. They're written into the fabric of existence. We perceive but we can't manipulate them. Death is one such law—a judicial cloth barring immortal adventure. We are all of the cloth, paying our unique servitude to its unforgiving circumscription."

"Death is not a final chapter," Mattie said. "You of all people should know that, Indie. We are more than temporary beings. We will one day exchange these bodies for others."

"But that exchange has no earthly good. That's why we've the laws of men, and specifically the United States, to guideline societal functioning with righteousness, and to preserve and enhance life. Law is beautiful when wielded righteously. It's worthless in the hands of men like Judge Fickle, who gives the law a mortal reading, whether warranted or not. Western anarchy is practiced by more than just outlaws. 'Righteousness exalts a nation, but sin is a reproach to any people.'

"We must break with mis-applied laws of society if in keeping them we would break with the laws of God and nature. I know Chaps would suffer an unwarranted death under the gavel of Judge Fickle. If he is to die, it should be by my hand. And I have set Chaps free. Mattie, you well know the parable of the servant who was forgiven much. His downfall was in not extending a smaller measure of forgiveness to another."

Mattie flushed. Indie stole a glance at her and rubbed his forehead. He saw again the other side of death, the exchange of old for new—a bright light illuminating a vast gray veil. The desert loomed as a vague shadow, an empty sky hurtling like a dream and hanging in the void.

"Death stands as a warning. She reminds me in my stiff joints of that moment when I sat up and felt the blood and bullet-wound pain for the first time. It was as though I awoke for the first time, too, and all the horrible and wonderful senses poured through me as cold water."

Indie gave Chaps the Tennessee pacer's reins. He helped Chaps mount the old horse.

"I thought you were dead," Chaps said. "When you revealed yourself to me at the bank, I thought I was dead, or would be. You had a direct shot. And then I hoped Fanny would escape. I suppose I never thought about building a farm or a life without him. Fanny could be terrible family, but he was family. Now that he's gone, I'm not sure I've the will to see it through. He always had more than enough boldness for the both of us."

Darwin scoffed. "A farm is a farm. You had better take this chance to live free. I would not extend the same token Indie has extended to you. I expect that he might be your only benefactor."

"Your devotion to your brother doesn't have to prevent you from living a good life," Mattie said. "Grief need not stop here. Fanny's death isn't the final resting place for your memories. You carry those with you."

"Am I not betraying him, leaving his body here while I go and satisfy my hopes?" Chaps said.

"What would you do with Fanny?" Indie said. "You can't stop his body from rotting."

"It would be betrayal, that he died and I turned my back on him."

"It'd not be betrayal," Mattie said. "Fanny chose his own destiny. You need to choose yours."

"A criminal cannot handle freedom," Darwin said. "You need criminality and to be on the run just as much as you needed your brother. What will you do without the driving need to *be* free now that you *are* free? You are on the cusp of gaining what you have always wanted, and it terrifies you. You can pursue your plans and it cripples you. I have seen many a criminal petrified by the thought of genuine freedom. A criminal knows the lawman, knows pursuit, knows a cell, knows confining purpose. We do not have enough jails for the lot of them nor enough lawmen to put them there. What a disservice to them and to our country." Darwin shook his head and spit more tobacco.

"What a treatise!" Indie said. "I suppose we're all delivering them. Chaps, be off. This is your chance. I won't be delayed. We've got to get a move on. If you don't go, I've got your eulogy." Indie tapped at his waist where he had stowed his notebook under his jacket and between his body and belt. "I'll shoot you if you stay."

"You are not only going to let him go, you are going to kill him if he does not go?" Darwin chuckled.

"I suppose I don't have much choice in the matter?" Chaps said. He winced and turned the horse to face far-off cliffs that rose purple-black into the pocketed sky. The sun dazzled between clouds and bore distant shafts of light in their void. Chaps turned the horse around. He walked it to the wagon, plucked an item from around his neck, and tossed it into the wagon. He cursed and kicked the old horse and sped away, out of reasonable pistol shot range, then slowed the old animal to a sustainable trot.

"Fanny and Chaps found some gold when they were young—small nuggets," Indie said. "Fanny kept one, Chaps the other."

Darwin picked up the gold. "Does it do any good out here?" Indie nodded for Darwin to pocket it, which he did. "Am I released from my debt?"

Indie smiled. "Yes, just get me to Fog's. He's my friend, as much as anyone calls Fog a friend, and he runs the station house you're heading to. I expect that you don't know Fog or anything about his station house. Why should you? It's not much, but it's the only station house between Racida and Cannonball Springs. I'll sleep there tonight and figure out the next steps in the morning. And I release you from your debt."

Darwin smiled. He urged the mule which lurched and moved the wagon, building inertia. It was little more than a walking pace but Indie said the house was not far away.

Darwin stopped smiling. "It will take us longer with just the mule."

CHAPTER 22

THE ARAPAHO WARRIOR HAD NOT told Slim to move on, and Slim had not. He enjoyed the fruits of the warrior's hunting and gathering, which proved excellent despite the sparse landscape. When he was not getting food, the Arapaho was polite to his guest and concerned with spiritual observations. Slim observed his host.

"Do you talk to spirits?" Slim said.

"What do you mean, 'spirits?'" the Arapaho said.

"Folks that's passed. Heaven and hell apparitions living among us." The Indian grinned and Slim continued. "All men have a spirit. I stay careful not to trespass against them; it's in the Lord's Prayer. You natives pray to the spirits all around us, in the rocks and trees and sky. You can put a body in the ground but its spirit remains."

"You have your religion. I have mine."

"That's just it, isn't it? We're separated by our beliefs. But spirits don't discern, do they? And how many spirits except in every man? I'm full of questions. I grew up believing in one God, taught by an angry school teacher that God was justice and the only way to heaven, or hell awaited. You can imagine hell, it's an awful place. And I didn't want any part of it. I became a convert, you could say, as good as almost any I've met. It was the Devil that scared me to God."

"Fear and obedience may link but there should not be terror in worship."

"Worship?" Slim swore. "I call a spade a spade. Worship's just appeasement by another name. My teacher said God's a spirit, and there's angels and demons, too. You Indians say everything's a spirit. So we agree there's spirits, and I think at least we're surrounded."

"We are all spirits."

"My point, exactly!"

"Consider them. Do not cower from what you yourself are. We commune with all things."

"Communing is one thing, disturbing is another. Can't you invite retribution? I want to pass without invoking wrath. Death is terrible and swift enough of its own accord. I don't need help to usher it to me."

"Spirits manipulate, but I think men more often exceed spiritual evil and without help. A chief once said to kill white men. They had settled our lands. I thought killing would bring more killing. I have seen the great river, what you call the Mississippi. Our people are great but we have no union strong enough to forever defeat a hungry people that conquered all land east of the great river.

"I wanted to believe we could win, but I saw the reprisals and new enemies flooding in while our men died without replacement. I knew your language; I sought peace for my village. They jailed me in their camp by a stream. The soldiers starved me trying to get me to say where my village was. I hated them.

"A priest visited. He stayed with me, improved my English; he showed me how words read and write. One day, he said the soldiers wanted to kill me. He freed me. I returned with warriors and found him dead. We burned the camp.

"The U.S. government pushed my village to a reservation. We live there locked away without chains. I left and came here for reasons I have said. I did not also say that I have come to ask your God about his people. The priest said He is good even when His followers are not. He does not prowl like spirits."

Slim sat silent for a long while. "Our old gang leader, Indie, said there's laws of God and nature, and to break them meant death. I have tried to not break a natural law. But if I stumble, repentance is all I have. I talked once with a theologian who told me godliness requires repentance. No one living or dead can forever hold a grudge. God is good. He only needs us to admit our shortcomings."

"Does He need us to do anything? Your theology is intentionality, observance, and repentance. The priest said God holds the key to unlock salvation. Do you believe this?"

Slim's voice echoed shrill off the cold rocks. He spoke about growing up on a New England farm with a profligate father. "He was drunk when I told him I would go to Harvard College; Yale?" Slim shook his head. "He said I'd never receive his blessing or money. I knocked him down, and he dropped a purse full of money. He was a gambler, it must've been winnings. I took the money and left for Columbia College.

"Do you fear your father?"

"Fear? It was bliss to study. And he didn't remember losing his money; he never figured out where I got the tuition money from. But damn the war which interrupted it all! After Lee's surrender, I was discharged and came out west. I met an old classmate, Indie Caloo, who introduced me to the rest of the gang. We gained quite a reputation. He couldn't have done it without me and my learning. My brain has saved me from a life of misery and thoughtless work. I've only to ensure goodwill from what spirits I might disturb. It's not easy, yet what other way can a man live?"

The Arapaho sniffed the air as the outlaw wrapped up his soliloquy. "You should go," he said. Without a word, the Indian saddled Slim's Appaloosa and furnished him with riding supplies. Slim rode away from the old warrior in the direction of Cannonball Springs. He cried.

When Slim had slipped out of sight, the Arapaho began to take down his camp. There was not much to tear down and he worked fast. He finished when two cow hands and Roberts appeared.

The outlaw whistled and his thugs dismounted and grabbed the Indian. They laughed and grunted and told him to hold still, even though he did not move. They pinned him down, kneeling, with his arms behind his back. Roberts savored the violence and clicked his tongue as he walked to the old warrior.

"What's a savage like you doing here?" Roberts said. "I thought they'd kicked your kind out and sent you to the reservations." He swore. "The only real solution is extermination. The west will never be ours while you remain. What other conqueror has ever left his enemy alive? Did Rome let Carthage thrive? It's plain benevolence; and yet, misguided." He stooped in front of the unflinching Arapaho. "Magnanimity, and what do we receive in return?" He spit in his face. Roberts turned to the Indian's dying fire.

The Arapaho swept his legs left and toppled one cowhand. His right arm cracked but he swept with his freed left hand and the other poke crumpled to the ground.

Roberts swung around with a stick, hot from the dying fire and glowing at an end. The Arapaho glared at him. The first knocked-down cowhand began to rise and the old warrior knocked him down again.

"Why have you come to kill me?" the Arapaho said to Roberts.

"I'd kill any of your kind given the opportunity. Like I said, the west will never be ours as long as Indians remain. But I didn't come looking for you to kill; I'm searching for another fellow called 'Slim.' Though I'll kill an Indian when I can."

The staying romance of hand-to-hand combat—exhibited in historic observations from amphitheaters to tournament grounds—stems from its unfettered competition between man and man. We admire combatants' skill and preparation applied in strategy, and we applaud victory fairly falling into the hands of the better or more determined. The Arapaho charged the bigger-bodied Roberts and slammed shoulder-first into his torso. The blow knocked Roberts down, his smoldering stick out of his hand, and his breath out of his body. He gathered himself and caught the warrior in the side with a fist before he could spring away. Then Roberts rolled over and stood to a crouch that mirrored his assailant's: elbows bent and hands ready.

Roberts broke the stare down with a smile. "I know you from somewhere?"

"Yes. You were a soldier, the leader of soldiers. I was a prisoner. I escaped and returned to your camp and killed you."

"Sauce Arroyo! I remember. I should've placed you straight away. That Catholic priest came proselytizing and I joked that you'd be as ready an ear as any." Roberts swore. "I didn't think an Indian could make a pupil. And you were a fast learner, too. How'd you learn reading and writing so damn fast? A learned man is more dangerous than an unlearned man. We had to kill you, but then you were gone."

Roberts reached for his LeMat revolver. The Arapaho rushed.

Bang!

Roberts fired a bullet through the Indian's dislocated shoulder. But the pair was too close to avoid a collision. The Indian bit Roberts' nose as they crashed to the ground. Roberts screamed.

They rolled and tussled. The Indian sprang away and held position between Roberts and the gun, which he had dropped in the collision. He twirled around and jabbed; he caught Roberts in the face, and he stumbled back. The old warrior held Roberts at a distance with a kick that almost caught him again in the face. Roberts lunged when the Indian bent for the gun and knocked him to the ground. The Indian slammed the pistol grip onto Roberts' head. He slammed him again and again until Roberts slackened his grip. Then the Arapaho gathered himself and cocked the pistol.

Bang! Bang!

One of the cowhands had recovered himself, too, and a pistol, and he had shot the native warrior in the back just before the warrior fired an accurate shot. The warrior's bullet penetrated Roberts. The cowhand's bullet penetrated the warrior. The Arapaho fell to his knees. The cowhand held his gun steady.

Bang!

The cowhand dropped. Slim shot him from his horse. He had turned back to the campsite when he had heard Roberts' gunfire. Slim dismounted and checked the cowhand: dead. He glanced at the other poke and at

Roberts. Both did not move. He ran to the Arapaho warrior who remained on his knees and upright.

"He is dead?" the warrior said.

"I'm sure he's dead."

"Then to rid the earth of such evil, we have lived well when it was most needed." The warrior smiled. "Bring peace." He died and fell to the ground.

Slim watched the old Indian's body for a long time. He closed his eyes and mumbled prayer on his lips. Then he shut the warrior's eyes. He surveyed Roberts and saw the outlaw king breathe shallow.

Slim swore. "He's not dead. But he won't live. I'll be damned if I'm the one to kill him. I'll not have his spirit haunt me."

One of the cowhands was dead, the other was unconscious and Slim saw him breathing. Slim checked the cowhands' mounts, both mules, and Roberts' brilliant palomino horse. He only found supplies except in Roberts' saddle, where he found a stack of letters bundled together. Slim untied them and read for a long time.

"I'll be! Judge Fickle, Clovis, a deputy in Racida, a dozen of Mormon Hyram's cowboys—so this is what you were about? Makes sense given the conversation at the dugout. But who would've thought it to be such an elaborate scheme?" Slim tied up the letters and put them in his saddle. Then he turned his attention to burying the old Arapaho warrior, but the ground was too hard to dig it out. He resorted to piling rocks over his body. He mounted his horse.

"This place is sure to be haunted." Slim spurred his Appaloosa and the pair disappeared.

CHAPTER 23

CLOVIS CHIDED SHERIFF BRICK. HE said they were on a fool's ride. "How do you know where they went? It's almost too dark to see anything."

"Who can tell what a fiend might do?" Sheriff Brick said. "I won't let Indie Caloo and his man take Mattie and the prisoner. I can still see the wagon tracks. We'll follow them until they disappear."

"What happens when they disappear? I can't see them now anyways."

Before Sheriff Brick answered, the wagon tracks spread out in a pattern of the earlier day's confusion. Sheriff Brick studied the ground and stopped himself and his deputy at Fanny's dead Sorrel. He dismounted to examine the remnants of struggle and told Clovis to have a look around. Sheriff Brick gauged the horse and even lifted it to feel under its earthward side.

Clovis had bragged more than once to crowds more than one saloon about his tracking skills. He had said he had grown up with a mountain man uncle who could find any animal he chose, including once a fish-stealing black bear after a five-day search through forests, lakes, and rivers. Clovis was a known exaggerator, and even if the story was true, association with a top-notch tracker did not make one a top-notch tracker. Clovis returned from his search, dismounted, and said he had found nothing else of interest at the scene.

Sheriff Brick shook his head. He was animated and walked Clovis through his interpretation. "The Marshal and Mattie left Racida this morning with the prisoner. Someone rode hard after them. Was he after Chaps? His horse was shot, here's the bullet wound. I'll bet it died straight away. I imagine the rider was thrown. Was he killed or hurt? Mattie and Darwin must've taken him with them because I don't see a body or a grave. And you can see that they drove the wagon back near his dead horse. They returned to see what happened."

"You think the Marshal or Mattie shot their pursuer?"

"Maybe, but not his horse because the wagon tracks run over here, close to the horse, but the entry wound is on the other side. You can tell where a bullet enters if there's no exit or if one puncturing hole is cleaner than the other because the projectile spreads after impact and does more collateral damage. There are two holes in the horse, one on either side, and I felt a lot more gore on its wagon-side, which leads me to believe it was shot hillside." Sheriff Brick ran away. And then he exclaimed.

Sheriff Brick turned to Clovis. "I saw other tracks leading from the hills: two horses, maybe a mule and a horse. It seems another rider either intercepted Mattie and the Marshal and their prisoner, or else he's following them. We need to follow the wagon. Whatever happened here and why, we'll have our answer with them. We've found a bit of luck because the wagon starts heading generally in the direction of Guilfoyle's station house which I believe is run by a man named Fog, though I've never met him. It's getting too dark to track well, but I bet they're headed to the house, which will save us tracking work."

Sheriff Brick spurred his horse and rode like mad. Clovis smiled evil.

Chapter 24

THE STATION HOUSE WAS A RUSTIC log cabin built better than it was maintained. It sat near the base of a large rock face. It was a welcome sight after a long day's ride in the sun and wind. The station house proprietor, a vacillating reclusive or welcoming hermit named Chester Fog, was, as far as anyone knew, a civilized and disgraced socialite from back east. Inebriation or the company of good friends spurred him to expound spectacular descriptions of lavish events he said he once organized or played a strong focal point in. Whether he hailed from the Great Lakes or Massachusetts, Fog was otherwise consistent in his origin story. He reveled in narrating his struggles out west, beginning with his initial fording over the Missouri River. And this narration is what he told Indie, Mattie, and Darwin as they sat around a roaring fire in the big fireplace of their patron's great room after a dinner of pork belly, pickled watermelon, and biscuits.

"I traveled west before the war between the states to Kanesville, now styled Council Bluffs," Fog said. "I carried a large assortment of luggage and $1,000. It could've been more than $1,000, too. I was mistaken for a follower of Father Pierre-Jean De Smet. He was organizing another mission trip to the Sioux or another tribe. I said why the heck can't I be a Cathy? And so, I converted!" Fog laughed and swore. He punctuated sentences with laughter and swearing. Mattie cringed at each instance.

"Two Potawatomi Indians ambushed me the night before Father De Smet's ferry was to leave for the western banks of the Missouri. Outfits spoiled, luggage lost—and what was their purpose? They wanted hooch. Booze!

"They quickly realized I was no Catholic, but I did have booze. We drank it all and I crossed the river a few days later to Omaha, which is much bigger now than then, I hear—a city! Yet I'm skeptical because you can't trust newsmen as far as you can throw them. Have you ever tried to throw a newsman? Omaha's got several of their ilk.

"I landed a job in the Herndon House hotel, named for Amazon expeditionary Lieutenant William Herndon. What a hotel! It's the best between Chicago and San Francisco. We were always crowded with westward-venturing settlers, and we were the center of society. Mr. Keith, the hotel's manager, took pride in presenting spectacular fare. I oversaw the collection of local game and fish. And if we didn't have it on our menu, we'd do anything to get it.

"One night, a brute ordered 'frog legs del Monaco.' I'd never heard of 'frog legs del Monaco,' and said that judging by his snickers, he'd never heard of them either. He was a sadist, I'd say. Without warning, he pummeled me sideways and upways and downways. I've never been so pummeled. I couldn't see, but I heard him laughing and howling as he fought expulsion from the hotel. I'll never forget that laugh. I left town the next week, as soon as I was able, carrying all I could on a westward-bound coach, all else be damned."

Fog then regaled his visitors with his journey farther west, a brief stint in the Colorado Territory militia, and chiefly in how he found his homestead. He finished his tale with a long recounting of the building of his home, which cost him nearly all his money. Then the travelers retired.

Mattie, under too many blankets, stared at her bedroom ceiling and moved her lips. Darwin slept. Fog, as was his custom, held an old Arapaho warrior's hatchet and serenaded his room off the strength of "warm milk." Indie sat on the edge of his bed fingering his Colt army model revolver in the near dark and admiring its glint in a window-sliver of moonlight.

Outside, The Milky Way painted itself in wide white strokes. A brilliant half-moon shined, its lunar surface like detailed ivory. Coyotes bayed in the distance. And the cold air settled in without struggle, unlike its usual roll down the rocks to rattle the funnel of Fog's settlement before exiting into nothing.

Bang!

A bullet flew through Indie's window and lodged into the wall. He jumped from his bed to beneath the windowsill. He cocked his pistol. More shots and more bullets crashed into his bedroom. Indie broke glass with his pistol barrel and fired a few shots outside. Then he ran to Mattie's room.

Mattie heard the shots and rolled out of bed to the floor, then crawled to a corner near the door. Indie burst through it. Mattie yelled when the door hit her. He checked her for injuries and sheltered her with his body as they both walked crouching into the great room. Two more shots were fired and bullets hit the south side of the house. He turned over a table, facing it against the door with their backs against the fireplace.

"Stay here," Indie told Mattie. He gave her his pistol.

"Don't you need this?" Mattie said.

"I've got to get my rifle. A pistol won't do any good holding them off. That's for if all this develops."

"Develops?"

"Into a gunfight."

"What do you call this?"

"A shooting."

Indie left Mattie. He opened and peered through the door to Darwin's well-lit room, which was next to his and faced south. Blood splattered the white bed sheets. He was dead.

Another volley of shots erupted in the night air. Indie reeled and slammed the door. He ran into Fog stumbling out of his room. He told him he would be safe with Mattie behind the table in the great room.

"No one's going to shoot at me in my house," Fog said.

"They're not shooting at *you*," Indie said.

"I'm here, not? And it's my house. I'll be damned before I let someone shoot at me in my house. Don't I know you're an outlaw! What do I care except that you pay? No other reason that men would be shooting at you this hour except that you're really an outlaw. I wasn't sure before. Newsmen be damned. Well, I know now, and I'll not warrant any trouble falling on *my* head. Where's that Marshal? Marshal!" Fog shouted. "He can handle this. He should handle this." He shouted for Darwin again.

"He's dead."

Fog blanched.

Indie brushed past Fog and returned to his room to get his Spencer repeating rifle. He also grabbed his leather-bound black notebook and gold pocket watch. He met Mattie at the door; she held Indie's pistol at him.

"Darwin's dead," Indie said.

Mattie gasped, then gathered herself. "Do you remember your riddle?"

Indie smiled. "You found the paper?"

Shouts rang from the yard. Fog had shuffled into the great room and thrown open the door. He walked outside to yell back.

Mattie lowered her voice and produced a folded paper. "It's half a map. It says 'Key Saddle' on the back."

"When I first met you—beautiful as you are now—I couldn't stop looking at you. My heart's still in my throat. If love's all that's needed for happiness, I'd give up misery."

Mattie's eyes glistened and she clenched her jaw as Indie walked by her to Fog. He had finished his yelling conversation and had re-entered the great room.

"They say they've business with you," Fog said.

"They?" Indie said. "Of course they do." He walked to the front door and outside. There, Chaps and the bounty hunter stood with guns. The bounty hunter swore.

"You missed me, but you didn't miss the Marshal."

The bounty hunter swore again. "The Marshal!"

Mattie and Fog crowded behind Indie and in the doorway.

"You'll put your gun down now, bounty hunter," Indie said. "You've no bullets left anyway, not after unloading on the house and killing the Marshal. Why'd you do that?"

The bounty hunter clicked his tongue. "It's surprising you made it as long and as far as you have—the infamous Indie Caloo,"

"I stay a step ahead." Indie smirked. "It's too bad we never played cards." He looked to Chaps. "You shouldn't have come back."

"I'd no choice," Chaps said. He coughed.

"You always have a choice. Some are just too unappealing to look like one."

"I was curious what your troupe would do with his brother's body," the bounty hunter said. "Is he still in the wagon?"

"We're going to bury him tomorrow."

The bounty hunter laughed. "Then you set *him* free?" He indicated Chaps then sneered. "What are you, Indie Caloo—saint, outlaw? Five thousand dollars will be the highest bounty I've ever collected. This fella will add to it, too. Notices say 'Dead or Alive.' And he's a member of your gang. It helps to have another mouth to confirm an identity."

"You're going to shoot me and have Chaps confirm it and then turn him in with my body?"

"You're keen."

"Being keen is how I've made it as long and as far as I have. I imagine it's how you've got on, too. But we all miss a mark sooner or later. I don't see how you plan to get out of murdering a Marshal. Not even Judge Fickle would believe whatever you're thinking, not with so many witnesses. You'd have to kill us all. I'm not going to let you do that. I'll explain quick for the good of us all, and then Chaps and I will get going.

"That's a Spencer like mine," Indie pointed to the bounty hunter's rifle. "It's got seven bullets in a magazine. I heard seven shots. You wouldn't give Chaps a loaded gun, certainly not his own Remington which I see he's holding. He's an outlaw and you're planning to turn him in. You wouldn't risk him turning his gun on you.

"Now, why you fired all your rounds is beyond me. Why fire at all? You should've taken the house under threat. But now you have no bullets, and I know that because while you were stealing my horse, you lost your reload magazines except one, which was empty. You didn't think it oddly careless of me that you found my horse?

"You're standing there with less firepower than I've got here. Your dragoon pistol might get me; your Derringer won't. But since you killed the Marshal, you'll need to do something about the witnesses. Thus, giving us reason to turn our guns on you, giving us a three-guns-to-two advantage at least, and I've got a rifle which is sure to kill you from where I stand."

The bounty hunter raised his rifle to fire at Indie and pulled the trigger. The hammer clicked. Indie raised his gun. The bounty hunter lowered his.

"Why do you think they'll back you?" the bounty hunter said.

"They've had opportunity to turn me in and they haven't."

The bounty hunter threw down his rifle and pistols as instructed. Indie instructed Chaps to bring them inside. Indie arranged for Mattie and Fog to hold up the bounty hunter in the great room, explaining to Fog three times what was occurring. Fog abandoned Mattie for his room and returned with "warm milk" in a brown bottle and his hatchet. Indie roused Chaps and they rode the Morgan and mule away and into the night.

Fog leaped at the bounty hunter. Mattie shouted Fog down, disarmed him, and held him and the bounty hunter with the pistol Indie had given her. She watched the men fall asleep. Horses approached and halted. Sheriff Brick shouted his name and greeting. Mattie answered with a yell which woke the bounty hunter and Fog.

"What's this!" Sheriff Brick said as he entered the great room. "Mattie, why're you holding a gun to these men?"

The bounty hunter jumped to his feet. "Sheriff, now we're even. She's holding us hostage. I'm on the trail of the notorious outlaw, Indie Caloo. She's his accomplice or worse. He's been here and she's covering his tracks, ensuring his escape. What a woman wouldn't do for the man she loves!"

Sheriff Brick's eyes widened. The bounty hunter grabbed his guns, stormed out the door, and disappeared.

"You shouldn't let him go," Mattie said. "Things aren't as he made them seem."

"Betrayal?" Sheriff Brick said.

"That's a nice ax you got there," Clovis said to Fog.

Fog had eyed the deputy from the moment he had walked in. "Thanks, got it off an old Indian."

Clovis laughed. Fog's eyes grew really big.
"He shot the Marshal," Mattie said.
Sheriff Brick sighed. "Are you well?"

PART V

ARREST

Chapter 25

"You're a fool," Mattie said to Sheriff Brick. "Arresting me?" She spoke between bites of an undercooked corn cake that Fog had made for breakfast. She grabbed an empty cup. "Fog said he was getting milk an hour ago, it seems. I've never heard it take that long to milk a cow."

"You had a gun to two men," Sheriff Brick said. "Indie Caloo escaped. You'd not arrest yourself if you were me? You obstructed justice by aiding and abetting a dangerous man, an outlaw!"

"I didn't obstruct anyone."

"Where's Indie?"

Mattie did not answer.

"The bounty hunter said you let him escape. Your loaded and aimed gun seemed to support his assertion."

"Should I have cooperated with him? I hardly see a bounty hunter as justice embodied. He fired on us. You can see the bullets for yourself in the other rooms. You can see them in Darwin's corpse. He's a murderer! He killed Fanny, brother to your prisoner, Chaps. He killed the Marshal. And he might've killed us, too, as witnesses to murder. You chastise me yet let him walk." Mattie stuck the rest of the cake in her mouth and chewed.

"The whole gang, I'll warrant—Chaps, Fanny, Caloo—no wonder that bounty hunter is out here. I warned him in Racida to not think of himself as law in himself. I don't trust him. I sent Clovis after him last night when he left, even before I knew about the Marshal, almost as soon as he'd walked out. Clovis didn't find him. He'd disappeared. But I'll get him. He must answer for what's been done. Two murders, criminal or not, and one an arm of the law. He'll give an answer. Arresting you doesn't pardon him. But his actions also don't excuse yours."

"You're still not convinced of his guilt."

"I'd need to talk to him. But though I were convinced one way or the other, I'm an instrument of the law, not the law."

"Yet you've taken me prisoner."

"You were holding two men on a couch with a gun. And what was your plan? You couldn't have kept them prisoner for too long."

"Fog wasn't right. I kept him from hurting himself. The bounty hunter, as I already told you, killed the Marshal. I was keeping him from doing the same to me. I didn't have a plan in mind, just waiting for daylight."

"You should always have a plan, Mattie."

"You sprang the most dangerous of our group. Chastising me!" Mattie scowled.

"Caloo was here and his gang—the dead body of one is outside in the wagon, and he escaped with the other, by your testimony and Fog's. *You* let them go. I tried to bring back the bounty hunter. But you let Indie Caloo go. Don't chastise me."

"I didn't—"

"Why didn't you hold a gun on him, too?" Sheriff Brick shook his head.

Mattie dropped the corners of her mouth and focused her eyes. "There are some things beyond law."

"If you're in league with Indie Caloo, the king of outlaws, I can't trust you."

"I'm not in league with him. Does he matter especially or is it the high price, the coup of his head? Indie's infamy is no greater of a misdeed than the hunter who slipped you last night while you assailed me to stand down."

"I didn't let him slip."

"You did exactly! I'm surprised. I shouldn't be, but I thought you were better than other men called 'Sheriff.' A murderer is a murderer, instrument of the law or not."

"I didn't let the bounty hunter walk! And I intend to get an answer from him about this affair."

"Affair." Mattie laughed. "*Murder*. You hesitated when he jumped up boldly and told his story. You hesitated and he was gone."

Sheriff Brick opened his mouth to answer. He reddened and turned from Mattie. She watched him and her cheeks crimsoned, too. Then Sheriff Brick spoke looking out a window to the farmyard.

"I was glad you weren't hurt." He turned to Mattie. "I'm glad you're safe."

Mattie smiled at Sheriff Brick. He turned around to the window again before she could see him smile, too. He stood there, watching the rising fall wind glide over the yard.

"Between us, I don't trust the procurator of this establishment, that Fog fellow. Something doesn't sit right. Do you know anything about him?"

"I know he's not a good cook. Credit him for trying, but it's overcooked or raw. And his 'warm milk' has a strong smell to it."

"I sent Clovis out with him to saddle up the horses." Sheriff Brick turned to Mattie again. "I intend to ride what tracks we can find. Men like Caloo and the bounty hunter know how to find each other. We've only to find one. First though we must bury the Marshal and the prisoner's brother. Fanny? The Marshal deserves a fitting resting place, at least.

"Clovis and Fog went to ready the horses and to start digging the graves. We'll join them when you finish breakfast."

"Is there a command in there? I'm your prisoner."

"All that," Sheriff Brick waved his hand. "I can't believe you let that outlaw, outlaws—*Caloo!*—how could you let them go?"

"It could happen to the best of us," Mattie said.

Sheriff Brick smiled.

"Don't think I'll forget this," Mattie began again, putting down her undercooked food. "You arrested me, and I'll remember it."

Sheriff Brick clicked his tongue and chuckled in rebuttal. He gathered his hat and the two went outside.

The morning air swirled with vestiges of the cold night warmed by the sun: a dry breeze carrying call but returning empty-echoed from the station house and grounds. Mattie and Sheriff Brick walked up dust which seemed to hang before it fell back to earth.

"Something isn't right," Mattie said.

The wagon mule and Dabney stood half-readied in the corral while a couple of other animals chewed hay.

"That's Clovis' mount and one of Fog's," Sheriff Brick said. "I thought Fog had two horses. Yes, accounting for the bounty hunter riding his mule out of here last night, there were two other horses besides mine and Clovis'. There should be five horses here now. Maybe one is in the barn."

"I recognize that saddle on the mule." Mattie paused. "It's Indie's—too fine a saddle and distinct with its Grecian key decoration to ignore. But why he didn't take it with him is beyond me."

When they reached the barn, Sheriff Brick called out into the dark, open doors. No answer. He held one hand back toward Mattie and one hand near his hip and holstered revolver. They entered. A hatchet-head-wounded body lay in a water trough filled with blood. Sheriff Brick ran at it and pulled on its shirt. It fell back against the dirt, eyes open and face ashen white. It was Clovis. Fog was gone.

CHAPTER 26

INDIE HAD RIDDEN ONE OF Fog's horses, gray and from mixed stock, through most of the night. He had led Chaps, hand-and-saddle-tied, and his old pacer from the wagon. They had struck little distance from the station house but had laid such twists and double-backed subtleties that their path would have been impossible to follow in the dark and probably in the light. Indie had said so with a dark smile. And then he had made a hidden camp, where he and Chaps had slept until sunrise.

"Mattie was pretty," Chaps said, over a rude bowl of breakfast grits. "She a good cook?" He coughed and spit blood.

Indie stared at embers of the fire he had made. He remembered Mattie showing him how stirring grits prevented lumping. Simple cooking had seemed like an illusion of complexity she had cut through. Not just bacon and beans, but biscuits and hash and grits and hot oats and tortillas and pancakes—the ease of a pot over a hot fire had empowered him. He had become a good cook. Mattie had lifted him up.

I wish I had your cooking now. What a fool I was! Was I really in the right to break off attachment?

"She's as fine a woman as any," Indie said to Chaps. "But I told her 'no,' because I couldn't marry her. She wanted to marry me. Can you believe it?"

"I suppose I'd do about anything for a woman like that." Chaps sighed. "You're a stronger man than me to walk away. I wouldn't have told her 'no' any which way; she'd have been mine." Chaps lowered his eyes and spit more blood in the dirt.

"You still spit when you're nervous?" Indie said. His cheeks were red. "You're spitting blood."

"I'm dying from that bullet you gave me in the bank." Chaps shifted, moaned, and swore.

"It's not the bullet."

132

"Why are we sitting here? You've kept me alive through the night, and warm, and fed me this morning. I don't understand why you don't kill me for double-backing, if you're going to kill me. You should've killed me last night, buried me with Fanny."

"I wouldn't have stopped you from joining him. But I wasn't going to kill you. You're going to help me chart my next move. You're no help dead. And I'm not sure I *am* going to kill you."

"I watched you and Fanny part ways with Slim over a week ago, before I caught you at the bank heist. He rode after Roberts. You don't trust Roberts, do you? There's always been a man above you, an authority to bite and fight though bridled. And then, you didn't have to worry about Slim if he chased after Roberts."

"He's a spook, more likely would've spoiled Racida than helped. And Roberts was up to something: figures, plans, messages, disappearing for days. Sending Slim to keep an eye on Roberts was killing two birds with one stone. We were to meet up in Cannonball Springs after Racida."

"Is he in Cannonball Springs now?"

Chaps shrugged. "Where's the Pioneer Bank money? We should've known better than to trust you. What'd you do with it?"

"Roberts was right, I did find a bunch of gold." Indie smiled. Chaps' mouth hung open. Indie continued. "I laid our ill-gotten gain with the treasure; someone else will discover it. I've sworn off gold. 'Lay up for yourselves treasures in heaven . . . For where your treasure is, there will your heart be also.' Riches must be used to have any worth. And they can only be used for good if I don't use them."

Chaps smirked. "Women, gold—you get your fingers on treasure and let it slip through! You should do what needs doing. And you should've killed me last night."

"'Whatever is done in the dark will be brought to light.' I gave you mercy you didn't deserve, just as we all have offered to us—grace and mercy beyond compare. But I'm not divine, only a messenger. You came back to kill me; now we'll settle man-to-man. There's nothing to be ashamed of, no cruel betrayal in the night, no leaving a body to bleed to death at the bottom of a canyon. You deserve justice, not a shot in the back. That's the other reason why I didn't shoot you at the house last night. It's light now. And you've helped me chart course. So, we'll duel."

Indie walked to his horse and grabbed two pistols, his Colt army and Chaps' Remington. He walked back to Chaps.

"Roberts killed Duncan, not me." Chaps said.

Indie's lips quivered. He tossed his Remington pistol to Chaps .

"You're aware of what dueling entails?"

Chaps shook his head.

"I've never seen one. But I've read about dueling—more common in older days and back east. Alexander Hamilton was killed by Aaron Burr in a duel."

"Walk-ten-seconds-turn-and-fire?"

"Could be—dueling randomizes skill to equalize footing as much as possible, with death or mutilation a deciding break to the grieving impasse. Gentlemen and savages alike have dueled to decide rights and wrongs."

Chaps laughed. "Suppose we both die. We've got good guns. I fail to see why you'd not just shoot me. I could kill you, too. Can't you just kill me?"

"Righteousness will prevail."

Chaps laughed again which turned to coughing. He ended the upheaval by spitting blood. He wiped his mouth. "How many men do you think we've killed?"

"Does it matter? The Lord can redeem any man willing—"

"Six, seven?"

"No man's unredeemable. The Apostle Paul—"

"I think seven. You might not remember. Me and Fanny and Roberts did the killings. Of course, we made it seem like we killed more. Papers can transform any molehill into a mountain."

Indie glared. "Paul abetted murder, more than once. God redeemed him on the road to Damascus. And Paul was redeemed. He went on to become one of the greatest apostles."

Chaps cursed. "An apostle? An owner's responsible for his dogs. You're an outlaw, a murderer, as much as any of us ever was. You may not have pulled the triggers, but you put the guns in our hands."

"I've never killed a man. And I didn't kill your brother."

"You've killed us all, Indie."

"He deserved death. Yet, he died trying to save you. He gave his life for yours."

"You're dealing in revenge, pure and simple."

"No, my work isn't personal, it's God's work. I'm an instrument of His hands. I wish I could change our past. The arc of history finds its right end in the hands of the Almighty. But who's to say how and by whom it's accomplished? I'd have liked to see your brother afforded a chance to repent of his ways. The Apostle Paul was, and to the forever alteration of history. Our gang raged against this new world's settlement. We should've left the west unbroken as we found it. And I slipped into outlaw madness believing I was preserving wildernesses—ruining men so they'd leave, and with them, their societal deprivations." He waved his hand. "Madness."

"Your ideals then as now cloud your eyes. Greed and revenge, you're like any other man." Chaps shook his head.

"That's Roberts. My greatest sin is that I allowed his menace to rise. He was my friend until he consumed our gang. He destroyed us. I underestimated him. We first met in a dirty saloon in Santa Fe, and he was drunk and pathetic.

"Even though we fought on different sides, we connected over the war. I was stuck in Paducah at the supply depot after some combat. I didn't like combat, but it was tedious working at the depot, until March of '64 when General Nathan Bedford Forrest brought 3,000 Confederate troops from Mississippi to raid and plunder western Tennessee and Kentucky. Our depot was the principal hub of supplies for the region and a fat prize. Colonel Hicks withdrew us to defend inside Fort Anderson. They sieged and charged but we held. And I'm glad we did. I've heard stories of how the Confederacy starved its prisoners. Roberts was also in Paducah, in Forrest's cavalry. He moved with the general to Fort Pillow where he helped massacre three hundred mostly black soldiers.

"Roberts told me about life after the war: coming west, enlisting with the Colorado Territory militia, fighting Indians. He commanded a small unit camped on the Sauce Arroyo until Arapaho scattered their camp and burned it. Isn't it strange when life connects, especially when it is beyond our power to connect it? Roberts participated in and fled from a massacre. I thought to myself, 'here's a man who's learned about life.'"

"Roberts fought in the militia?"

"He's not an idealist—neither confederate nor territory man. He's a killer, the kind of man who looks for a gun and a reason to shoot it. If we had clubs, he'd use clubs. The weapon doesn't matter. I saw it too late and to my detriment.

"But he's also bold. And I needed a bold man if I was to change the west. We partnered and stole from the crooked and to preserve the glory of the wild. I heard that Slim was out here, he was an old classmate, and we enlisted him. We enlisted you and Fanny. We gained capability and embraced capacity. We were great, unquestioned and unstoppable. But we got out of hand. That's why I'm disbanding the gang."

"Why disband?" Chaps smiled

Indie laughed. "Roberts killed me. And my death was a new beginning. Rebirth signaled the Caloo Gang's end. I thought that meant killing you, but I think I don't have to kill everyone in the gang to destroy it, even though I've written eulogies for everyone in case I do kill everyone. Fanny is dead and he has his eulogy."

Indie grabbed his black leather notebook, opened it, and ripped out a page which he folded and gave to Chaps. Chaps held it in his hand, his right hand.

"I put one on you in the bank, too," Indie said. "This is your second eulogy. It's better than the first."

The wind started to pick up and the horses were restless. They swatted their tails. The sun was above the horizon and its orange glow bathed the two men in full light. Their fire burned low.

"You can read it before we duel," Indie said.

"No, I don't suppose I will. Sheriff Brick said he'd a eulogy from the bank. He didn't tell me; I heard him talking about it. I didn't read that one, I won't read this one unless . . ." Chaps waved his arm. "I'll put it in my breast pocket."

Chaps and Indie put away their food before meeting near the dead fire to turn back-to-back. Indie counted paces as they began to walk, free men, away from each other for ten paces, as they had agreed to do. They turned and raised their guns.

Bang!

CHAPTER 27

Slim's frantic ride from the fight between Roberts and his thugs and the old Arapaho warrior carried him though rough highlands and downslope into another valley. His rein-grip loosened and Lazy's pace slackened as he veered nearer to green vegetation. Slim muttered to himself when the Appaloosa meandered to a stop. He slid off the saddle.

"Why'd the Indian send me away? We could've ambushed Roberts."

Slim did not make camp. He settled into the grass with a blanket over his body. He complained about mosquitoes and topped his face with his hat. Lazy grazed well, and when finished, laid down beside Slim. The grass hid man and horse, unnoticed in the fading light by three traipsing cowhands who camped at a nearby clump of Pinyon Pine trees. Their guffaw awoke Slim and Lazy. Lazy twitched his skin and fell asleep. Slim stalked and crawled to the small gathering and large, warm fire. The cowhands were the same rabble of body carriers who had chased Slim out of his boots at the dugout.

"Roberts is a mean cuss," one of the men said. "But he's a bold boss—bolder any way than old Mormon Hyram. He's a tight one, and that's about it. He's the man with the talent, as the Bible says: buried and taking from other fields, tares he did not sow."

"You've got that story wrong," another man answered. There was a third, too, and they continued their conversation. Slim listened.

"There were three servants, each receiving talents. The master was the hard one."

"Two servants doubled their talents. One buried his."

"The details don't matter. My point is that he's going to notice them missing. We could slip away with twenty, thirty head, maybe fifty. Hundreds?"

"It won't be the same brand. Hyram won't prove they're his; he can't."

"A brand's a brand, not law."

"There's a telltale sign. A good eye can always tell when a brand's been changed."

"Who'll be looking?"

"You can't spot a good alteration."

"Seen or not, it doesn't much matter. The law settles disputes. And Roberts said he has the law on his side."

"He's got nothing but hot air in his side." The speaker laughed hard and alone at this.

"He's no lawman, naught to boast. And what's he boasting of?"

"He's got Judge Fickle on his side!" The speaker swore. "And the judge handles disputes in these parts. Mormon Hyram would take a matter to him, no doubts, first thing."

"Judge Fickle wouldn't handle a case like that—not brands."

"Who else is there?"

"No judge in Stanchion or Racida."

"Judge Fickle's the only justice of the peace in the region."

"We're lucky to have him. This is a dangerous world for men of the law. You should make it to town more for gossip."

"What town?"

"Any town. A man can lose himself to the wild if he stays out here too long without civilizing influences."

The men chuckled.

"I wouldn't mind seeing one lawman pass who hasn't passed yet, and that's that sheriff over in Racida."

"He's a constable."

"They call him 'Sheriff.'"

"Slave fella!"

"Yeah, he was a slave. He was a Union soldier, too, I hear."

"Can you kill him for that?"

"Men have died for less."

"He doesn't know his place, is all. And no man black or otherwise is law unto himself. We're a country of laws." He swore. "Slaves don't know that. They've got to be taught on what's proper, that you can't just do whatever or talk to whoever you want."

"You're talking about Mattie!"

"That pretty preacher's daughter over in Racida?"

"Your ears pick up when you hear her name."

"More than his ears." Two men laughed.

The other man swore again. "That Brick or whatever he's called, he shouldn't be even looking at her. And I've heard they've been alone nights.

It's wrong, plain and simple. If God had wanted mixed races, he'd have mixed them."

"You're just jealous, as any single man in the valleys is, that Mattie's never mixed with you."

"You keen for an outlaw woman? She's an outlaw woman, sure, I don't see why else a woman would disappear into the wilderness. A woman only despises reputation for love. And who could she love in the wilderness except an outlaw? There's many a person's got the same theory."

"I think you're getting red."

Oaths and curses followed sheepish disavowals. The company spit and spat and muttered.

"Brick don't got long. Roberts said he was going to take care of him."

"Clovis, right? He's a lying son of a gun and a sadist."

"Roberts has his time. I don't know why he wouldn't just pull the trigger. A black lawman doesn't have friends out here."

"A black lawman doesn't have friends anywhere."

"Except Mattie."

"Cool it."

"Sheriff Brick is a stickler for the law, too. He's a dangerous man for us. Roberts is a fool for not having Clovis do away with him already."

"He hired you, so maybe you're right; maybe Roberts is a fool." The speaker laughed.

"Rumor is, he outlawed with Indie Caloo."

"No one knows who outlawed with Caloo except Caloo. That's how he played it. When you give the public its man, they don't care to see accomplices, not enough to go looking for them. But I'll be damned if it wasn't Roberts with Caloo when they held up the bank in La Junta. I was in the saloon when someone yelled about a fire outside of town. I was too drunk to go. But I stumbled outside, and what should I see but five men and a boy breaking into the bank! They all wore masks, save one, and I saw as I watched that it was Indie Caloo. They made off without anyone noticing, save me. And as they rode away, one of the masked riders' masks flew off and I remembered the face—I remembered it when I saw Roberts again when he was fixing to enlist our services!"

"You should've ridden after them."

"I did ride after them. I gathered who I could and rode after them, in the direction of abandoned Bent's Old Fort. But we didn't find hide nor tail."

"Caloo had five men, no boy."

"I saw a boy. You could've scrutinized him and known. But La Junta was two years ago; boy grew, or perhaps they enlisted another hand. I think it was the same guys always in the gang. No way you could keep a stable and not have one or two turn coat."

"It's a wonder the Caloo Gang evaded capture. Half the country is trailing them. I even hear there's a legendary bounty hunter came back from Mexico looking."

As if on cue, the bounty hunter stepped into the cowpokes' discussion. Slim stirred when he heard his voice and the men yell.

"Couldn't help hearing you fellas. Anyone within a quarter mile couldn't help but hear you." The bounty hunter walked into the men's firelight. He looked them in their eyes. He laughed hard. "It's like you've seen a ghost! I'm no more a spirit than Indie Caloo. You're right about the boy. Duncan was his name. He's dead now. Indie's culling them. Would you believe I saw him in the flesh just last night? But I underestimated his hold on this land—his girl Mattie held me at gunpoint as he rode away."

The bounty hunter swore and helped himself to the last bit of the cowpokes' stew. Two of the pokes laughed and explained to the bounty hunter the other's consternation.

"I don't reproach you," the bounty hunter said to the smitten poke. "She's beautiful. I've never seen a woman her equal. She's a modern-day Medusa." He chuckled. "A modern-day Medusa! How Caloo ever sunk his hooks into her is a mystery. Her father couldn't have approved it. No father would approve of an outlaw. And he's a preacher besides. Doubtless Caloo had his way with her, and there no woman goes against a man once he's had his way."

Two of the cow hands chuckled, one really trying to laugh, but he choked instead and coughed.

"How can you be sure?"

"Saw it with my own eyes!" the bounty hunter said, "just last night, like I said. She held me at gunpoint for him to escape."

"You know a heap about Indie Caloo."

"I've been hunting him for a long time. The longer the hunt, the better you understand your quarry. You learn habits, accomplices, likes, dislikes— you learn how they think. Indie Caloo and I are linked through dogged determination, and we'll be the death of at least one of us, maybe both.

"There's no escaping an inevitable resolve. We've spent too much of our lives chasing and evading each other to escape it. I am Indie Caloo and he is me, friend and foe, neither without the other. And when you're on the trail as much as I've been, you notice little things, like how there's a man listening to us now in the brush."

Slim had almost nodded off to sleep to the philosophical and otherwise ramblings of the cowpokes. The bounty hunter's entrance had awoken him, yet Slim had not completely shaken his exhaustion listening to the mysterious man. But Slim heard the bounty hunter's last words. He fidgeted and rolled.

The bounty hunter enjoyed his cruel joke on the cowpokes with a strong laugh. The pokes grew uneasy and muttered about checking the near-camp thickets. No one rose to the challenge. Slim began to crawl to Lazy, who still slept.

Who can tell when a man will rise to unrehearsed mastery? There is practiced perfection, apart from which a man may hobble into action—the more difficult, the more hobbling. But there are rare instances of impeccable capability, when the doer does not understand how, yet performs beyond imagined hope. And this is how Slim woke up Lazy with one rising gesture, crawled on his back, and rode away from the three cattle hands and the bounty hunter with little more than a stirring noise. The hands drew pistols and fired in Slim's direction, charging the night with explosions, but missed, though they never knew one way or the other. The bounty hunter doubled over in laughter.

Slim cursed and cursed. He rode for a long time, before at last quieting to the trance of Lazy's rhythm and ride. Then he even fell asleep against Lazy's neck as the horse walked. The Appaloosa found a trail which turned into a road which turned into Cannonball Springs. Slim awoke before reaching the town limits.

CHAPTER 28

HISTORICALLY, NON-INDIANS HAVE LEFT THE WESTERN United States to itself. It is the rugged back spine of North America. Some have called it the "Great American Desert." Desert could be called desolation. The steppe bears deserted resemblance, but it teems with life. The sparse bounty has beckoned animals for as long as there have been animals: bison, deer, prairie dogs, coyotes, elk, bears, gophers, badgers, birds of every sort, snakes, bugs in seasonal deluges. The land could not flourish without them, and they could not flourish without it. Little rain strikes a delicate balance with the foragers, so, too, predators which keep too many mouths from eating too much. Feeding cycles stabilize the endless grasslands from perpetuity to perpetuity, constant and new like rolling waves.

Prosperity and ingenuity, foolhardiness and grit, have changed this natural dynamic. Ambitious men have tamed the untamable, predators and grazers have dwindled. But the land is not lost to itself. Spurred by natural opportunity and the bounty of endless growing grass, men have introduced an intrinsic caretaker: cattle. Its lumbering ways, sharp cloven hooves, and heft strike deep into fertile but dry soil, giving it air. Its wandering graze trims the brush, allowing new growth. And cows poop. There is no more reliable fertilizer.

Sheriff Brick soiled his boot in just such a patty off an unaware dismount. He gritted his teeth then looked up and over his horse's croup. Mattie, still mounted, looked at him and laughed.

"I won't swear because you're here," Sheriff Brick said.

"You shouldn't swear at all," Mattie said. "You should look before you dismount."

Sheriff Brick gathered his teeth. "What're the chances?"

Mattie laughed again and eyed her dismount. She and Sheriff Brick sat on a dead log to eat and drink. They had not stopped for repose since they had set out from Fog's station house to search for him and Indie and Chaps and the bounty hunter.

"We've been traveling northwest," Mattie said.

"I would've said north," Sheriff Brick said. "You know this land."

"None other. And I know it better than you do. You're mostly right, we have come north, also a little west. We're on Mormon Hyram's land, I think. He's a wealthy cattle baron. Most Mormons live in Utah territory or 'Deseret,' which is the state the LDS church proposed for admittance into the union, an area even larger than the territory is. I've read about it. That proposal didn't include southeastern Colorado. But Hyram's a convert. He's had this land going back two generations, so he's here even if other Mormons aren't. He's cruel and very possessive. He'll kick anyone off his land he feels doesn't belong there. I've heard folks say he's even killed trespassers."

"That's what folks say?"

"That's what folks say."

"Have you met him?"

"No."

"Judging a man can be dangerous, especially if you haven't met him. I've met him. And he didn't seem cruel. He seemed concerned, said he's been missing cattle and cowhands."

"I'll bet he didn't mention Jenny Sewart! She was riding out this way and she never came back."

"You think Mormon Hyram?"

Mattie reddened. "I don't think it's out of the realm of possibility."

Sheriff Brick shook his head. "Whatever you heard, you need proof before you accuse a man. It's just supposition without evidence."

"How many cattle and hands is he missing?"

"A hundred or so cattle, enough for a small ranch. He said he misses some every year, but that it was early for him to be missing so many. Did your outlaw man and his crew ever strike Hyram?"

"Indie's not my outlaw man."

"Perhaps he never told you."

"Don't insinuate about me and Indie. It was never push and pull with us, drive and attract. We were drawn to each other, but not tethered. We were free, and in our freedom, more independent. We saw this land in all of itself—rocks and trees and sky—and that's what drew us together, the idea of it all.

"Of course, I'm ashamed now, like my father of my mother's passing, for the whole idea that I was swept up in what it was, what we were. Make no mistake, I behaved honorably and I'm proud of my conduct. The shame, embarrassment really, is that I believed Indie Caloo loved me like I loved him, and I mean not only deeply, but for all abandon, all else as chaff in comparison. Gossip, reputation—a brave woman should trade what she can't control for bliss. I regret thinking that I'd summited a great mountain when I hadn't. I don't have a care for the talk shaming me for loving Indie. But I'm ashamed that I might not have the stomach to climb into love again."

Sheriff Brick watched Mattie wipe her eyes and sniffle. He watched her for a long time. At last, he put his arm around her; she leaned into him.

A stir of dust swirled in the distance. Three figures appeared over a ridge.

"We should leave," Mattie said after watching the distance. "I'll bet it's Hyram's men or worse."

"I'm an officer of the law," Sheriff Brick said. "We've nothing to be ashamed of."

Mattie shook her head. "You or me alone, I doubt they'd care. You and me together, I doubt anyone would leave us alone. They've seen us, and they're riding this way."

"Spoken like an outlaw's lover."

Mattie shook her head again. "I'm disappointed you said that. But haven't I earned it?"

"You're agitated. I wouldn't back down even from a greeting. Certainly, I've had my share of unpleasant ones. Even as I rode from Pecker's farm yesterday afternoon, ruffians rode up on me. They meant harm. You can taste a thing like that on your teeth. We used to taste it back in Mississippi when the master had a mind to whip.

"Running can't secure. You've got to face what's coming, else it'll chase you, and that can be worse than facing death."

"I see no good will come of a meeting. Stay if you like. I'm going."

Sheriff Brick called after Mattie. "Of course, no gentleman would let you ride thus away and alone. Do I ride with you as a gentleman and a coward, or do I stay as a ruffian though brave?"

Mattie returned to Sheriff Brick and grabbed his face. She stared straight at him. "You're a gentleman now. And you will be, stay or go. I want you to come with me. I can't see good in staying. A man can't prove his courage. He *is or* isn't. You've got courage, Solomon. You don't need to face these men to prove it to me."

When unexpected bliss steals buried joy, it can direct a man with more force than a cannonball. Sheriff Brick held himself strong as Mattie kissed him. They closed their eyes and lost their breaths.

Mattie whirled with a wild look in her eye and bounded to the Morgan. She mounted it and rode off.

Sheriff Brick wiped his lips and smiled. He looked at Mattie ride away. He looked at the far-off, closing riders. He ran to Dabney. He spurred the quarter horse until it caught Mattie and the trotting Morgan. They matched pace. Mattie, sitting on Indie's beautiful saddle, smiled.

"Canyon," she said over the din of the horses' hooves. She pointed at a growing division of land under gathering storm clouds. Sheriff Brick nodded and glanced back. The three figures were riding after them, now faster. He urged Dabney to push ahead faster and Mattie clicked for the Morgan to follow speed.

CHAPTER 29

"Do you think the dirt's red because of all the blood that's been spent fighting over it?" Indie said. "We're new to this country but we act like it's been ours always. Pioneers first, miners, farmers, ranchers, riders, lawmen, entrepreneurs—is this land big enough? I don't mean physically; of course it is. But does it satisfy with what each party obtains? It doesn't seem it'll contain us and the Indians as they were before us. Clashes are worsening. It'll be a wonder if they aren't all wiped out, only by God's grace.

"But when has a great civilization not taken all that it could, not conquered its doorsteps and those vulnerable? History is full of examples. Only when the weak joined together were the strong beaten back. Napoleon ruled Europe until alliances brought him low. That's what keeps these Indians from autonomy: they can be and are each other's enemies as much as ours."

Chaps looked up. He drew his wincing eyes tighter together. He breathed shallowly. He had fallen when he had fired his gun. He had missed. "Dueling in the desert," Chaps said, one or two words at a time, "I would've supposed one man lucky, one man dead." His week-old gunshot wound bled.

Indie smiled. "Dueling, you have to hit a man to kill a man."

"When have you ever killed a man? I suppose that's why you kept us around. You didn't even fire your pistol. How're you going to finish me now?"

Indie shook his head. "I laid an obvious trail. Then I double-backed. It's too cold and dry for any discernible trail other than an obvious one."

Chaps swore. "I'm about dead." He groaned and he bled.

Indie nodded. "'God's will be done.'"

Rustling captured the two men's attention. Fog appeared from behind two boulders.

Fog swore and spoke. "I've been watching your queer shootout. I couldn't hear much of what you said; Indians, killing, God's will?"

"How'd you follow us?" Indie said.

"Follow?" Fog swore. "I was making a trail of my own. I'm on the run of sorts. No sense playing cagey with two wanted outlaws: I killed the sheriff's deputy. I killed him! He was the scoundrel who ordered frog legs del Monaco back when I worked at the Herndon House in Omaha. You'll remember, he pummeled me when I said I'd never heard of it.

"I confronted him in the barn when we went out to saddle the horses." Fog regaled in explicit detail how he had killed Clovis. "I thought it imprudent to stick around for the sheriff and that woman. I've been running. And I stumbled into you and watched you do whatever the hell it is you're doing; looks like dueling. But why didn't you shoot?" Fog asked Indie.

"He can't kill a man," Chaps spoke in sputters.

Indie blushed. *Or won't,* he thought, and then he thought such a reply could only denigrate him. Two murderers, and one a recent murderer, stood before him. These were brute men unafraid of themselves and God, wicked to terrible consequence. And then he saw again in his mind Roberts with his Lemat revolver pointed at him, ready to shoot if he persisted to not disclose the gold he had found. How had Roberts discovered his secret? *He tracked me, no doubt. But I'm a better tracker than Roberts.*

Then Indie saw Fog again through clearer eyes. The deranged station house manager was more than a lucky fool. *He found us. How? But he found us.*

"How you found us beats me" Indie said. "No doubt you left a trail. They'll be on us."

Fog started laughing. He laughed and laughed. "They? You hoping to be found?" Fog wiped his eyes and continued. "I was in the militia, remember. We tracked many a man, only ever found the ones who *tried* to hide. You always hear about disappearing Indians. They're good at hiding because it's habit to disguise routes, followed or not. White men aren't good at it because we don't usually hide our tracks, and then when we do on account of being followed, we try too hard to hide! If only we'd make it a habit and not give a damn when we're scared!" Fog broke into another round of belly-laughing.

He asked for a drink from Indie's canteen. He surveyed Chaps' bleeding wound. Fog whistled, "That looks bad. I don't mean to scare you, son, but I think you're going to die."

Chaps moaned.

"Maybe a doctor can save him," Indie said.

"You're no doctor," Fog said. He laughed when Indie did not reply. He addressed Chaps. "If it was your arm or leg, I'd chop it off with this hatchet and burn it shut. That's what I did in the militia. I was a doctor of sorts."

Fog turned to Indie. "Didn't I tell you? I got to liking it—mostly making heat salves and concocting cures for bad food. The militia wasn't a bad life, not until an Indian we captured escaped.

"We were camped by the Sauce Arroyo. He came back with a band and we all followed Captain Roberts and fled. They probably let us flee. They could've caught us. They burned the camp."

"Captain Roberts?" Indie said

Fog nodded. "Meanest cuss I ever met. Know him?"

"We were in the same outfit," Indie said. "Roberts told me he'd been a captain after the war; must've been the militia. What a tangled web!"

"We were the Caloo Gang," Chaps said.

Fog reddened. "You two were outlaws together, with that dead man in the wagon, and with Captain Roberts?"

"That dead man was his brother," Indie said. "There were two others, too: Duncan, who's dead, and Slim."

Chaps sputtered. "We killed Indie, or tried to, and he's killing us for it. Fanny, now me if he ever can, then Slim and Roberts." He coughed blood.

"I received a wake up call," Indie said. "For the first time in my life I've got purpose. I have a reason to live! I'm going to dismantle what I built: the Caloo Gang."

Fog laughed. He lifted his hat and wiped his brow. "If that don't beat all."

"Eye for an eye," Chaps said.

"No, it's not a personal vendetta," Indie said. "God told me to restitute. He told me to destroy the evil I set in motion and to restore what I destroyed."

"Sounds noble enough," Fog said.

"Chaps is going to start a farm."

"He looks in bad shape." Fog walked over to Chaps, who had stopped moving. "He's dead."

Indie felt lightning go from his head to his toes. He said nothing but picked up the pistol from near Chaps' body. He returned it and his own pistol to the saddlebag on this horse.

"We both know he wasn't going to make it out of here alive," Fog said. "It's for the better. You're a wanted man. I've heard about the reward, though I don't believe it, not a word. You can't trust newsmen as—" Fog sneezed a violent sneeze. He excused himself. "I sneeze when I see or do something terrible. You should've seen me this morning." He sneezed again.

"You're a wanted man now, too, killing a deputy of the law," Indie said. "You can't go back to your station house and ranch."

Fog damned it. He broke into a swearing tirade and said he never wanted to see his farm again. Tears fell down his cheeks.

"If not your farm, what'd keep you here?"

"I want to see the rest of America, to take a first-hand part of something new. This nation's steaming ahead on her new inventions—railroads, telegraphs, gins, factories—and the west is her best endeavor. It's the creation of a new society. I've always fancied being a creator, an inventor myself."

Indie scratched his head. He saw the whole world as the gray horizon of mountains, a forever sky, dry earth and rock, and a madman with his oral manifesto. He looked at Chaps' body.

"There's nothing new about killing and death; it's not an American invention," Indie said. "It's as old as Cain and Abel. I came west for reinvention after the war. I served in the regular army, as a quartermaster in Paducah's supply depots. But we had fighting there, too, when Confederate General Nathan Bedford Forest swept in for a raid. Talk about invention! I came west to reinvent myself. I thought I had, with the gang—an enterprise to correct societal inequalities. But now I see it was a worse enterprise than what I embarked on before. That's why I intend to fix it."

Indie knelt beside Chaps' body and took the eulogy paper from his bloodied shirt pocket. He unfolded it, cleared his throat, and took off his hat.

"Chaps' real name, like his brother's, we never used. Fanny and Chaps—it was a play on words I came up with. Fanny was a real ass pain. We would've called him 'Ass,' but have you ever met a man called 'Ass?' And Chaps wouldn't go anywhere without Fanny. He stuck close, like a pair of chaps."

Fog took a moment to laugh. And then he really laughed. His face turned purple.

Indie chuckled, then waited until Fog stopped laughing. "I was going to read this eulogy." Indie held the paper then folded it and put it back into the shirt pocket. He walked to his horse and readied to ride. "What's your plan?" he asked Fog.

"I was going to turn you in and get a reward," Fog said. Indie glanced at him and Fog chuckled. "If I could do it, why wouldn't I try?"

"If you *could*," Indie said and snorted.

"I'm in trouble with the law now, so that limits my options. It was passion. Damn passion."

Indie mounted. "That's why I stay away from killing. Passion is too dangerous; it carries you beyond intentions. I know mine: Slim and Roberts to handle."

Fog paused, looking at the ground. "Where are you headed?"

Indie twisted in his saddle. The leather moaned. "This land is beautiful. It's the inevitability that's got me itching to leave." He turned to Fog. "Chaps said he and Fanny planned to meet Slim in Cannonball Springs. It's not unlikely Slim is already dead. But if he's alive, he'll be there."

Chapter 30

"You lead the way," Sheriff Brick said. He and Mattie had slowed their horses to a walk on reaching the canyon.

"But I'm a prisoner," Mattie said. She cupped her hands and put them to her chest. She screwed up her face to a half-smile.

Sheriff Brick hissed. "I see you're not going to let it go. I was only deliberating."

"The revolutionaries in Paris only deliberated, until heads began to roll. Then they couldn't get enough of it." Mattie crimped her nose and jostled her hair. She moved the reins back and forth. She clicked and her Morgan cantered in front of Dabney.

The canyon's red rocks echoed at their entry. Temperamental waters had smoothed the canyon bed and hollowed and sculpted its sides. Established vegetation clung to higher ground while young shoots greened the path of disappeared waters. The gray storm overhead kept gathering like a living beast, with brilliant and impossible columns and heights.

"That storm's got me worried. It's getting colder. Is that what's on your mind, Mattie? You look like a dog that's spotted food it can't get."

She pulled out her riddle paper with the half map and words "Key Saddle." She gave it to Sheriff Brick. "You might as well know that I'm following Indie, in a way. The riddle at the end of the eulogizing letter from the bank? That paper you're holding was under the saloon, where Indie used to stash letters for me." Mattie blushed.

Sheriff Brick took the note. He shook his head and studied it.

"There's a map to this canyon. And then the words 'Key Saddle?'"

Mattie shrugged and shook her head.

The pair continued in silence. They rounded a corner to a crossroads: a large shaft running left and two smaller shafts running to the right, the farther-most disappearing quickly behind a sharp rise and bend and the other obscured by boulders and a sharp turn. The view of the large shaft's run was obscured, but it was clear for longer and less pocketed with boulders and loose stones.

This was a gathering place for water. The more abundant green foliage of the three-shoot meeting-ground indicated lingering fresh water. Parted reeds indicated animal life and frequent passage through this funnel-gathering. Closer examination would have yielded abundant life clues like scat and fur and trails.

Mattie pointed to the canyon walls and said the discoloration between one layer and another showed the maximum height of water that would flood the area. "We won't want to be caught here when it's raining." She looked at the dark sky. "We've maybe minutes."

She turned to Sheriff Brick. He was smiling ear-to-ear.

"You might as well spit out that toad." Mattie swung her head sharply, tossing her full curls. Folks said she had the prettiest hair, and that she knew how to use it to her advantage to turn a man's head.

"Look at your saddle. It's decorated with Grecian keys. Some folks call them 'meanders.' I read about them in an art book; they were common in Greece and Rome. Is that Indie's saddle?"

"Yes. Key saddle, of course!"

Mattie and Sheriff Brick dismounted. She took off the saddle and they both examined it. Sheriff Brick said it was a fine saddle, maybe the finest he had seen. Mattie said it was comfortable.

Rain drops began. Thunder rolled. Mattie shivered and mumbled "maybe minutes."

They looked and looked. Then Mattie found leather sewn onto the underside of the back housing. Sheriff Brick cut it loose, and a paper slipped out of the makeshift pouch. It was wrapped around a coin.

The rain fell harder. The drops were big and fat. Small hail struck the canyon rim.

"A Spanish doubloon." Sheriff Brick pulled from his pocket the coin he had picked up at the old Pioneer Bank and matched it with the new one. "Same cast."

Mattie took the paper. It bore a map. "We're here. And the map shows that there's a passage," she looked at the canyon wall and pointed, "there."

The rain intensified. Sheriff Brick and Mattie became soaked. Dabney and the Morgan became soaked. Lightning flashed and thunder split the air. The horses reared and ran away in panic.

Sheriff Brick yelled after Dabney. Mattie yelled at him.

"It'd be foolish to leave the horses," Sheriff Brick called. "We've got to bring the horses!" He squinted hard against the rain, which was coming down in waves in a stiff wind. His voice was quiet compared to the raging weather.

"We can't catch them! Follow me!" Mattie scrambled up the canyon wall as Sheriff Brick watched. Mattie called back. "From here I can see a cleft concealed by a huge boulder! We don't have much time before the canyon fills. It's too much rain. Flash floods will tear through here with deadly force."

The liquid sky reared and rang. Thunder crashed again and again, deep to deep. Sheriff Brick looked in the direction of the vanished horses.

Bang! Bang! Bang!

He exclaimed at the gunshots. He began scrambling after Mattie. Loose rocks sputtered from under his boots. The storm lulled but still fell heavy.

Suddenly, the three riders that had been following Mattie and Sheriff Brick appeared. They were Roberts' hands, the same that had haunted Slim, and they were drenched and angry and paranoid from the bounty hunter's fireside visit the night before. They had shot at Dabney and the Morgan but missed in their hysteria. They whooped when they spotted Mattie and Sheriff Brick. They whooped like madmen.

Bang! Bang! Bang!

Bullets whizzed by Sheriff Brick but one grazed his shoulder. He yelled and hurried up the slope toward Mattie. She had gained the huge boulder and cover. He presented an easy target, still exposed on the slope's face.

Then a terrible rumble, not from the sky, shook the air and earth. Mattie grinned a terrible smile and walked from behind the boulder to see a surging flash flood round a bend. "A Red Sea," she whispered, unheard under the crash of muddied waters. She hurried to help Sheriff Brick, whose burning cut slowed him.

The cowhands turned to their doom. Two of them spurred their mounts to flee from the inevitable. The other looked at Mattie. She was beautiful in the gloom and in her concern for Sheriff Brick, a black man running to her.

"I'd give all if it was me," the cowhand said.

Water crashed onto the riders, the stationary one first, and dragged them from their saddles. It plunged them and their horses screaming under its brown surge. The water also slapped Sheriff Brick's feet and knocked him down on his face. But Mattie had just grabbed his hand and she pulled him from the crest of water. He arose bleeding and finished scaling his climb with Mattie. He had not turned his face from her.

He sighed, sweating, "No horses, then."

She hugged him. They held each other in the rain while the flood raged beneath their feet. Then they turned from the deafening storm to the crevice behind the boulder. It turned into a dark cave with no end. Mattie said their eyes would adjust, but soon it was too dark to see.

"This is a cave in the canyon walls?" Sheriff Brick said.

"More a tunnel, according to the map from the saddle," Mattie said. "I saw that this opens up on the other side. It's actually a shortcut to Cannonball Springs. Riding through that canyon would've taken us all day at least, maybe two, it winds so. And if the map's accurately scaled, we'll now be able to come out near its end in only a few hours. There's an offshoot, too, clearly marked with the word 'find' and circled."

The tunnel grew low and narrow. Sheriff Brick led with a torch he made with old clothes and a stick, sparking the cloth with gunpowder from a disassembled bullet. The torch burned well. They continued slowly on the twisting trail, steadily downwards, until they came to a bend where outside light penetrated the dark. It was enough light to outline a shallow pond. The water reflected immense rocks above it which dripped water from some opening high above. Mattie and Sheriff Brick drank from the pond before continuing. The trail led down and the air grew thick. Mattie asked to lead. Sheriff Brick resisted but she insisted and so she led.

"How long do you suppose this trail is until we find the 'find?'" Sheriff Brick said.

"The map seemed scaled," Mattie said. "I would say some miles. But I don't know how far we've come."

"You said you found the first part of the map under the saloon. Have you been in cahoots with Indie this whole time?"

Mattie stopped and turned to Sheriff Brick. She held the torch near his face. She squinted her eyes. Folks said Mattie squinted whenever she was about mischief. Then she smiled, which folks said was a dead giveaway for mischief. Mattie squinted and smiled a lot. "Yes, of course." She turned and walked on.

Sheriff Brick didn't speak again until they reached a fork in the cave path. They consulted the map and determined which fork was to the "find," and took it.

"Mattie, I shouldn't have—I've never believed rumors about you or anyone else. People talk. They can say whatever comes into their heads. Too often they don't have sense enough, and so they do say whatever comes into their heads. And saying something is halfway to believing it's true, even if it isn't true at all."

"I'll forgive you, Solomon, if you tell me the most outrageous story you've heard about me."

Sheriff Brick held Mattie's words. "Frida with five kids, sits in a middle pew in your father's church, she told me that you had children hidden in the hills and you'd disappear to feed them."

Mattie snorted laughter. "I hadn't heard that. No wonder Frida would never have her children say 'hello.' That rumor is as bad as any I've heard, mostly eavesdropped. No one would tell me much nonsense in person, except Mrs. Guilfoyle, and that's because she doesn't know better.

"Alright, the truth, though I've told you as much before. I liked Indie as soon as we met; he's a way about him. He's inspiring though troubled. His outlawing is part ideal pursuit of adventure, part rebellion against a society he feels betrayed by, and part boredom for not having worthwhile opportunity to ply a pursuit. He's stubborn and smart and stripped of history, yet full of life, listless in the wild. He fell in with a bad man, Roberts, and I think thievery was Roberts' idea."

"I came across an evil man once, named Roberts. He was evil, too," Sheriff Brick said. "But then, I really didn't know him, just his name and what he did. When I was still in bondage, I witnessed the murder of a supposed runaway slave; he was really a free man, our pastor. I pleaded for his life. Roberts—I never saw him but I heard his name called, 'shut him up, Roberts,' they said—he knocked me out. I heard later that he killed the preacher, too."

Mattie gasped. "An innocent man, a preacher?"

Sheriff Brick spit. "We were all innocent men, maybe not preachers, but innocent. Birth should not compel a man to bondage. If I were to ever find him, I'd kill him. I don't suspect I'll ever run into him or that if I did, that I'd know it was him. But if I did and if I did?" Sheriff Brick's voice drew low. "I'd kill him. It'd be justice. Even imagined justice is one sort."

"The last time I saw Indie, the last time I saw him before this most recent episode, he said he thought Roberts was planning to kill him," Mattie said. "And now Indie tells me Roberts did kill him. Indie said he was dead and now he's alive. And now he's killing them all; he says for God. Well, not Duncan, because they shot him after shooting Indie—so all the rest. Fanny's dead. You saw his body in the wagon at the station house. Did I tell you that Indie tried to send Chaps away to farm? He's with him now, or at least he rode away with him last night. That leaves Slim and Roberts."

She continued. "My part in all of this is history: I loved Indie. And I'd run away, too, for brief periods. It wasn't girlish cupidity, but it certainly looked like it, which I regret. But he turned me away like an old mare, in denial of his love and mine. I've always believed a first love is more powerful than any other. I'm scared that's true, and that I'll never forget Indie. My story's at once too little and not enough, but there's nothing more. I'm not working with Indie, certainly not in cahoots."

Sheriff Brick held silence. The tight passage they walked opened up into a large space. Their footsteps echoed. Mattie raised the torch higher and its light glinted off objects along a far wall.

On February 1540, Spanish conquistador Francisco Vázquez de Coronado y Luján left his governorship of Nueva Galicia in Mexico to lead an expedition of around two thousand troops, allies, clergy, slaves, and others in search of the rumored golden cities of Cíbola. The two-year expedition traversed what is now the southwestern United States and onto the Kansas plain, guided by Indians. But instead of Cíbola, Quivira, El Dorado, or any of a number hoped-for cities of gold, Coronado found giant, naked Indians—probably the forebears of the Wichita and Pawnee peoples—living in straw-thatched villages surrounded by rich land, the best he had seen on his journey. He returned disappointed to Mexico.

Yet Coronado's expedition, though uniquely large and crown-sanctioned, was not the only quest in search of Cíbola. But few stories of the other expeditions have been preserved as many of these other would-be conquerors were never seen again. Rumors of gold still percolate, and even now of Spanish gold.

Sheriff Brick darted ahead to the glint and slammed his boot into objects which clanged. He called Mattie closer. She shrieked as the torch's light caught human bones and skulls under dim conquistador armor.

"I've not seen a man scare you like that." Sheriff Brick laughed. "But there's more here than bones." He took the torch from Mattie and revealed gold and silver in its light. He picked up a coin and matched it to his collected coins from the bank letter and hidden saddle pouch. "Now we know where Indie got these."

Chapter 31

Cannonball Springs was a small town "Two hundred people a hundred miles from anywhere!" townspeople said with smiles, which did not reflect geography nor perhaps actual population figures; no one knew how many people lived in there. It had once been an annual wintering spot for a band of Arapaho in addition to a white settlement. The town had also once been named "Sweet Springs," until it had received a visit from the "Bloodless Third" Colorado Cavalry on the unit's journey home from massacring Chief Black Kettle's Arapaho band along Big Sandy Creek. The calvary had confronted the "Sweet Springs" Arapaho band. Many had died, and survivors had left. After the troops had left, too, residents had renamed the town "Cannonball Springs," though no cannons had been used in the cavalry's activities.

As in Racida, Cannonball Springs notably held a church, though just one and half-attended and a bank that some said had never been robbed because it shared a wall with the jail, though others said to mark their words and that the bank would be robbed. There was a general store with a proprietor who refused to sell pickles and a saloon which had burned down six times, each time rebuilt as before, with no mandated changes in smoking behavior, except finally with a hotel added over the saloon.

Hank Beyer owned the building, and he called it Beyer's Hotel and Saloon. The new building dominated Cannonball Springs' main street. Bright wood siding, yet unpainted, covered its three stories. The saloon occupied the first floor, and the hotel's ten rooms the top two.

The saloon was large and open but dark despite its windows; its pine paneling was dark from tobacco and fire smoke as well as a dark stain that had been applied to new boards in an attempt to blend them in with fire-salvaged ones. The floors were decorated with spittoons and littered with near-misses. The heavy-hanging smoke emanated from a few good smokers.

Wooden columns supported the ceiling. The ceiling above the bar—on the left on entering—opened overhead and an "L" shaped second floor balcony overlooked it. Stairs began at the end of the bar; a second set began at the end of the balcony and ran over the first stairs, necessitating a clockwise-pattern traverse of the second floor to reach the third. The third floor held the biggest and best rooms, one of which was occupied by a prostitute who said her name was Delilah Rudemore.

Not unlike other western hotels and saloons, rooms were vacant during saloon operating hours, which was as long as Beyer could stand to work, or about 12 hours. He was a stickler for payment, and to ensure debt collection, he kept a Colt revolver under his polished bar and an eight-gauge shotgun he called "Rattlesnake" near a large mirror behind the bar and above hundreds of liquor bottles. He was a good shot, as exemplified by an impressive elk bust mounted on the wall across the room and opposite to the bar. Rumors said Beyer had shot and killed people, too. The most often circulated tale was that he had threatened three men from Lonesome Dove on a cattle drive, famously saying, the story goes, that they "better not dirty the tables or feel eight-gauges of wrath," and then he had pointed at Rattlesnake hanging like sleeping death behind the bar. There was no proof for the story besides Beyer's habitual and offensive threats. Crazed looks added to his compelling reputation. No one forgot to pay him.

Beyer did not tolerate fighting nor the display of any guns but his own. Beyer also insisted patrons stick to his establishment's proper name. Frequenters referred to it as the "Spig," referencing a spigot, as no saloon in the region served more alcohol, and to infuriate Beyer. He often got hot and threw bottles at insubordinate patrons.

Roaring card games drew Spig patrons around tables packed around the saloon, and specifically one table covered in green baize, which Beyer said he had brought by wagon from Denver or Golden or maybe Santa Fe. This table was reserved for gambling, and though it always seemed full and surrounded by rowdy men, the baize remained in excellent condition and clean because Beyer insisted it stay so and prohibited anything but cards and chips and money to be placed on it.

Faro, also called "Bucking the Tiger" for the early tiger-backed cards it was played with, was the Spig game of choice, as throughout the west. Its French inventors dubbed it *Pharaon*, and it dominated European gambling halls before varying and finding even more enthusiastic gamblers in America. Faro is fast, simple, and has good odds for any number of players or "punters." A suit of cards is laid out on a table. Punters place chips on a number or face to bet; each number or face has four corresponding cards in a deck to be drawn two-by-two by a "banker." A full deck is placed in a box or "shoe." The first or "soda" card is flipped and discarded or "burned off." All flipped cards remain exposed for the game. The banker then flips one card which is called the losing or "banker's" card, and any chips bet on the corresponding number or face go to the banker. The banker flips a second card which is called the winning or "English" or "player's" card, and any punter's chips placed on the corresponding number or face are doubled. If the banker flips a pair, he collects half stakes. Complications include betting that the player's card will be the "high card;" reversing a bet's intent by topping chips with a penny or "coppering;" and the last flip or "calling the turn" of the deck, which can result in a 4-to-1 payout if a punter predicts the order of the three final cards which are called the banker's, player's, and "hock" cards.

Gambling savvy is unnecessary to discern the unusually precarious betting position of faro's banker, called the "house" position in other games. And this difficult position has contributed to a falling opinion of faro and the rise of games with better house odds.

But the dismal integrity of faro's players, both punters and especially bankers, has been the chief reason for faro's waning enthusiasm, raising poker's almost by default. Hoyle's Rules of Games begins its section on faro saying that one cannot find an honest faro bank in the United States. Bank cheating is often more elaborate, but a good punter cheat is no less effective.

Slim played faro at the baize table, and he was joined by an Irishman named Shamus Callaghan, two seedy characters, a rough cattle hand, and the bounty hunter. Slim did not know the bounty hunter by sight. But after he had sat down to play faro and spoke, Slim had paled at the bounty hunter's voice—the same as from the campfire the night before. The bounty hunter had tracked Slim to Cannonball Springs. And now as the banker, he was winning.

"How's one get so good at bucking the tiger?" one of the seedy characters said to the bounty hunter.

"Yeah, so good?" the other seedy character said.

The bounty hunter smiled. "How a man gets good at anything: practice. It can take a degree of intelligence, too."

The seedy characters did not like that comment and wriggled in their seats. Shamus laughed. Slim shivered. The cattle hand wore a stupid look on his face. He served as "coffin driver" to watch the bounty hunter for cheating.

"Yes, I think a man can get good at just about anything if he keeps at it—cards, drinking, thieving." The bounty hunter looked at Slim. And Slim, for the first time since they had sat down to cards, returned the gaze. "Say like Indie Caloo, he's kept at thieving—and wow, has he gotten good at it."

Slim gasped. The bounty hunter called the turn, drew the last three cards from the shoe, and laughed: one dead bet and a pair. He settled all bets again and quit with more than he had ventured. The bounty hunter excused himself, but first raised a glass of whiskey in toast to himself. The whole saloon joined him except for Slim, who slinked away to his room. Then the bounty hunter disappeared, too.

"Whiskey!" Callaghan said. "In the old country, we drank more beer than spirits. Americans drink a lot of rum, gin, ale, and beer, but nothing as much as whiskey." He spoke with a heavy accent and his words were difficult to understand. His sharp voice ground the syllables one by one.

"I think just about anyone who knows me knows I don't like Irishmen," Judge Fickle boomed. He had watched the game table from the bar. He was heavy-set with broad shoulders and a barrel chest covered in a rough and loose suit. He had blonde hair and a long brown and gray beard that obscured his turkey neck like a scruffy donkey mane. Folks talked about how much Judge Fickle liked to gamble; they said he only drank at the bar when his money ran out because he was a terrible card player. He was not always aware of the rules, or at least he did not always heed them, and he was too-aggressive a gambler to boot. He engaged in boisterous conversation even after losing, sometimes shouting here or there to no one and closing his eyes and nodding his head as an actor might do for raucous applause.

Rumors also said the judge lived off scraps and charity due to his gambling losses, that he maintained a constant degree of waking intoxication, and that he visited the prostitute Delilah on the third floor once a week. The judge had heard the rumors and had said they were "truer than hell," and he had laughed his big laugh. He laughed now. Before he interrupted the faro players, he had been talking to Fog and drinking from a larger-than-regular shot glass. Beyer liked to spoil his best patron.

"I don't like Irishmen," Judge Fickle repeated. His voice carried through the room. "I don't care for their thieving and drinking." He took his shot glass and emptied it. He tightened his eyes and breathed a rasping breath through his nose. "They think they know a good drink. Yet they can't handle our hooch." He laughed and turned back to Fog.

Callaghan did not speak. He kept his attention on a new game of faro. The cowhand assumed banker duties. He smiled wide as he flipped the soda. "Ten."

Callaghan reddened and smashed his fists on the table, upsetting his and the other punters' chips. He whipped from his seat which fell backwards onto the floor. He stood there, shorter than his long upper body suggested, and pointed a cocked-pistol hand—index finger a barrel and thumb a hammer—at Judge Fickle. "You'll take those words back!"

Judge Fickle turned from Fog. He curled a smile on his cheeks, and said quietly, "Words?" Folks said Judge Fickle was quiet only when he was up to something or about death at his gavel. As a judge, it struck many folks odd that he could be mixed up in mischief, but mixed up he was, and proud of it, too. "I'm proud as hell," he would say. And then he would laugh his big laugh.

"You know what they say of you!" Callaghan said. "You're an evil man, an unfit judge. Folks are scared of you. People don't want to appear in your court because it's conviction after conviction, hanging after hanging. You won't get away forever with what you've done, with what you're doing. There's an end to the rope you've wound; a noose is tightest when strung by your own hands."

Judge Fickle played with the rim of his glass. He laughed a breath from his bulbous belly. "You threatening me?" He swore.

Callaghan lunged and was caught by the arms of his tablemates and other saloon patrons. They secured him. Judge Fickle laughed his raspy, full-bellied laugh, which had often reverberated in his courtroom. Mexican prisoners called it *La risa del diablo*, or the devil's laugh. Judge Fickle pronounced especially harsh sentences, usually hangings, for Mexicans. He said he liked Indians but he did not like Mexicans. He also said he did not like black people, Chinese people, Catholics, people who were too religious, people who were not religious, and Irishmen. It is possible Judge Fickle disdained other people, too, but he had not said so.

Beyer swore and ordered the ruckus outside "Or it'll be Rattlesnake!"

Judge Fickle's protectors dragged Callaghan outside which drew the whole saloon. The swinging saloon doors knocked together as the men passed through them, and then fell off their hinges to the ground. Beyer swore and said the ruffians would need to fix them.

Judge Fickle wore a wicked smile and excused himself from Fog with such grace that the old man was visibly disturbed. The judge walked to the fallen saloon doors with measured step. He turned to Beyer, "your place is falling apart." Then he laughed and left the room.

The great scene had emptied the establishment except for Fog, Beyer, Slim and the bounty hunter, and Delilah. The latter three were upstairs while Fog and Beyer occupied the bar. Beyer searched for tools to fix the doors. Fog whistled and Indie slipped into the saloon unseen because Beyer's back was turned to him. He crept along the back wall, under the impressive elk, and upstairs. Fog chuckled and drained his glass.

"To the scene?" Fog said to Beyer.

"I can't find my tools," Beyer said. Then he cursed his tools, grabbed Rattesnake, and acquiesced.

Bright sunlight kissed the saloon's graying siding. A mob gathered in the street. Beyer and Fog stood in the saloon entrance. Beyer was known for his entrepreneurial acumen, and he began canvassing the growing crowd for bets on a presumed fight to unfold between Callaghan and his handlers. Judge Fickle was the first to wager, though it was for credit, which Beyer rebuffed.

"Whatever time he needs," Fog said under his breath.

Slim had retreated to his room, number 9. His third floor window overlooked the street, and he watched the outmatched Callaghan begin a losing effort to best eight peers, to cheers from the crowd.

Indie entered the room without the door sounding its opening or closing. "Hello, Slim."

Slim turned to Indie, screamed, contorted, and would have fallen out of the window except that Indie dashed and caught him by his belt and shirt. He threw him onto the bed, which well-exampled the hotel's best furniture. The dark furniture was reserved for the best rooms and was made by a local craftsman. Beyer liked to say the furniture pieces would compare to the furniture in any San Francisco hotel. Beyer had never visited San Francisco and had only received one traveler who had been there, and that traveler had said Beyer's furniture did not compare. In Beyer's mind, which he boasted about, this meant that his furniture was better.

The bed buckled and broke under Slim's sudden weight. He gasped out pain from the fallen, straw-stuffed mattress.

"The Lord repays the sins of the wicked," Indie said. "He's tasked me to repay good for the evil I've done. That begins with disbanding our band."

"Ghost!" Slim's face paled and he convulsed.

Indie shook his head. "Reborn."

Slim repeated himself and cried.

"Quit crying. I'm not a spirit to haunt. I came on the Lord's work." He pulled Slim up. "Sit like a man." Slim sat on the mattress like a shell of a man. Indie pulled up a chair across from Slim, sat, and smiled.

Indie spoke again: "You can imagine I'd some time to think about our reunion, this moment, and meeting again. I thought initially it'd be the whole gang together, that I'd catch you all out on the steppe or riding through a canyon and we'd have a shootout and that'd be the end of it. I imagined ambushing you at night and leaving your corpses to the rising sun and whatever came after. It was always murder I came back to." *Righteous, satisfying murder.* "But I stayed my hand at the crossroads where you separated from Roberts. I'd opportunity to fight you all. I didn't.

"I was intrigued. I wanted to see the end of your schemes. I wanted to see them unravel and to watch you fail. Fanny and Chaps rode for Racida;

I knew they were headed for the old Pioneer Bank. You all never got over leaving the money back there.

"You were rightly suspicious. I ferried the money out behind your backs. That was my plan the whole time, to keep your hands off that money. I wanted to see what Fanny and Chaps would do when they didn't find anything."

Indie regaled Slim with his adventures, with Fanny's death and Chaps' conundrum to live or die. Slim looked like a ghost watching Indie. Indie surveyed the room and found brandy. He gave some to Slim.

"I set him free!" Indie said. He narrated the way an actor narrates a monologue. "But Chaps didn't go. And now he's dead, too." Indie took the brandy bottle and a drink. "I think now it was God's will to kill you at the crossroads or on the road. It would've been direct. It would've been easier. I hesitated. But you can't flout God; His will will be done. You and Roberts are all that's left."

Slim shook his head. "Roberts is dead. I tracked him to a meeting with Mormon Hyram's hands in a shack by a creek. They discussed stealing cattle, changing brands, mentioned Judge Fickle; they've got the whole thing tied up with lawmen including the deputy in Racida.

"I left the meeting in a hurry and ran into an old Arapaho warrior in the hills. Maybe a week later, the Indian sends me away suddenly. But as I'm riding away, I hear gunshots." Slim sounded a gunshot. "I come back to see one man down, Roberts down, the Arapaho warrior with a revolver about to shoot the prostrate Roberts, and another man about to shoot the Indian. And then he does shoot him! So, I shoot the man.

"The warrior wasn't clean dead. 'Bring peace,' he says, and then he dies. I've never seen a more holy sight."

"That's blasphemous, Slim."

Slim swore. "It's true."

Indie asked him what happened then. Slim swore and asked for brandy. He drank and swore again.

"Roberts wasn't dead," Slim said. "I could see him breathe, just barely, but he was alive."

"Did you stick him?"

Slim shuddered and shook his head. "I'd be a fool to bring his spirit's wrath on me. He was bad off though, real bad. He's certain to be dead. A man couldn't survive it."

"I survived it. You'll remember, you killed me."

Slim moaned and bit his finger. He shook his head.

"You're probably right though," Indie said. "He's probably dead. But what's this you mentioned about hearing a connection to Judge Fickle, lawmen, and Mormon Hyram's men?"

"Yes, and more than just hearsay. Slim rose and retrieved from across the room the same bundle of letters he had taken from Roberts' saddle. He gave the letters to Indie. Indie read a few.

"Roberts must have been at this work for a long while, planning it even before he killed me."

"Are you going to kill me?" Slim said.

Indie put the letters away and addressed his quaking companion. "Ever since Roberts shot me, since I was reborn, I've been at God's work. I'm weary. It might all seem a sort of vengeance. But I loathe seeing men die. My mind's clearer than it used to be, I can see it all clearer: clearer and harsher." Indie pulled a folded piece of paper from his pocket. "I have your eulogy." He held it to Slim.

Slim gathered his hands to his knees and breathed hard. He looked up at Indie. Sweat matted his wiry hair to his forehead.

"After Chaps died," Indie said. "I felt life's sacredness. It hit me like little has hit me before, save Duncan's death and Mattie's kiss. I've seen plenty of folks die but no death except for Duncan's has hit me between the eyes like Chaps dying. When I was resurrected, I thought my purpose was to bring retribution. I think now that my purpose in being brought back to life is to bring a message of repentance. I died in sin; I was reborn in light. God didn't unleash divine retribution, he didn't chain-whip me. I was reborn without grand gesture. I breathed life again. And this—as I think about my purpose now, more and more—I realize that I wasn't sent to murder the gang. I was sent to set you free.

"That's why I'm here, Slim, to set you free from what I've put you to—free from misery, free from your past sins and griefs and guilts." Indie swelled his cheeks and sighed, fury to sadness playing on his eyes. He held silence for a long time before continuing. "I can only offer what I've been given: the clean washing of life, inexplicable, unwarranted, complete. 'Go, and sin no more,' the Master says. Your eulogy is yours."

Slim, shaking, rose to a stooped height. His arms hung by his side. He took the paper Indie held out.

Smash!

The door exploded. The bounty hunter kicked it in. He had been listening in the next room to Indie and Slim talk and he had decided on this spectacular trap—to kick down the door and take Indie prisoner.

Door Splinters flew at Slim and Indie. Indie turned to save his face.

Sheer terror, like courage, can rise like a strong elixir through the bones and propel impossible feats, courageous or foolhardy. In madness, Slim screwed up his face and threw his shaking limbs forward. He screamed "Spirits!" and lunged for the window. He tripped, and as he stumbled, he turned to Indie. Their eyes met. Slim beheld an old classmate and the man who had brought him into his gang, who had guided him through life and death, to riches and infamy, and who had now offered a promise for life without vengeance. Indie saw it all and reached to help Slim.

But Slim pushed away. He hit the ground and rolled with tremendous speed then leapt before hitting the wall and window. Though the bottom sash was open, Slim's unclean fall sent his feet into the upper and raised window sash, smashing its frame and glass, which cut him. He hit the boardwalk overhang with his neck and rolled off into the dusty street, landing with a thud. Glass and wood followed. Callaghan and his assailants stopped fighting and turned towards the violence. The crowd quieted and encircled Slim's body. He had almost landed on top of some of them.

"Doctor!"

"He looks real bad!"

"I'm not sure he'll make it."

Slim did not make it. He was dead. And he held Indie's eulogy in his right hand.

"Indie Caloo!" the bounty hunter shouted from Room 9. The sound filtered down to the crowd.

Indie had rushed to the window to watch after Slim. He gazed down at the spectacle. The bounty hunter's shout and a point from the crowd turned attention. Indie's implacable features changed as he saw Mattie and Sheriff Brick. They had walked from the canyon and had just joined the crowd, with enough time since arrival for Sheriff Brick to find and arrest Fog. Thus, as Indie stared, Mattie, Sheriff Brick, and Fog stared up at him, too, along with the crowd.

Fog swore. Indie smiled.

"No sudden movements," the bounty hunter said to Indie. "Gun's loaded this time."

PART VI

TRIAL

CHAPTER 32

"ARE YOU SATISFIED NOW THAT you've killed them all?" Mattie said to Indie.

"I didn't kill a single one, Matilda," Indie said. "The world may be a better place without them, but I didn't kill them despite my intentions. Though does it matter? It only matters what folks believe I've done. Judge Fickle would hang me on reputation alone and to raucous approval."

Fog snickered from the corner of the cell he and Indie shared in the Cannonball Springs jail with two other criminals—one who disavowed wrongdoing and another who gloated in it. Mattie talked through the bars of the rectangular holding cell built along the back wall of the room. Cannonball Springs' Sheriff Jeb Boone fiddled with papers he did not know how to read. Folks said he often pretended to read but it was just antics. Indie's Spencer repeating rifle hung in a gun cabinet and Indie's gold watch lay on the cabinet's table ledge next to his black leatherbound notebook and the stack of letters that Slim had taken from Roberts' saddle. Indie had been holding the letters when he was arrested.

"You didn't kill Slim?" Mattie said.

"I killed him as much as I killed Fanny and Chaps, and maybe less."

"But you didn't—"

"Kill Fanny, no."

"Chaps neither," Fog said. He laughed. "He just died."

"But you shot Chaps," Mattie said.

"He was healthy enough when I found you wagon-riding and heading for this town," Indie said. "It wouldn't matter if I'd killed them all or not, my reputation is enough. Sheriff Boone has a bill on his desk with my name on it: appearance, description, list of evil deeds. I was always going to stand trial if I was caught. My sins could only have led me here, under the law. I broke with society. It'll break me. We both know Judge Fickle's trials end with a man hanged, doubtless for me. There's a mob waiting for my corpse."

Indie rubbed gathering sweat from his brow. "At least God's will is done. I've completed His task. The gang's been undone: Fanny, Chaps, Slim, Roberts—all dead." Indie chuckled. "Before he fell to his death out the window, Slim told me that he saw Roberts dead, or nearly dead."

"Weren't you dead, or nearly dead?" Mattie said.

"There was a reason for my resurrection. What purpose could there be for Roberts? He's dead, same as the rest of them."

"Will they bury Slim's body or burn it?"

Sheriff Boone interrupted with words mucus-thick from chewing tobacco. "We burn them." He coughed and smiled at Mattie, who, like the prisoners, glanced at his interruption. "We burn unclaimed and unwanted bodies, criminals usually, vagabonds, drifters. But if you'd like to see a burial, we've a first-class undertaker." Sheriff Boone snickered.

Mattie smiled at the old bachelor sheriff. He blushed and returned to his papers.

"Let him burn," Indie said. "They're dead now, the will of the Lord! But I wonder, did I complete God's will or did He complete it for me?"

Mattie replied. "God's will is always accomplished, Indie— 'On earth as it is in heaven.'"

"Then why bring me back?" Indie gripped the cage. "I was resurrected for a purpose. What purpose other than to undo the wrongs I committed? My past mistakes have been undone but not by my own hand!"

"You're sulking! You completed your resurrected purpose. You should be happy."

"Don't tease a man about to die," Fog said to Mattie. He laughed, coughed, and spit.

Indie watched Mattie. He squinted, blinked, and shuffled.

"Why didn't you leave with your new life?" Mattie said. "You had Chaps and freedom. You're a wanted man in these parts, but not everywhere."

Indie laughed. "I came back to do the Lord's work."

"That's not the truth, not all of it, maybe not even any of it. I think you came back because you wanted to kill them for what they did."

"Haven't I said that? Yes, sometimes our desires align with God's."

"And you thought of Duncan, too?"

Indie's face dropped. "They shot him in cold blood. I expected as much. I thought maybe I could save him."

"And me, you came back for me?"

Indie's eyes swelled. His lower lip quivered.

"I'd have moved heaven and earth to come back for a pretty woman like you," Fog said. He swore.

Indie shook his head. "You tethered me against the darkness. My soul is black. 'In me, nothing good dwells.' I may not deserve to die but I've lived wickedly. I was pulled this way and that.

"You were a light of goodness guiding me away from pure destruction. But I was pulling you down with me. I couldn't hurt you anymore. Look where I've ended up. I would've brought you down with me." Indie looked at the ceiling, around the jail and cell, at Sheriff Boone and Fog, and then he settled his eyes back on Mattie.

She shook her head and whispered. "You're a coward. You need this melodrama. A quiet life wouldn't suit you. It can be the hardest thing to live content and anonymous in the eyes of the world, living good, doing the right thing. But you got it wrong, Indie. Heralded deeds, good or ill, don't make you more of a man. And they certainly can't bring you happiness."

Indie's eyes hollowed. His face paled and he clenched his jaw.

"Why'd you send for me?"

Indie composed himself. "I know you and Sheriff Brick are close."

Mattie blushed.

"He's not a sheriff," Sheriff Boone said. "He's a constable; jurisdiction's Racida and thereabouts. I'm a sheriff, and the only one in the region." He sucked in and then spit.

Mattie turned back to Indie from Sheriff Boone. She opened her mouth to speak but Indie waved her off.

"Even if I'd a measure of influence in opinionating on your friend-ships," Indie said, "I wouldn't. At least, I'd like to think I wouldn't. But you and I both know you well enough, with all that's happened, that I've no influence anymore. And you're also not really the sort of girl who gives a damn about what other people think."

"Do you mean to drivel and dig at ashes?" Mattie said.

"No, I mean just this, Sheriff Brick is a good man, from what I hear. He served in the war?"

"His real name is Solomon Bragg. And yes, he fought at the Battle of Fort Blakeley."

"He must come from up north. He's too good a lawman to have been a slave."

"No, he was enslaved in Mississippi, a place called Loess Manor north of Vicksburg."

Indie straightened. "Loess Manor?" And his mind raced. "I'm sur-prised. He seems like a learned man."

"He is a learned man."

"And important to you?" Indie raised his eyebrows. "You're still impor-tant to me, Matilda. And if he's important to you, that lends him a degree of importance in my eyes, too." He shook his head. "But what I'm getting at—Mattie, you sure can make me ramble."

"I'm sure I can't make you do anything."

Indie dipped his voice into whispers. "Slim told me about a conspiracy. And he had a stack of letters. They're over there on the table next to my notebook. Sheriff Brick's deputy, Clovis, was planning to kill him. Roberts was going to rustle cattle by stealing from Mormon Hyram's stock. He had Judge Fickle in on the affair to stamp it with legal authority or at least hedge against challenge. Clovis was awaiting word to kill Sheriff Brick."

"Fog's in there with you because he killed Clovis," Mattie said. "Sheriff Brick arrested him for Clovis' murder."

"But there's still the proof," Indie said. "And Sheriff Brick should have it. The letters Roberts and his accomplices wrote prove it all. They're over there on the desk."

"Stop your whispering," Sheriff Boone said.

Indie cleared his throat and continued audibly. "The trial's tomorrow morning. Judge Fickle said I'm to be last, after these three." He gestured to his inmates. "I'll be hanged and my body will be burned and that'll be the end of it. But I have personal effects which I want you to have." Indie intimated for Mattie to move closer. She leaned in and Indie grabbed her face through the bars and kissed her.

Fog and the other prisoners exclaimed. Sheriff Boone protested and rushed to break up the pair. Indie let go. Mattie reddened and backed up across the room and took the pile of letters from the table. She hid them in her dress.

Sheriff Boone smacked Indie through the bars and yelled at him. He stumbled over apologies as he walked to Mattie.

"Did you find the canyon?" Indie said before Mattie left the jail.

Mattie turned back. "Yes. Sheriff Brick and I found it."

"Canyon?" Fog said.

Sheriff Boone swore and said Sheriff Brick was not a sheriff and that he would be damned if Sheriff Brick was referred to again as a "sheriff." Sheriff Boone told Indie to be quiet. He apologized again to Mattie.

"Can you trust Brick?" Indie said.

"He's the most honorable man I've ever known," Mattie said.

Indie laughed. Mattie walked out. Sheriff Boone swore. Fog swore. The two other prisoners swore.

Indie sat down. *It's all clear. Sheriff Brick doesn't stand a chance on his own word, but maybe with Mattie's to back him. And the letters are indisputable proof. Maybe things will turn out right. And they found the canyon. Mattie will be a made woman. I've given her more in death than life. So it must be with all truly great works.* Indie wished his good deeds could be as well known as his bad ones, and he did not look up for a long time.

CHAPTER 33

SHERIFF BRICK NURSED A WHISKEY shot alone at the saloon bar and listened to the bounty hunter expound to a full house how he had tracked and caught the infamous Indie Caloo. The bounty hunter was excited. Everyone listened hard with alcohol in hand.

"I figured he'd show up again in Racida," the bounty hunter said.

"How'd you figure?"

"The old bank robbery?"

"Good guess!"

"I'd never show up dead in Racida."

"Pioneer Bank don't hold a candle to Settler's Bank."

"It's all government anyway."

"Ain't government."

An argument broke out about the government and someone said Andrew Jackson was a damn hero, someone else said he would be damned, and then Beyer shouted for calm and mentioned Rattlesnake which gleamed dull like any well-kept shotgun would in the low light of an evening saloon. The men did not calm much but their arguing did not intensify. And then someone said it was a good thing that outlaws like Indie Caloo could be brought to justice, to which the room drank health and quieted for the bounty hunter to resume his tale. He resumed his tale.

Mattie walked in and up to Sheriff Brick.

"Did you see him?" Sheriff Brick said.

"Yes," Mattie said. "He's sulking. I think he half believes he's there by choice, still a free man if he wants to be. He could escape but hasn't decided yet if he wants to. He's not yet faced up to the death that awaits him."

"You sound as though it's certain he'll be executed."

"You don't think he will be?"

"Many witnessed his evildoings. It'll be hard for him at trial. But there'll be a trial. A man's innocent until guilty in America. Isn't that beautiful? You might not imagine, but that's beautiful."

"Judge Fickle should see it your way."

"I'm sure he does. He's a man of the law, and the law is a pillar of democracy and the self-evident truths we hold dear."

Mattie cocked her head and twisted her lip. "I'm impressed. You're always impressing me, Solomon."

Sheriff Brick blushed.

"You're wrong about Judge Fickle, naïve or obstinate. He doesn't deserve your faith in him."

The bounty hunter's voice brought interruption from across the room. "And then he, right there, Sheriff Brick stopped me! I would've had Caloo on the steps of the old Pioneer Bank, too. He didn't trust me."

"Boos" echoed from the audience. A man muttered punishment but he was shushed. Eyes glared.

"Who's to say your own sheriff would have acted differently?" The bounty hunter said. "Lawmen are peculiar, and bound by jurisdictions and commands. That's why you need men like me!"

Applause.

"Do you expect it'll be a long trial tomorrow?" Sheriff Brick said to Mattie.

"You've never been to one?" Mattie said.

Sheriff Brick shook his head.

"He's efficient. There are four criminals to stand trial including Fog and Indie."

"We'll witness at Fog's trial, I don't doubt. Isn't it odd that all four trials are tomorrow? I would think each one too complicated to lump together with others. Certainly, Caloo's will be complicated."

"Four is hardly the record. Like I said, Judge Fickle is efficient. He may have missed his true calling, whatever it could've been, and he atones for deficiency by opportunity. And by that, I mean he's a butcher."

"He's not—"

The bounty hunter broke in again above Mattie and Sheriff Brick's conversation. He pointed at Mattie. "There she is there, one of the wagon party that killed, I suspect, an outlaw associate of Caloo's. They put him in their wagon. I caught a whiff of a trail!"

The bounty hunter's saloon audience echoed "whiff," and he began again in detailing his work.

"Did he want anything else?" Sheriff Brick said to Mattie. She asked if "he" meant Indie. Sheriff Brick nodded and repeated his question with different words.

"He granted me his personal effects after he dies—really just clothes and a notebook," Mattie said.

"Notebook?"

"Yes."

"Significant?"

"I saw him frequently write in a black, leatherbound notebook. I assume he means now to give me the same or similar. He told me once that he sketches the west in words, folding the wild into rhyme. And I took that to mean poetry. He also draws. There's probably more than one picture of me in any notebook he has or has had."

"Pictures?"

"Of course. And yes, of course!"

Sheriff Brick blushed and Mattie shook her head. She slapped his shoulder.

"He has his eulogies now," Mattie said. "Oh, and he asked me if we'd found the canyon. I said we had. And he said he was glad I had but he wasn't too sure about you."

"He doesn't trust me."

"How's that, a criminal who doesn't trust a lawman! I suppose it stands straight enough. And it also stands that his opinion doesn't matter much."

"What should we do about the treasure?"

Mattie shushed Sheriff Brick. "You'll be careful using those words, Solomon. Men are greedy, especially when there's," and she dipped her voice to silence and mouthed the word "gold." She shook herself. "You've got to be careful."

At no time in American history is greed more conspicuous than in rushes for gold. The North Carolina gold rush began soon after a jeweler swindled Conrad Reed's father out of an unidentified 17-pound doorstopper gold nugget the boy had found on a school-skipping fishing trip. That rush spilled over to a fuller realization of gold mining in South Carolina and Georgia, including a "Great Intrusion" into Cherokee Nation, and culminated in the building of a federal mint branch at Dahlonega and a forced march of the Cherokee on a trail of tears to Indian Territory. But the Georgia gold rush soon downturned and a discovery at Sutter's Mill in California kickstarted the largest mass migration in American history. There have been gold rushes at the Comstock Lode in Nevada, along Cripple Creek and Pikes Peak country in Colorado, and in Dakota, Idaho, and New Mexico Territories. While each rush has held unique riches and challenges, all have followed similar patterns of greed and desire culminating in enrichment for a few with moderate and mostly no success to speak of for the rest.

Mattie and Sheriff Brick had not stumbled on a lode but a treasure of gold. If men stoop low for opportunity to work hard in recovering gold, what limiting expectations prevent slaughter for easy-picked spoils? Indie had kept his secret for a reason, and had taken pains to preserve it.

Sheriff Brick gave Mattie a nod. "You're right," he said. "There's a proper time to discuss such things. Better not on a trial's eve and in such company."

The saloon patrons cooed again as the bounty hunter spoke. He was arriving at the point of his story where Sheriff Brick had given him his freedom from Mattie, though he described her person as that of a huge man with six guns. The bounty hunter raised a glass to the sheriff. The audience turned and most lowered their raised glasses on seeing him.

"You've still not told me all, Mattie," Sheriff Brick said. "I can see you've still got—what'd you say—a frog in your mouth?"

"A toad to spit." Mattie sighed. "Indie said that Slim, the man who fell from the window and died on the street, told him before he died of a scheme involving Indie's old partner, Roberts. It appears Roberts was setting up to rustle Mormon Hyram's cattle. Judge Fickle, and Clovis were in on it, too."

Sheriff Brick moved back and exhaled. He smiled. "A dead man, by all accounts an outlaw, told an outlaw, the worst we've seen, about a devious plot involving law-abiding, law-upholding individuals?"

"Yes."

"And you believe him?"

"I believe that's what he was told. He also had proof." Mattie pulled the letters from her dress.

Sheriff Brick shook his head without looking at Mattie. He looked at the letters.

"Do you think Clovis was capable of such mischief?" Mattie said.

"I sometimes caught him visiting unlawful retribution. And he had a reputation for sadism. I believe the best in Judge Fickle."

"You don't know him well enough to say what he could do."

"Same could be said of any man."

Mattie shook her head. "Many men, maybe, but not any. I know what the judge will do. Anyway, I'll leave you those. I've already read some of them, enough to draw conclusions. They're straightforward. And I think Indie was right about Roberts and Judge Fickle. Although it seems like they were introduced to each other. Their writing back and forth to each other is awkward at first, like neither proposed the ideas they agree to. Maybe there's more in there to explain it. I'm tired." She said goodbye and insisted on walking alone to her boarding house. Sheriff Brick said it was maybe for the best and Mattie said it was.

Then he was alone again at the bar. He read the letters. The bounty hunter finished his story and joined the sheriff.

"You're drunk?" Sheriff Brick said. He folded up the pile of papers and excused himself.

"I'm drunk," the bounty hunter said, not letting Sheriff Brick leave.

"That was quite a story."

The bounty hunter smiled. "It *was* quite a story."

"You got Caloo. That's what you wanted. You're happy?"

The bounty hunter's face dropped. "I should be. I'm not. I am and I'm not. I've been following Caloo for a long time now. I left for Mexico. But I never forgot Caloo! He's a fiend! I could've made a good go of it there. I couldn't though, not knowing if Caloo might be alive. So, I came back. And he was alive! And I caught him!" The bounty hunter chortled.

"You did what many a lawman's tried."

"Yes, and he'll hang tomorrow!"

"Trial's tomorrow."

"Judge Fickle's a hanging judge!" The bounty hunter chortled again. "You might not want to believe it, sheriff, but that's how it is. The judge is damnation itself."

Sheriff Brick did not answer. The bounty hunter turned to stare at a game of faro. After his speech, patrons had started games of intermittent contest.

The bounty hunter made a move and stumbled. He fell on Sheriff Brick. Sheriff Brick offered the bounty hunter assistance to his room, and the bounty hunter assented. The bounty hunter fell onto his bed when they arrived. It creaked violently under his sudden weight.

"Sounds like it's going to break," Sheriff Brick said. He shook his head, and turned and left the bounty hunter to sleep.

After the door closed, the bounty hunter opened one eye and then the other. He saw no one and smiled. He pulled one of the letters and laughed. "What sort of business you up to, sheriff?" He laughed again, then rolled to his side, the letter still in his hand, and fell asleep.

CHAPTER 34

TWO MEN GUIDED A HORSE-DRAWN wagon down Cannonball Springs' main street at midnight. Dust billowed off and around the huge tires. The fall weather had set in, which meant rain had left and the air had chilled. It dipped to near freezing at night.

"Been riding a long time," the wagon driver, an old man, said from his spring seat which he shared with a young man.

Bud Jeb, Mormon Hyram's head hand, urged his mount to level with the drivers. He shushed them. "The wagon's loud enough as is. We can't allow for more racket, not until we're safe. Secrecy is important."

They stopped the wagon in front of the general store. They pulled out a stretcher from the back. It bore Roberts.

"Damn near killed me." Roberts said, and he swore.

Bud and his companions carried Roberts to the general store door and knocked. The proprietor opened it with a candle stick in hand. They disappeared inside.

"Got any food?" the old wagon driver said.

"At this hour?" the general store owner said.

"Doesn't have to be nothing fancy. A pickle would do nicely. I'm craving a little salt."

The general store owner frowned. "No, I don't have pickles. I don't sell them. I hate pickles!"

Bud told the general store owner to quiet down. He told the old wagon driver to be quiet.

They set Roberts down on one of two cots in the storage room in the back of the store. The general store owner had set them up. There were no windows and the cold dark cast a gloom on several candles burning low in the room and on the candle that the general store owner held. Bud paid the owner and the two wagon drivers. They left Bud and Roberts alone.

"Things in place for tomorrow?" Roberts said.

Bud nodded. "It's a fool thing. You're barely alive. A wagon ride is bad enough. I don't think you should go to the proceedings. You might not make it. We've too much to risk."

"Remind me to wipe my ass next time I poop." Roberts swore. He coughed blood. "This trial's bigger than anything we could cook up, and I won't miss it—the trial of Indie Caloo!"

CHAPTER 35

"COURT WILL BE IN A few hours," Sheriff Boone said. Indie and Fog languished in the prison. The other prisoners were a juxtaposition: one clung to life, the other was all spit. Outside, a crowd gathered.

Trial days were exuberant affairs. People would travel from miles around to watch the proceedings, pack lunches, and hold picnics in the dusty patches of grass surrounding the center of town before the proceedings began. It did not matter to parents if mortal sentences were executed, they brought their children. Some children cried. Parents shushed them or beat them. Justice inspired the populace.

When there is little else that makes sense in a large and empty land with beautifully ferocious and humbling features, justice can create a sense of sense. Chaotic Indian wars and outlaw ramblings—of which there were few, though notorious—had callused the psyche of settler pioneers. Scratching hard soil just to live off the land wears a man down, and it can break him, too. Meanwhile, trials were spectacle, a welcome relief from unwelcome circumstance. Even Baptists and Catholics participated.

Hangings held greater amusement than trials. There is little worse than a philosophical judge, folks in Cannonball Springs said, and they used as an example a justice of the peace in Bullwhip that had been run out of town. He had insisted on criminal rehabilitation. Yes, they said, Judge Fickle was the only reliable judge to deliver hangings; he could be counted on. Entertaining the crowd was his specialty, and his near perfect trial-to-hanging record delighted the populace, which delighted him. His courtroom was always packed.

"How do you think this will go?" Fog said. "Will we get off free?" He spoke in spurts. The few folks who knew Fog said his speech would staccato whenever he saw a skunk and whenever he got spooked.

"How familiar are you with the law?" Indie said.

"Well, *habeas corpus*, and fair trial, and something else I can't remember."

"Yes, those are facets of the law and how it should work. In most places, even rural outposts, the law works and it can be depended on. But in these parts specifically, the law, like whatever else folks do, is subject to interpretation. We're a sort of dream, I think, of what we imagine the west to be. We take pride in manifesting that dream. And our society and civilization reflect that.

"The United States—we belong, and yet we belong to ourselves. You won't see Philadelphia or New York here. And even if the federal government did care, there's war bills to pay. Judge Fickle's law works a little different than I imagine the law's intended to work. It's accepted practice in these parts. Men will always be able to kill a man, and law can be used to make it acceptable. I think most everyone's heard what happened up in Bannack."

Fog nodded. "We're doomed then?"

Indie raised his chin. "There's always the possibility of living even in the face of death. If Fickle has his way? Yes, I think we're doomed."

"I did kill a man."

Sheriff Boone said Indie and Fog needed to quiet down. He walked outside to address the crowd. They cheered.

"There might be a jury," Indie said. "Fickle uses juries. That's about our only hope for leniency. But judging by the mob I hear outside, we might be out of luck any way."

"When those Indians attacked our militia unit, I thought I was going to die," Fog said, "I ran. I was scared, and I ran until I fell on my face. But since then, I haven't given much thought to dying."

"When you're sure you'll die but don't, you don't pay it as much heed," Indie said. "Before I was transferred to the supply depot in Paducah, I was assigned to the Army of the Southwest. I was in an advanced munitions supply unit. We fought at the Battle of Pea Ridge in Arkansas. I thought I was going to die. We were outnumbered. The Confederates tried to surround us. We beat them back but they came again. There was a line near Elkhorn Tavern pushing in on our position. We had good cover but not many guns, and not much in the way of experience to use guns anyway. But we did have ordnance. And that's when I got an idea to explode it.

"Sergeant Wilhem Blocke, a German immigrant son from Champagne, commanded our unit. 'Sergeant,' I said 'we should feign retreat and explode gunpowder on our unsuspecting conquerors!' And Sergeant Willy—we called him 'Willy' because he didn't like it—said to use his Christian name and that he liked my idea.

"We poured piles of gunpowder around a barrel which we rigged to explode with a fuse. I ran the fuse and the other boys around me formed sort of a human wall as we abandoned our position.

"Our pursuers were either horrible shots or didn't care much for shooting. They only shot Billy Jones, a boy from an Indiana pig farm. He died behind my heels. The rest of us made it out. Some continued running but I and Adolphus Benneker didn't go far because the fuse wasn't long, maybe twenty yards, into a massive hole that just covered our heads. We ducked and I lit the fuse. We watched it burn. Fuses don't always burn well, but that fuse burned well.

"While I watched, I saw the battlefield. It was more vicious than I could've imagined. I thought then that war is horrible, hell even. And I still think that—men killing men, God must look down in disgrace. And then the gunpowder exploded. Men's bodies flew in pieces into the air." Indie stopped talking.

Fog cleared his throat. "That's quite a story."

"I have a gift for explosives. I realized it then. Black powder can be beautiful. And I enjoy pairing surprise and destructive force. But I transferred out of active combat because I hate war."

CHAPTER 36

"DISMISSED!" JUDGE FICKLE BOOMED.

The disavowing prisoner, one of the two that had shared a cell with Indie and Fog, stood before the judge. He peed himself.

The gathered townspeople gasped. The judge repressed a smile that deepened his cheeks. The courtroom rang with murmurs.

A small call punctuated the bravado. It remained steady as the guffaws subsided, thus clarifying even though it did not louden. It was Sheriff Boone, serving as bailiff, and he was sounding a peculiar call he reserved for criminals and drunken revelry and to calm uproarious courtroom proceedings. It was a high note akin to a continuous pig call. Folks said it was obnoxious.

"All right, all right," Judge Fickle boomed, "be seated, ladies and gentlemen. Be seated."

The assembled, who except lawmen were unarmed in accordance with local ordinances, began finding their benches which creaked under the weight, like a large gathering of grasshoppers chirping louder and louder and then dying away. Judge Fickle's courtroom had moved more than once over the years to bigger and bigger buildings to accommodate the popular attendance his work inspired. The current venue, the general assembly building, was the biggest building in town but it proved to be too small for the packed crowd which stood against the walls. More people gathered outside.

The general assembly building was little more than a rectangular room with a tall ceiling and paneled in pine. It looked like a church sanctuary, but it was bigger than any church in the area. An aisle divided rows of benches down the middle to permit egress and regress. There was a low wall and a wooden gate that separated the public from the official proceedings. Prosecuting and defending lawyers shared a table and chairs, with another chair for the accused; they were arranged on the left-side of the room and perpendicular to the elevated and partially enclosed stand where Judge Fickle sat. A witness chair sat to the right of Judge Fickle, with farther chairs, two rows of six, occupied by jurymen and backing against the wall of the room's right side. Sheriff Boone sat in front of Judge Fickle in the center of the room. A courtroom reporter sat in the other centered chair.

Sheriff Boone turned to Judge Fickle after the courtroom talk subsided: "Your honor." He gestured. He then eyed the recorder. Judge Fickle also eyed the recorder, a spectacled man with close eyebrows and big ears. Rumor said he had come from Fort Lyon.

Folks said there was only one person who could worry Judge Fickle and that was a courtroom reporter, whose written case transcripts were supposed to make their way to a probate or district court. There was even a possibility that, if received, another judge would examine these case transcripts. Judge Fickle tried to ensure that his work appeared in good order. He swore whenever he saw a reporter. He had even been known to intimidate them. There was a different reporter for every court session because folks would run them out of town. The Fort Lyon man was new, too.

"Let the record show that the judge heard the accused first."

Sheriff Boone unfettered the criminal and sent him down the aisle to his freedom.

Judge Fickle spoke while the sheriff worked. "The facts of the case are known to me! Would we destroy a man's bright future for an honest oversight that might not even be corroborated, thus perhaps unfounded and untrue?"

The audience was shocked. Some booed. Judge Fickle smashed his gavel and ordered silence. Then he called for the next prisoner.

"He can't set a man free thus," Sheriff Brick said to Mattie.

"It's his courtroom," Mattie said. "He's been afforded such great authority. And he wields it."

"It's not justice."

"Certainly, it's unexpected."

Sheriff Boone escorted the next criminal before Judge Fickle. The criminal was a gloater. His night behind bars with the notorious outlaw Indie Caloo had emboldened him. He stood with a wry smile.

"You should hang me, judge," he said.

"I should?" Judge Fickle said, drawing out the words.

Sheriff Boone kicked the prisoner. He grimaced and snickered. "You'll only speak when addressed," the sheriff said. He turned to the court. "Accused stands accused of horse thievery and larceny and reckless endangerment."

A full-boned man, white-bearded and red-faced, rose in the crowd. "He killed my chickens and a prize hog! And my horses and barn—"

Judge Fickle slammed his gavel. "I'll have him bear witness, Nicholas! In turn, in turn—every man will have his say." He cleared his throat and nodded to Sheriff Boone.

Fellow spectators urged the angry farmer, Nicholas, to sit, and some even helped seat him. He shook and reddened.

Sheriff Boone asked the criminal's name, which the recorder noted. He then noted that he had a right to a jury trial.

"Let's expedite this; what do you say?" Judge Fickle said. "I can read it fair. A judge is a diviner. I can spot a recalcitrant or a penitent a mile away." His smile enveloped his face.

"Witnesses—" Sheriff Boone began to say.

"What's it matter?" The criminal said. "You can hang me. You're the judge. I'll leave it to you."

"Excellent!" Judge Fickle boomed. "Ladies and gentlemen assembled; it is obvious to the court a grieved party is in attendance. And it is equally obvious that the accused before us presents himself into our assizes without any personal predilections. That is to say, as the record will reflect," Judge Fickle glanced sideways at the recorder, "that he lays himself at the mercy of the court, forfeiting his right to a jury trial, thus disposing himself to my determinations." Judge Fickle's smile almost broke his face as he leaned down and said low, "mercy."

He slammed his hammer and pronounced that the captive be set free. The audience really animated. Angry farmer Nicholas jumped up from his seat and exclaimed. The prisoner gasped. Sheriff Boone un-shackled him and escorted him down the middle egress aisle, all while beginning his crowd call to silence. The farmer broke out of his surrounded seat. The prisoner ran out of the courtroom doors. The farmer followed in a run. The crowd cheered them on.

"Why even have a jury?" Sheriff Brick said. He began to rise but Mattie steadied him.

"Steady, Solomon," Mattie said. "Is this a moment to erupt?"

"What better?"

Mattie shook her head.

Sheriff Brick resumed his seat. He slapped his knee and folded his arms in front of him. "He has a jury but doesn't use it."

"It's his way. That is, it's not usual, but father says the judge likes to use other men in well-known cases, collaborators. The judge is at his best when eyes are on him."

"Your father is a philosopher."

Mattie glared at Sheriff Brick. "He's a good preacher."

"Fog!" Sheriff Boone called when the din subsided.

"Read the charges," Judge Fickle said. He looked really alive and full of spirit and spirits.

Sheriff Boone cleared his throat and began. "Accused stands accused of murder in the first degree."

"Who accuses?"

Sheriff Brick rose. "I do, your honor."

"Constable!" Judge Fickle motioned for Sheriff Brick to walk to the front.

More than one person asked why Judge Fickle had called Sheriff Brick "constable." A few were correctly answered with a clarification that Sheriff Brick was officially Racida's constable, that Sheriff Boone was the only area sheriff, but that folk referred to Sheriff Brick as a sheriff anyway.

Sheriff Brick walked to where Judge Fickle sat, watched by the sun-tanned faces filling the courtroom. But not even the most leathered complexion approached Sheriff Brick's deep black skin. He held his head and especially his chin high. Whisperings rose in a din above even the random coughing and spitting. But Sheriff Brick did not look any way but straight ahead.

There is sterling beauty which cannot be mocked, its transcendent strength immune to jest. Sheriff Brick did not flinch and his solid features cut deep as if from obsidian. He was black in a room full of white faces. He was strength and resolve in a courtroom of jesters. His presence did not permit for the humiliation and mocking he had endured. Sheriff Brick was a man of the law, and no one could take that from him. Not even Judge Fickle's long record of wielding the law's nooses seemed much compared with the resolute stone of this man. Sheriff Brick was an overpowering song of sun in the midst of dreary barroom light. And the revelers, who had come for blood as they always had, dumbed in silence at the sight of a good man.

So it seemed to Indie Caloo as he waited his turn for judgment, seeing the glory he had chased, embodied and out of reach for him now. Tears fell from his eyes as he watched Sheriff Brick. Indie looked to the back of the room and Mattie.

She loves him.

Sheriff Boone swore-in Sheriff Brick. His voice left something of a pall on the congregants.

"You have any other witnesses?" Judge Fickle said when Sheriff Brick had sat down in the witness stand chair.

Sheriff Brick reddened. "My word is sufficient. I'm a lawman. Matilda Schroeder—her father is the preacher over in Racida—she also saw," he nodded at Fog, "this man's victim, my associate."

"Clovis?" Sheriff Boone said.

Sheriff Brick nodded. Sheriff Boone looked at Judge Fickle and they both smirked.

"How can you be sure he killed Clovis?" Judge Fickle said.

"There were only four of us at the station house," Sheriff Brick said. "Me, Clovis, Mattie, and him."

"Fog?" Sheriff Boone said.

"Fog, yes; he ran the station house. Five days ago this morning, Mattie and I were in the house and Fog and Clovis left to saddle the horses."

Judge Fickle shook his head and waved off Sheriff Brick. "I'm sure it's a good story, good as gold. Your reputation for honesty and lawful vigilance proceed you, constable." The judge raised his voice so the whole court could hear. "The criminal will speak for himself."

Sheriff Brick obeyed intentioned gesture and walked from the stand back to his seat next to Mattie. He was eyed for his return. She smiled at him and opened her mouth to speak. He shook his head and gestured to Judge Fickle. "We'll see."

"It's his courtroom," Mattie said.

"Law should be law in any room."

Fog spit and swore after being brought forward. "It was my body that carried out the attack, so it follows that I killed the man. Certainly, I hold no ill will against the esteemed sheriff." He turned around and nodded at Sheriff Brick.

"Constable," Sheriff Boone said.

Fog nodded and then turned back around. "I am sorry he wasn't served by a more honorable deputy."

Sheriff Boone, red in the face, corrected Fog. He said that Sheriff Brick was not technically a sheriff, so Clovis was not technically a sheriff's deputy. Fog said that was fine by him, and that he could go over his story again. Judge Fickle said that would not be necessary, and asked the reporter if it would be necessary. The reporter said "no."

"That Clovis," Fog said, "whoever the hell he was, he was evil. He spurned me years ago at the Herndon House hotel in Omaha, asked for frog legs del monaco and then roughed me up. You can imagine I had time to stew on the slight. And how could I not feel indignation seeing the fiend in my own establishment? It was pride took ahold of me, and drove me insane."

"Temporary insanity!" Judge Fickle boomed. "Criminal wasn't himself. Can we hold a demon accountable? We are not the Almighty." He slammed his gavel and ordered Fog's release.

Fog mumbled and gaped as Sheriff Boone unfettered him and urged him down the aisle to the exit. And then he was gone.

Sheriff Brick gripped the bench with both hands and shifted his clenched jaw. Mattie rubbed his hot back. Folks were talking.

The whole courtroom buzzed when Indie Caloo was called. He walked before Judge Fickle, who wore a big smile.

"He rushed through the others to get to him," Sheriff Brick said to Mattie. "This is all about Indie Caloo. He may have an important case, and justice should be done, but not at the expense of justice. What about—"

Nearby court attendees shushed Sheriff Brick. Mattie raised her shoulders.

Sheriff Brick whispered, "Clovis, that farmer?" He shook his head. "Mercy is for the Almighty, not a lawman. Justice deferred is injustice to the victims of crime."

"Hang him now!" someone yelled.

"We know what he's done!"

"Robbed the Pioneer Bank in Racida!"

"Killed Tall Jim Payne!"

"Killed Uncle Elbe!"

And the shouts continued until Judge Fickle quieted the crowd. "I know well this man's reputation. But you can't hang a man on reputation alone. We must conduct a trial. I'd give the Devil himself a fair shake, a chance to hear and be heard. If we don't supply justice here, on the edge of the world, who will?" Judge Fickle cleared his throat and bade the crowd sit. He played with his beard and smiled his mischievous smile.

"La risa del diablo," some Spanish-speaking spectators whispered under their breaths.

Judge Fickle turned to Indie. "How do you plead?"

"Don't you want to give further parameters?" Sheriff Boone said.

"Boone, sit. This is my courtroom. I'm no lout."

"But perhaps a fool," Indie said.

Judge Fickle told the recorder not to record Indie's comment, which he called "insubordinate." Judge Fickle ordered Indie to sit and he sat.

A squirrely lawyer named Felton acted as prosecution against Indie. He rose and delivered his first comments: long and poorly organized though delivered with conviction in an effeminately high voice, which caused two rascals in the fifth row to snicker. Felton ended by saying Caloo was evil and that the jury should absolutely convict him or they were not good Christians. Folks murmured that unbelief already characterized jury members.

"Why didn't the lawyer prosecute the other criminals?" Sheriff Brick asked Mattie.

"Lawyer Felton can be spectacular," Mattie said. "But he's not flexible. I've not heard of him prosecuting more than one case in any session of court. And I think you may have been right about case prioritization, and so Judge Fickle has appointed Felton to where he's needed most."

Felton was wrapping up his soliloquy and about to present the charges. Then Indie would defend himself, like anyone facing trial in Cannonball Springs.

"Let the prosecution present their case," Indie said. "A man has to live, and I have. I'll defend my actions as questioned, not simply presented as a devil to hate."

"Silence!" Judge Fickle said. "The accused, this Indie ruffian, shall have a chance to defend himself once the charges have been levied. You, sir," he said to Indie, "can speak when spoken to, but not until then, or I'll have you hanged before the words run dry." He cleared his throat and nodded to Felton. "Proceed." Folks said Judge Fickle would yell "proceed" whenever he was unsure of what to do next.

"Murder!" Felton said. "Gentlemen of the jury, this profound blackguard you see before you is death embodied. He has killed six, nay, seven men, and more women and children besides, if reports are to be believed."

Some audience members murmured that reports weren't always to be believed. They were shushed.

Felton continued. "He is an excellent shooter, so he had no difficulty dispatching innocents—sheep to the slaughter. And where is your wolf?" Lawyer Felton gestured with both hands at Indie. "Wolf!"

Courtroom spectators applauded. Judge Fickle rolled his eyes as Felton bowed. Sheriff Boone urged calm. Indie indicated no rebuttal.

"First case," Judge Fickle said, "is the falling death—or was it pushing?—the death of that out-of-towner in front of the saloon yesterday. Let's deal with the immediate; perhaps we can come to a decision sooner. Is the bounty hunter here?"

The bounty hunter was not there, which Judge Fickle noted with an oath. "Damn him. But there are other witnesses. First, Beyer!"

"I'm supposed to call, not?" Felton said.

Judge Fickle swore. "Proceed!"

Felton called. Beyer rose from the crowd and walked to the witness stand.

"That last fellow—Fog?—he was talking with you, judge, at the bar," Beyer said after several cross-examining questions, one from Lawyer Felton and the others inappropriately from Judge Fickle. Beyer cleared his throat and continued. "Then Callaghan rose up, exchanged words. He attacked you. And the boys at the table all shoved him outside." Beyer nodded to Lawyer Felton and winked to Judge Fickle.

"Where is that devil Callaghan?" Judge Fickle said. "He should be gracing these proceedings."

The sheriff indicated that Callaghan was recovering in the town doctor's home from his street brawl bludgeoning. The reporter indicated that the line of questioning had gotten off track.

Judge Fickle glared at the reporter. "Proceed," he said to Beyer.

Beyer stumbled into recollecting his thoughts but then recounted how the doors fell off his saloon. He cursed, which made ladies blush. Then he said he thought about grabbing his gun from behind the bar. "Rattlesnake's a swell gun, a real fine piece. I've shot birds with her before and she does the trick. She'd saw a man in half if you needed her to. But she's a real fine gun. That's why I keep her behind the bar. That's why I keep her away from folks."

"The gentleman, Fog," Lawyer Felton said, "was speaking with the honorable," Felton nodded at Judge Fickle, "and then the brawl?"

"Yes! And it was the two of us at the bar. The honorable had left with the mob. I think the bounty hunter had gone upstairs to visit Delilah. And I saw the fellow, who fell out of the window, he went upstairs, too. And then Fog, yes, we went outside to see what all the fuss was about. I decided against bringing Rattlesnake."

"Did you see anyone else enter the premises, such as this criminal outlaw?" Felton indicated Indie. "He was found by the bounty hunter and cuffed by that Racida lawman they call Sheriff Brick in your upstairs room, the room from which the deceased fell and died." Felton stopped his slow stroll around the witness stand and squinted his eyes at Beyer. Folks said he squinted his eyes when he wanted to be intimidating. "How did he get there?"

"I'll be?" Beyer said. He shrugged.

"He followed him upstairs!" Felton opened his eyes wide and turned to survey the packed courtroom, then the jury. "And then he pushed him to his death!"

The collected assembly murmured. Judge Fickle boomed for order. He smiled as he gaveled.

"Objection, your honor," Indie said.

"Overruled!" Judge Fickle boomed.

"Your honor," the reporter said after clearing his throat. "The defendant should be allowed to voice objection since he's representing himself."

"I'm no lout!" Judge Fickle smiled at the reporter then turned to Indie. "Let's hear your objection. Proceed."

Indie said, "I was in the room, but I didn't push or coerce Slim, the man who died. Insinuation isn't implication, and the prosecution can't jump to a conclusion it hasn't presented proof for."

"Then how did he end up dead?" Felton said.

"Slim? He tripped and fell."

"You were seen having pushed him out a window!"

"Who saw me push him?"

"Don't be surprised!"

"He fell out the window."

"After you pushed him!" Judge Fickle roared. "Ladies and gentlemen, I see no need for continued examination. This man is guilty, he said so himself; he was in the room when the poor gentleman's soul was carried from this earth—in the room! Many saw him. He said he was there! I see no need for continued examination or witnesses. We have a confession. We have a confession!" He smashed his gavel while the audience began cheering.

Someone whistled. "Hanging!" The sentence was met with uproarious applause.

But the reporter indicated that the sentence was premature and the jury had not been consulted. Sheriff Boone and Judge Fickle glared at him. Judge Fickle blushed red.

"Have you anything else to say?" Felton asked Beyer after a long pause.

Beyer said he did not and left the stand with the same earnest expression. He had served as a witness before and folks said he had become really good at it.

Lawyer Felton cleared his throat while grasping his shirt as a general might on review. His clearing turned harsher and into coughing, then one final heave and he relieved his throat into a spittoon.

"Your honor," he said, "gentlemen of the jury, there are other witnesses." He cleared his throat again. "There was one man who saw the whole thing happen—who burst in on the scene after the murder. Sheriff Brick!"

Sheriff Boone muttered again that he was the only sheriff in the area. Sheriff Brick walked again to the front of the room, watched again by all. He took another oath, as Beyer had, and sat down in the witness stand chair.

"Is it your . . ." Lawyer Felton scratched his head. He then bulged his eyes. "Did you see this gentlemen here," motioning to Indie, "attacking the deceased?"

"No," Sheriff Brick said. There were audible gasps.

"Surely, he was—if not attacking, he was present?"

"Yes. He was standing behind, watching it all. I saw him from the street looking out the window after the other man had fallen—"

"Was pushed!"

"Perhaps. But in any case, he tumbled out of the window. And then I saw Indie standing in the light of the window and watching the scene which unfolded quickly, as you can imagine when a man falls and dies in the street. I'd cuffed Fog. But I didn't want Caloo to escape. So I ran upstairs. The bounty hunter was in the door. Caloo was beyond him, still looking out the window. And I rushed in and apprehended Caloo."

"But he did kill the deceased?"

"It may be, but from my point of view, I didn't see any actual work in the affair as to having directly killed him."

Lawyer Felton sighed and did not have any follow-up questions.

Judge Fickle reddened, then shook his head and cleared his throat. He swore. "Take that bounty hunter, doesn't show up to court when his talking might actually make a bit of damn difference. Jury, note that the sheriff said 'it may be' that this Indie assisted in that poor soul's death.

"But this unfortunate bloodshed on our doorsteps is hardly the only the offense Caloo stands charged with. Felton, present the next murder charge."

Felton retreated to his papers on the table he shared with Indie. He rifled through them. His face turned bright red.

Sheriff Brick was excused from the witness stand. The whole room, except panicking Felton, watched him return to Mattie.

"You were right, Mattie," he said loud enough for the whole courtroom to hear, "Judge Fickle doesn't care for justice. This may be a court, but it's not a court of law."

And then he walked out of the building. Mattie walked out after him.

There was no life in the general assembly building. *Sheriff Brick and Mattie withdraw themselves and the vestiges of propriety. What does it matter anymore if the best of us object?* But though Indie felt the weight of dignity alight, he broke the spell.

"Where's the bounty hunter?" Indie said.

Judge Fickle exploded. "Why isn't he here? He could've given a most excellent witness."

Murmurs highlighted the mob's snap back into violence. They asked around for the bounty hunter. Then Sheriff Boone spoke up. "He gave a rousing tale at the saloon yesterday."

"I heard about it," Judge Fickle said. "I was hoping he'd tell it here, too, testify in our court where his words could be recorded and verified, purified by—"

"Soiled by your airs," Indie interrupted.

Judge Fickle left his seat, swung his arms and gnashed his teeth. "Contempt! Contempt of court! If we cannot respect even our last vestiges of humanity—must we put ourselves at the mercy of blackguards and dogs?"

Felton exclaimed. "Yes! I have a witness to another case of murder. It's signed by a Mr. John A. Boothe of Stanchion: brother was killed on a Tuesday, a Tuesday in November, a Tuesday in November of last year." Felton looked up from his papers and saw that some in the crowd nodded. He smiled and read on. "He says the accused, this Caloo—he saw him blow away his cousin over a disagreement at a game of faro. He says Caloo was cheating. He confronted him about it. And Caloo killed his cousin; killed him with a Henry rifle. Blood and guts everywhere. It was heinous. Only God could pity such a man."

The courtroom gasped. The jurymen twitched and coughed.

"It's signed, your honor," Felton said, holding the affidavit up. He handed it to Judge Fickle as a mortician might hand a shovel to a digger.

"What kind of rifle did you pull off me?" Indie said to Sheriff Boone as he began his defense.

Sheriff Boone said it did not matter what kind of rifle it was. He said men like Indie should not be allowed rifles. But Judge Fickle stroked his chin and glanced at the reporter. Folks said Judge Fickle stroked his chin when he was intrigued. He told Sheriff Boone to indulge Indie's question.

"A Spencer repeating rifle," Sheriff Boone said.

"A Spencer repeating rifle isn't a Henry," Indie said. "Second, Stanchion's saloon proprietor isn't fond of faro because he thinks there's too much cheating goes on, so he's banned it from the premises. Third, Stanchion doesn't allow for guns to be openly carried around town without approval from the local magistrate, Parsons. You can ask him yourself; I saw him shuffling in here."

Parsons raised his voice to declare his presence.

"Parsons is a good man," Indie continued, "and he loves to talk—maybe about as much as the telegraph operator over in Racida. So you can be sure Parsons would know a criminal like me even from my poor description on wanted bills and proclamation warrants. I couldn't walk into a saloon with a gun without being confronted by Parsons, and Parsons would know me straight away, and not allow me to get away, especially with murder, especially with a gun I don't even own."

Judge Fickle gasped while the jury mumbled to themselves.

"Surely the dead cannot speak for themselves!" Felton said. "Who are we to believe, this devil's instrument or the voiceless innocent?"

Judge Fickle swore and rubbed his hand down his head to his chin. "Voiceless innocents are immaterial, Felton." He gathered himself and rebounded. "But this blasphemer hasn't killed but one man only—many!"

Felton swallowed hard and dug into his papers again. He found one, exclaimed, and read: "Mr. Heckle Few!"

"Heckle Few?"

"Yes, your honor. Heckle Few."

Judge Fickle nodded. He gurgled. "Ah, for the good of the court, a little background on Mr. Few."

"Well, he's dead. He was shot. Few was a rancher with cattle on a thousand hills or a thousand cattle on a hill, or how it says it in the Good Book—he was richly blessed. And he ranched not fifteen miles from where you're sitting. One night, he's sleeping, door locked, windows locked, and a demon slips into his home and *boom*!" Felton imitated shooting a rifle.

Women gasped. One covered her eyes.

"It was never solved who did the killing. But being a bachelor with no inheritor, Few's whole lot was sold off. The money—well, Sheriff Boone's kept it in public trust. Some was used a year ago this week to buy a potbelly stove for the school."

Sheriff Boone blushed. Judge Fickle cleared his throat. Women whispered on the fineness of the school's potbelly stove.

"Caloo killed Few!"

Indie rose to defend himself after allowing the community's qualms to quiet. "You've served as judge here for how long?"

Judge Fickle screwed up his lips. He turned his head right then left. "It's been, let's see—six years, and a month since I left New Orleans. I remember reading President Johnson's proclamation recognizing Texas' state government, declaring that, as anyone could plainly see, hostilities had ceased in the war between the states; and I remember *that* because it was an affront to me and all southerners.

"I ventured to Kansas where I met Guilfoyle, who said he wanted to start up a courier business—horses and carriages. I came to Racida with him and then I continued here, to Cannonball Springs. And that was I'd say five years and two, three months ago."

"I commend you, your honor, for your memory. And if mine is still in working order, Heckle Few was found dead five years ago next month. Which means you would've arrived just before his death. You forgot it, forgot him?"

"Slip of memory. Of course—"

"You're going to deny, too, that you've been working with rustlers and my former partner, Roberts, to rustle Mormon Hyram's cattle. But I have secured proof! Letters that plainly state the affairs and your role in them." Judge Fickle paled. Indie smiled and continued, voice rising. "The man who died yesterday, Slim, told me all about it. He saw your partner Roberts and heard him conspiring with Mormon Hyram's cowpokes.

"Should Hyram bring a cattle brand dispute before you—as he'd have to since you're the only justice of the peace in these parts—you'd say that the brands are genuine, haven't been tampered with, no doubt to the benefit of the outfit holding the cattle in question. And that outfit is providing payment or stake in whatever eventual cattle sales, not?

"What are you speaking of?" Felton said. Murmurs echoed through the crowd.

Sheriff Boone tried to talk but Indie cut him off, shouting.

"Where are the funds from Few's legacy?" Indie said. "They're gone! Did you steal them or was it just Judge Fickle?"

Sheriff Boone turned to Judge Fickle, who had retreated into himself. The jury mumbled among themselves. Everyone did, all in attendance.

"Guilty!" Judge Fickle boomed. "This man is clearly guilty! The court doesn't need—we're all well aware of what he's done. And the jury will side with me. We don't need more talk. I'm God here. String him up!"

Bang!

Judge Fickle's chest exploded and he slumped forward.

Roberts laughed from the back of the room. "God is dead," he sputtered.

He fired again and Sheriff Boone's head exploded. His body slumped into its seat.

"And so is justice."

Twelve men jumped to their feet and brandished pistols. Roberts gave an eye to Parsons, the only other armed individual in the room. Parsons dropped his gun in a show.

Roberts holstered his pistol and hobbled on rude crutches to the front of the room while his henchmen held the crowd at gunpoint. "Indie," he said several times, almost moaning, as he neared the front of the room. He clicked his tongue and labored breath. "You know why I came, don't you?"

"I don't suppose you came to kill God and justice," Indie said.

"Better off without them."

"Roberts, why don't you leave the people here out of this. Your quarrel is with me."

Roberts pushed Judge Fickle's body aside. He assumed his seat. "I'm here on your behalf, Indie. I'm here to make sure you get the trial you deserve."

Roberts coughed. "Ladies and gentlemen, you're all aware that this gentleman before you, this criminal, is Indie Caloo. I should know, I was his victim, a forced accomplice.

"Somewhere, a banker rolls in his grave at the sound 'Caloo.' Indie's a thief, a killer. Lawyer, whatever papers you've got in your pile won't tell the half of it. God as my witness, he's guilty and deserves to die!"

"Who are you?" someone shouted from the crowd.

Roberts stood and flashed his Colt .45 pistol. He fired, *bang*—flare, roar, smoke—through the crowded court.

Women screamed. Men swore and jumped. The bullet hit an exposed rafter. The dozen armed men trying to control the crowd yelled for order.

"Anyone else?" Roberts said. "I won't miss next time." .

The crowd was silent. Roberts resumed his seat.

"You're a coward, Roberts," Indie said. "We're both cowards for what we've done. But I've seen the error, and I've quit it. I'm going to stand up for what's right, and that's in your way."

"I understand from what I've heard that Slim is dead. Chaps? Fanny?"

"They're dead. And you know Duncan is dead, too. You're the last of the gang. Well, you and me."

Roberts drew his face back and rubbed his chin. "We were the bold and free, society's bane, and proof that no man can tame the wild and other men. Isn't that something like what you used to say?"

"If a man can conquer himself," Indie said, "he has no need to conquer another. I couldn't see that before, when we jaunted juvenile through this beautiful land. Yes, I had a notion that our unhindered escapades brought balance to what men like us—pioneers and settlers—had upset by pouring themselves into God's unspoiled land. I was wrong. *We* were the filth of civilization that I wanted to burn away."

"Debauchery of war, crime, hate, lust." Roberts laughed. "Yes, I can see that. It's an evil to live at the mercy of fate. We were set to take hold of destiny. And make no mistake, we took hold."

Indie gaped. Roberts stood, strained, and smiled. The courtroom buzzed with the energy of a suppressed curiosity but remained audibly quiet for fear of the brandished pistols. Someone coughed as someone always does in a quiet room.

Indie smiled. "You came here to tell me that I'm as guilty as you are."

"No, you're guiltier than me. You talk of me and the dead judge and cattle branding conspiracies, while what you've done!" Roberts scoffed. "But I interrupted your trial." Roberts clicked his teeth again. "And since we are sans judge—since God and Justice are dead—I'll have to step in."

Roberts picked up the gavel and slammed it. Indie flinched. Roberts slammed the gavel again and again.

"It's supposed to explode, not, this whole thing? You told me that you were a munitions expert in the war between the states. You worked in a supply depot. You fought at Pea Ridge near Leetown." Roberts swore and leaned over the mantle. "I remembered this morning how you set up the Racida heist, the stagecoach robberies north and south of here: gunpowder! And I thought, what would you plan for your master trial?

"You're too smart to get caught, only let yourself be caught. These fools," Roberts gestured to Judge Fickle and Sheriff Boone, "they couldn't see beyond their own ambitions and pleasures. But you always had a bigger picture in mind.

"Duncan is dead." Roberts spoke low. But Indie did not flinch. Roberts laughed and spoke again, "You already know! So you must've been on our trail then?"

"I should've killed you when I had the chance," Indie said.

"I heard about Chaps' capture. I knew Fanny would be near, too. You know their brilliance, but revisiting that old, boarded up bank wouldn't draw attention. It was a damned good idea of yours to fake the heist at first, get away, then go back later without quarrel."

"It was my ruse. I stole the money and hid it."

Roberts stopped, and laughed. "Good! And I was thinking you'd gone soft. But you know, that's not why we killed you."

"You didn't kill me."

"I can see that. Except, I know you were dead. You're not dead now, but you were." Roberts swore and spit. "There's a story there. But I want to know this, you let yourself get caught knowing that if I could, I'd hear of it and come? You risked your neck to confront me."

"I know it now: if I'd only killed you when I had every opportunity, or killed you at the crossroads, my work for God would've been satisfied. As it stands—Slim, Chaps, and Fanny are in the grave, Duncan, too. But not you. Though my work is mostly finished, it's the least complete."

"Work for God! He brought you back then to kill me? And not just me; you've been set like a dog to kill your own gang." Roberts clicked and shook his head. "I'm the last of your coerced henchmen, the final pawn to execute. You were going to build on your own myth, too, and blow me up here in this courtroom?"

Indie stared and his eyes watered. A tear fell down his cheek.

Roberts pulled out his LeMat revolver and put it on the ledge in front of him. "My men captured your man stationed outside this building. He had flint. He stood next to a fuse that disappeared under where I sit. He said he was waiting for a signal to light detonation. That's a very complicated plan. The more complicated the plan, the poorer. You outsmart yourself."

"What's your course of action?" Indie asked. "You've killed the judge and sheriff, but there's all of us. We're too many for you and your thugs. Even if you had one bullet for each person, you couldn't kill us all quick enough before we'd get you."

"I'm going to leave and no one will follow me or my men. Who will organize a posse? These people are ready to hang you. Let them! But I'm going to quit this country. If you let me leave," Roberts announced to the assembly, "you'll never see me again.

"But before I leave, I'm going to kill you." Roberts picked up the revolver. "Only a few hundred of these LeMats ever made it past Union blockades in time to make any difference. But they're a unique caliber; you have to cast the ammunition for yourself, except for the buckshot which goes in the barrel underneath. I've only shot the gun a few times for practice. I've been saving it for a special death. I'll enjoy—"

"Stop!" Sheriff Brick shouted from the door. He pushed Fog as a human shield with his left hand and brandished his Colt Army model revolver with his right, pointing it from standing thug to standing thug. Mattie followed with a rifle and covered the young men, too.

Bang!

Bud Jeb yelled and fired a bullet over Sheriff Brick's head.

Bang!

Sheriff Brick returned fire with a bullet that tore into Jeb's revolver. He swore and dropped the blasted gun. Sheriff Brick did not even smile.

Roberts raised his LeMat revolver and then startled with a fit of coughing. He spit blood. He coughed and coughed. Then he vomited and fainted. Blood began to seep through Roberts' shirt, from the wounds the old Araphao had inflicted days before. He gasped and fell and breathed his last.

Murmurs rang through the audience. Everyone looked at Sheriff Brick and Mattie and breathed. Then the crowd chaos ensued as the crowd attacked their would-be masters. The trial audience beat up Mormon Hyram's cowhands, especially Bud Jeb, and the other worthless fellows Roberts had enlisted to hold the court hostage. Two misfires tore small holes in the roof. One intentional shot lodged into a wall. The assaults lasted minutes.

Then the mob marched the ruffians to the town square where gallows stood. One rope hung from the cross bar. It had been intended for Indie. The gallows creaked mercilessly under a cold afternoon wind. Parting clouds revealed the sun, still brilliant and hot though spectators shivered in shade. The world was big and grand and beyond the little struggle.

The crowd readied to string up each young man. They affixed the first noose to a gulping neck.

"Stop!" Sheriff Brick shouted. He raced up the gallows. "We must allow for justice."

"We all saw what these men did!"

"They threatened us all."

"If they'd had their way, we'd be dead."

"Guns on us!"

"Kill them!"

"Ruffians."

"Hang them!"

"String them up!"

Sheriff Brick raised his voice and silenced all others. "No matter the witness, we must bear the burden to prove and process offenses. I won't allow a lynching mob."

Mattie joined Sheriff Brick on the gallows. The air played around the now quiet square.

"Where's Caloo?"

"Caloo!"

"Murderer!"

"Fiend!"

"Devil!"

Men, women, and children forgot the captured fellows and began a frantic search for Indie. Even the Roberts' ruffians, so recently free, joined in the hunt. They searched the square. They searched the courtroom where the bodies of Roberts, Judge Fickle and Sheriff Boone sat slumped in their seats or on the ground. The mob searched the entire town. They formed posses to ride and search the surrounding countryside. They found no one. Indie was gone.

PART VII
RESOLUTION

Chapter 37

"Must be a lot of folks itching to get to Kansas City if it takes all morning to get a couple tickets for tomorrow." Fog said to Indie. "What time is it?"

Indie sat down across from Fog at a table in an eating house in Denver City. They had found each other after the trial, and they had banded together. They had decided to leave Colorado Territory, and over several months, they had made a slow but safe way north. Indie had insisted on this slow and safe travail.

Indie smiled. "We leave mid-morning, tomorrow. I thought I'd find you feasting. I didn't know where. And here you are."

"At least I've been busy filling my belly with victuals."

Indie asked what there was to eat. Fog gave him a litany of foods that Indie said sounded like nothing good.

"I didn't think you could get skinnier," Fog said. "Yet you keep passing over nourishment. You've barely eaten enough since you escaped Cannonball Springs to keep a jackrabbit alive. Had I not gone back to my station house and found you, who knows if you'd be alive?"

"My body's too stubborn to die," Indie said. "My mind's made peace with death, but my body hasn't."

"You're trying to kill it?"

"I'm not trying to keep it alive."

"Sounds like the same thing to me."

A fat woman with greasy hair slapped down a tin plate with thick bacon still steaming from the fire. The hot grease bubbled in thin edges like foam over the red flesh and the tanned fat that curled in waves. Indie grabbed two pieces and ate them. Fog gestured surprise.

"Bacon's something I can always eat, hungry or not," Indie said.

Fog grinned like an old horse. Then his eyes dropped and half-chewed bacon fell out of his gaping mouth.

"Bacon's a hell of a thing!" the bounty hunter said. His sudden voice carried over the assembled cacophony and directed attention to him and Indie and Fog.

"It is," Fog said, and resumed masticating the rest of his bacon bite.

Indie reddened but otherwise chewed without betraying his surprise. He did not even turn himself to face the speaker. "You're going to sit, sit," Indie said to the bounty hunter.

The bounty hunter laughed. "I will!" And he sat next to Fog. "I'm going to sit across from you, you old devil, so I can get a look at you." He looked at Indie.

"Beside me, too?" Fog said. "I can be devilish."

The bounty hunter laughed again. "Yes! Doesn't surprise me, the company you keep. You're a cagey one, Indie. If fools didn't get in my way!"

The bounty hunter called for drink and enough food for three men. Then he rubbed his whiskers, took off his hat, and rubbed his bald head. He cleaned his spectacles while he chatted about nothing with great enthusiasm. "Dinner-talk first. We can't just dive into it."

His food and drink arrived and he dove into them. He insisted and prevailed on Fog to dive in, too. Then the bounty hunter leaned back in his chair, burped, swallowed again what had almost come up, and then he talked.

"This is what I really want to talk about, what I'll proffer you really want to talk about, too. To transpire, we require a good bit of preparation, greasing if you will. You wouldn't just slap a pony for a sprint. It'd kill itself, likely, and you with it. You wouldn't take a woman—" the bounty hunter interrupted himself by laughing.

Then he knotted his eyebrows, which effect was heightened because he had no head or face hair except his eyebrows and whiskers. "Ah, and now I'm ready; we all are. It's been a long time I've tracked you, Indie, longer than I should've allowed, no other man would've lasted like I have. I've nearly impoverished myself, killed myself, humiliated myself—all chasing you." He shook his head. "I had to go to Mexico just to get the hunting funds so I could continue my pursuit.

"You can imagine, then, my excitement capturing you in Cannonball Springs. You must've let me catch you, that's all I can think, and that ate at me after I saw you behind bars and I got a reward—only $200 because Sheriff Brick put the cuffs on you and Sheriff Boone didn't have $5000. But I'd been hunting you so long that I didn't care much how much I got to bring you in, just that *I* did. And I had!

"I couldn't stay for your trial. But I heard about it. Who hasn't? And I heard that you were gone. Someone said 'gone' and I took it to mean ultimately. Come to find out, he meant you'd flown the coop. The official word out of Cannonball Springs is that you had one of your men, Roberts, kill Sheriff Boone and Judge Fickle and a court reporter!" The bounty hunter took a swig. "Then folks said the lawman from Racida, Sheriff Brick, busted in; he exchanged gunfire with one of Roberts' men; and Roberts keeled over dead. The crowd tried to lynch the hooligans holding them up. But Sheriff Brick stopped that, too. I wish I'd seen it!"

"The Sheriff used me as a human shield," Fog said, and he snorted. "I intended to take the judge up on his freedom offer. But Sheriff Brick wouldn't let me go."

"Would you believe there was more to it, too? I grabbed a letter off Sheriff Brick, and in it, the writer, Roberts, discusses a cattle rustling operation; he addressed it to Judge Fickle! Could it have been the same Roberts as died at your trial? It must've been the same judge, how many 'Fickles' do you know? I think it was the same Roberts at the trial as who wrote the letter."

"It was the same Roberts," Indie said. "Do you still have the letter?"

The bounty hunter nodded. He produced the letter and unfolded it in front of Indie. "I never read Roberts' writing, and I'm no expert judge of handwriting, but he writes very similarly to how you write. I've read a heap of your correspondence, and it looks similar in style."

"It looks like my writing because it is," Indie said.

The bounty hunter chuckled. "What mischief were you working? When I saw the letter, I figured that if I ever saw you again, I'd ask you. You were working mischief?"

"You're not so bad, bounty hunter. And I mistook you for a fool. Yes, mischief, you could call it, of a sort. Roberts and I saw eye-to-eye. I don't remember when it happened, but he changed his tune, and I knew it'd be him or me. So, I planted a seed of destruction. And my middle name is Roberts, so it was easy for me to write in that name."

"You proposed cattle rustling to Judge Fickle?"

Fog chuckled.

Indie nodded his head. "I knew if it took, which it did, that Roberts would keep it up and to himself, which he did. I planned to expose the affair and the gang would kill him for it. But he found out one of my secrets and got the gang to turn on me first."

Fog swore. "You're devious." He pointed his hand at Indie like a gun. "How you plan so far ahead beats me. It's almost as if you've got eyes on the future."

Indie briefly opened his eyes wider, then smirked. "I think about what's right in front of me, which is more than can be said for most."

The bounty hunter laughed. "How your plans ever work is beyond me. They're so convoluted!" Then he swore and drank and ate and burped and said he was finished eating. "Help yourselves to the scraps." Then he eyed Indie. "How does this end?"

The hum of eating hall patrons clashed with their plates and cutlery. Sweet and especially salty smells hung in the air as did the question. Fog hummed. Folks said Fog hummed when he was nervous.

Indie was not nervous. But he was tired. He had seen a great many men threaten and hold him with their teeth. *I've escaped them all to run into them again. Will it end? There is no end to the pursuit of blood. And he's the worst. What would he be without me? I am his source of energy, his inertia and drive.* And Indie looked with pity on the bounty hunter who had followed him across desert and hunger and thirst. But pity wouldn't save him. It was the pity of a rat before a trap, an undeniable truth that had to be taken care of despite itself. *If it could only all be avoided.*

Indie lunged across the table, which upset it—food and drink and tin thrown asunder—and he crashed into the bounty hunter. He had anticipated assault. Both men flew backwards over the bounty hunter's chair and onto the grimy floor, grunting and squeezing and grabbing for each other's neck, face, and soft spots like armpits.

Eaters put down their fare and watched the fighters. Fog shouted. The crowd cheered both on, and cheered for more violence. A waitress shouted for order, but her shouts were unheard for the other shouts.

Then Indie shoved away and kicked the bounty hunter in the body. The men rose in fist position. The bounty hunter jabbed and Indie ducked. Indie brought a fist to bear on the bounty hunter and caught him in his ribs. The bounty hunter winced. He swayed and knocked Indie on the bottom of his jaw. Indie slammed his head into the bounty hunter's. Both men reeled and swore. They looked like madmen, with death in their eyes.

"I wouldn't have it any other way," the bounty hunter said during a pause, blood dripping from his eyebrow. "One of us must die. It's been too long, too much travailed for it to end but with one of us dead!"

Fog called for peace. He smiled when his call had no effect.

Indie spit and drew himself ready with the crowd's encouragement. The bounty hunter pulled a derringer. Indie ran at him.

Bang!

The bullet ripped into Indie. But his momentum carried him into the bounty hunter. Both men fell backwards and the bounty hunter smashed his head into a table.

CHAPTER 38

INDIE AND THE BOUNTY HUNTER were taken to a doctor's house to treat their wounds. Fog went, too. Indie ran a fever and fell in and out of consciousness. The bounty hunter was unconscious and stayed that way.

"You're the one who got shot," a Denver constable said to Indie the next day, after gathering the story. He clicked his tongue. "How you're awake and even alive, and the shooter's still out, beats me." Indie sat stunned and nursed his gun-shot shoulder.

"I'm free?" Indie said.

The constable nodded. "But only if you promise you'll leave town."

"But don't you know who I am?"

"Who are you?"

Indie didn't say. He was amazed at his luck of anonymity.

"That was a fight!" Fog said as he came into Indie's room. "I haven't seen such viciousness even out of savages, save one, and I almost didn't live to tell tale. Now it's twice—such viciousness!" He addressed the constable. "You can count on my word; this fellow won't trouble you or the good people of Denver again. We're going to the train station now."

The constable warned that Indie had better not trouble Denver again. Then he left.

Fog regaled Indie with the story of how the fight had been received, what the talk of the town was, and the fact that Indie would need to confine himself if he could not control himself. "That was a stupid thing you did; almost got yourself killed!"

Fog talked as Indie dressed. Indie winced as he pulled the shirt over his shoulder. They left the doctor's.

Indie walked the wet Denver road with purpose.

"Where are you going?"

"To the hotel."

Fog shook his head. "That won't do. Our train will be leaving soon. You were out most of yesterday. Perhaps you don't remember. But today is the day for our tickets. It felt like you were held up for a long time. I didn't even know if you'd make it. Can you imagine? You can be glad you had *me* here. Other folk would've left.

"I sold your narrative of innocence, too. I said the bounty hunter was harassing you. He instigated the fight. And they went along with it—not worth an investigation. The constable here's seen drunken revelry before. And he's sick of it. He wants the rabble to go somewhere else."

"I can't believe he didn't recognize me," Indie said. "I thought any lawman would. I guess—I can't make sense of it."

"Cannonball Springs folks declared you dead, satisfied your bounty."

"Yes, but still, there was a bounty. And every lawman would've known about it."

Fog laughed. "Suppose you're not the infamous man you think you are?"

"And the bounty hunter?"

"He'll recover, I think. He hit his head pretty hard."

Indie shrugged his shoulders and sighed. Spring air carried commerce songs and moisture over the mud. Wagons and carts and people and horses stomped and rolled and moved fast.

"If not the hotel, are we headed to the train station?" Indie said.

Fog pointed to a dense group of buildings and bustle and smoke.

"The train to Kansas City."

CHAPTER 39

PROSPERITY IN THE WEST IS linked with effective transportation, especially as vast open spaces lie between it and the rest of American civilization. Boomtowns come and go, but sustained societies require connection, especially with the coasts and ultimate destinations of market and trade. Cattle cannot heat a home in winter or sweeten coffee; a gold nugget cannot harness a horse or fire a bullet.

Colorado Territory provides a good example of societal interdependence. As in California ten years earlier, gold brought crowds of "'59ers" to the Rocky Mountains; some settled on the threshold of the Front Range, at the confluences of the South Platte River and its tributaries like the Cherry and Sand Creeks. They called this new "Queen City of the Plains" Denver. And steel, not gold, secured its ultimate fortune.

Denver faced economic marginalization when the Union Pacific Railroad built its transcontinental railway one hundred miles north through Cheyenne as the line ran west to Promontory Point and California. Denver businessmen packed their belongings to Wyoming Territory to profit from what would be railroaded into and out of the region.

To compete, Denver needed a rail line. Who can say how the population reached this conclusion—perhaps a proposed railroad from rival Golden to Cheyenne; foresight by prominent Denver denizens like John Evans; or a Union Pacific star promoter's rousing speech—but they did. And thus, the Denver Pacific Railway and Telegraph Company was created to construct a railway from Denver to Cheyenne. Yet while the new company sold $300,000 of stock in its first three days, its fundraising fell short of the estimated $2 million needed to complete the work.

A lobbied Congress played savior by approving the transfer to the Denver Pacific of 977,994 and 96/100ths acres of land (of which 821,822 57/100ths acres were ultimately acquired) from the Union Pacific Eastern

Division, which was later called the Kansas Pacific. Construction of the new Denver railway quickly proceeded on the back of land sales, and in June 1870, the first train arrived in Denver—an event marked by ceremony featuring a papered spike to resemble a silver one that had been pawned for booze (the silver spike was later found and redeemed). Two months later, the Kansas Pacific finished another line connecting Kansas City and Denver, securing Denver's place as a prominent transportation and distribution hub on the doorstep of the Rocky Mountains.

The city prospered. Two railroad stations—the Denver & Rio Grande's at Nineteenth and Wynkoop Streets and the Denver Pacific's at Wazee and Twenty-First Streets—skirted the bustling downtown. The Denver Pacific station was busier as it served three railroads: its namesake; the Kansas Pacific; and the Colorado Central Railroad, which ran west to Golden and Central City. The stucco-brick station building was set by paralleling first-and-second-floor windows that terminated in raised keystone arches. A wide archway on one side offered entrance and exit. Three chimneys stood above a roof decoratively railed at its precipice.

"I'm amazed at such impressive displays of industry," Mattie said. "It's been a long time since I've seen a railroad station, and never in Denver."

"Man can be awesome in his inventiveness," Sheriff Brick said. "The iron horse, some call it, and it has no equal on land in reliable, inexhaustible movement."

"I hope it's more comfortable than Guilfoyle's coach." Mattie looked at Sheriff Brick and they both laughed.

The couple stood on a low hill near the station which overlooked the yard and its trains. Steam swirled and spit from a huge engine preparing to depart westward, and black smoke began spurting from its chimney. The engineer sounded the whistle. The train wheels began to turn.

Mattie wore a red dress that drew the compliments of many passersby. The dress was remarkable, an expensive purchase from her father. Sheriff Brick wore a gray suit which fit well and became him. His gray top hat of dyed beaver fur set him in preeminent fashion. And though men feigned not to notice him, he struck a near sufficient compliment to Mattie's overwhelming beauty.

Someone bellowed from before the station house that the train to Cheyenne would leave within the hour and the train to Kansas City would leave within the half hour. A crowd gathered and descended on the Kansas City train. Mattie and Sheriff Brick shuffled toward the station. Then Mattie gasped.

"What's it?" Sheriff Brick asked. He looked in the direction of Mattie's eyes.

Indie stood in front of one of the Kansas City train's coach cars. He was narrow and stark, like a marble visage bursting from a flat canvas.

"Wait here," Sheriff Brick told Mattie.

She cocked her head and raised her eyebrows. Sheriff Brick exhaled and the two walked together to Indie. He noticed them and stopped his surveillance of the iron horse that he was preparing to ride. He nodded his head. He wanted to dip into the ground and disappear or rise like an eagle and fly away. *If only I were already on the train to Kansas City.* Were they together? Mattie and Sheriff Brick stood like two gold nuggets in a sluice pan of gravel.

"You're not supposed to be alive," Mattie said. She drew herself into Sheriff Brick as she spoke.

Indie wiped his brow. "Sorry to disappoint."

"How're you alive?" Sheriff Brick said.

"Simple as any man, woman, or child."

Sheriff Brick snickered. "Dodge me if you'd like. You're a free man now. You've been tried, even if not exactly right. The folks in Cannonball Springs pronounced you dead to the world."

"I guess to save face," Indie said. "Would you disgrace them?" He looked fierce at Sheriff Brick. "If you're fixing to take me in, I should point out that you don't technically have jurisdiction in these parts. I also just came from consultation with a lawman. The lawman didn't recognize me or care to. He let me go. I guess this is the civilized world."

"Racida was civilized, too," Mattie said.

Indie shook his head. "Thank God, not like Denver. I miss the wild, a quick ride into nothing but empty land watched by empty sky."

Mattie agreed and said the country was beautiful. Sheriff Brick said there was lots of beautiful country, and that this was certainly special land.

"I'm curious why, it looks like you're leaving it?" Indie said. "That's what I'm about to do. I'm not sure I'm ready. But you can imagine my reasons. Why are you leaving? Have you had too much of this land or are you striking out to see where your new wealth will take you?"

"Oh, the gold," Mattie said. "Yes, we have a lot of it. Thanks to you, I guess. We returned the robbed goods to Racida. Solomon piled the wealth in the jail and opened opportunity for claimants, but only a few had ties to the contraband. We gave a quarter of what was left to father's church and even some to the Catholic church. Solomon bought liquor and food and held a dinner for the town. Then with the rest, he established an account at the new Pioneer Bank for the town to use. I think Solomon is as popular in Racida as anyone could be."

Indie laughed. "That's more than I could bring myself to do with it, and to better purpose, too. But there was more gold besides. You didn't leave it in the cave?"

"No," Sheriff Brick said. "We gave some to Reverend Schroeder so he'll never want again. We brought some with us. We left the rest. We're heading to San Francisco. I've read that I can put gold to good use there."

"You should be careful what you read, Sheriff." Indie winked. "Even with this wonder carriage on iron rails, it'll still take some time, I imagine, to transport yourselves to California. And then disposing of gold? I imagine that'll take some time, too. I don't think a lawman should abandon his post so cavalierly."

"I gave up the badge," Sheriff Brick said.

Indie clicked his cheeks. "Too bad for Racida. You were a good sheriff."

"Some would say I was only a constable." Sheriff Brick, Indie, and Mattie smiled. Sheriff Brick continued. "Maybe again, but I'll leave others to look after the law for the time being."

"I hope not on my account," Indie said.

"No, though maybe you had something to do with it. I learned that the law in the hands of determined and unchecked men isn't entirely free of their own desires and perspectives. America wasn't built on law in the hands of men, but institutions, checks and balances. Men must carry it out, of course, but the law is intended to be separated from individual ambition and opinion by implacable standards.

"A man like Judge Fickle violates the public's entrustment. Justice without due process is hardly different from vigilantism. He was involved in a scheme; Clovis, too. I read those letters you gave to Mattie." Sheriff Brick sighed. "Who's a man to trust? I wasn't given much grace by Racida anyway. They'd suspect a decent man, thinking he has motives other than seeing righteousness done. I lost appetite in helping establish order. Let someone else take a turn to protect Racida. I took care of its outlaw problem. And without that, there's hardly enough to keep a body busy."

"You look hurt," Mattie said.

"I am hurt. I got into a tussle yesterday with the bounty hunter. He shot me, and I blacked out. But it seems I whipped him."

Mattie gasped.

"Yes," he said. "I didn't even intend to. He shot me yet I'm the one up and about. But that's that. Fog is here. I think he might've talked me out of jail."

Sheriff Brick sneered. "Fog's been tried, so I'll leave it at that." He shook his head.

"You should've left a long time ago," Mattie said to Indie.

"With this new iron horse—the railroad has brought Denver practically closer to parts of the country that are much farther away than that country which lies at its doorstep," Indie said. "I could travel for weeks and never pass through those mountains." He gestured to the Front Range holding its winter's snow as the peaks climbed white to heaven. "In a day, I could be in Omaha; in two, Chicago."

"Where are you planning to go?" Mattie said.

"To Kansas City—at least, if you won't stop me—as soon as the train's ready."

"I don't know how I'd stop you."

"*Why*, maybe, but not how. I hardly think I could escape Sheriff Brick, especially on your command, Mattie. I know his name is Solomon, too, and I should call him by it.

"Solomon, your stature merits your name. And doubtless you're capable of restraining me. The crowd may help, too, when you tell them who I am. I'll bet more than one has heard of Indie Caloo. The question is not how but why would you stop me."

"You should explain it to me." Mattie puckered her lips and dipped sideways.

"You're dead," Sheriff Brick said, "at least as far as they could be concerned. You had your day in court."

"More famous in death even than life!" Mattie said. "At least in Racida. and Cannonball Springs and Stanchion—you're larger than life. And that's a remarkable feat, Indie. I imagine that if any in this crowd knew who you were, they would press for autographs not cuffs. 'The Trial of Indie Caloo' was big news. Of course, you'd have to explain how you're alive and not dead as you're supposed to be. You did it once; you can do it again. But wouldn't that just sensationalize it if a resurrected villain returned?" Mattie held her hands up then arced them out and down like she was bowing to Indie from the waist up. She laughed. "You're a legend."

"I don't care for legends," Indie said. "I prefer the truth. The constable here didn't even recognize me. I can see when it's a mockery."

Mattie snuffed and shook her head.

"But you are a legend," Sheriff Brick said. "And legends, especially of the west, have a way of outgrowing the truth. And we're not going to stand in your way except to keep you from any new mischief."

Indie repeated the words "new mischief" and laughed. He rubbed his nose. "Some might say it's mischief that brings you two here, and especially together, and especially with so much wealth. I know you wouldn't leave Racida, Mattie, except for something extraordinary." Indie studied the couple. "You didn't get married or something?"

"Yes," Sheriff Brick and Mattie said at once. They wrestled with smiles that overcame them. Indie smiled, too.

"I know a bit of your histories," Sheriff Brick said. "Mattie's told me. While I'll always be glad to claim her, my enthusiasm is tempered knowing it might pain Mattie, perhaps the both of you, to announce our nuptials in your presence."

Indie laughed. And he really laughed. People stared as his laugh rose above the general din. Sheriff Brick and Mattie did not laugh.

"You're not kidding! Sheriff, you're a greater thief than I ever was." He shook Sheriff Brick's hand with both of his. "How you stole Mattie's heart, I'll never know."

"He didn't steal my heart," Mattie said. "You can't steal a gift. We're for each other. What am I but fading years? I've the heart of any woman. It's he," she intended Sheriff Brick, "who doesn't have the heart of just any man," and she winked at him.

"I'm surprised no one objected."

"Don't be, folks did object," Sheriff Brick said.

"The wealth Solomon distributed softened any dislikes," Mattie said. "You can imagine that folks like a man a lot more when he's giving out free money."

Indie laughed. "You sound like a politician. What about your father?"

"He's a good man, and hardly ready to stand in the way of his daughter's happiness," Mattie said.

"And public obstinacy, tempered or not, can only go so far," Sheriff Brick said, "especially when one's chief enemy becomes—not friend exactly, but certainly he gave up the fight. Pecker's not the same man since his barn fire. He's no longer an antagonist. I suppose I've you to thank? You started his barn on fire."

"You've only yourself, your hard work and generosity, as source for gratification."

"But you did burn down his barn."

"Yes and no. I planned it, yes—a magnificent explosion, I'd imagine, and probably a strong fire to boot. But I didn't execute my plan. Pecker's an enemy to many men. I found one that'd light a fuse."

"Gunpowder?"

Indie nodded. "I learned how to use the stuff in the war, though I'd be fine with forgetting it all."

"There are many things a man would like to forget, especially about war."

"Mattie told me you served, too, Solomon—Battle of Fort Blakeley?"

Sheriff Brick grunted and nodded. "I was glad to play a part in securing freedom."

"She also told me that you were a slave in Mississippi."

"Well, I don't hold that I told her that in confidence," Sheriff Brick said, blushing. "However, it's something I've not told many people." Sheriff Brick looked at Mattie. "It was called Loess Manor."

"I know it," Indie said.

"You know it?" Sheriff Brick said, taken aback.

"Yes. I was a slave hunter before I enlisted and the war. I wanted to make quick, good money, at least that was my thinking. It wasn't long that I hunted slaves like you, runaway slaves. It wasn't many. I couldn't stomach it. In a venture like that, there must be violence. It was awful. That's why I quit.

"This may sound strange, but my last job was at a place called Loess Manor in Mississippi. I'll never forget the place, even though I don't remember names. Funny how you can remember places but not names. Aren't people more important than fields and buildings? I remember Loess Manor, and I remember a giant oak tree stump.

"We caught a runaway and brought him to the plantation yard. I remember him saying he wasn't a slave, to let him go and that we had the wrong man. I asked him who the right man was and where he was. But he wouldn't tell me. He just said that he was a preacher. We took him to the tree stump, 'Slave-killer,' the foreman called it. It couldn't have been long in being chopped down, it was still green in parts, but it was splattered with blood from whippings.

"The man who hired us—I get such a headache trying to remember, but I guess he must've been the master—he was clapping and smiling. Then someone ran past me from behind, a young man like myself, and he said 'that's not a slave, that's our preacher.'"

Sheriff Brick's chin shivered. Tears pooled in his eyes and dripped down his cheeks. His cheeks reddened.

"The foreman was mighty upset. 'Roberts,' he said—because Roberts is my middle name, Indiana Roberts Caloo, and down south it's common to use your middle name—'Roberts, shut him up.' I hit the young man with my pistol, not hard, but the grip must've caught him just right because he fell to the ground, knocked him out. That shook me up. Then, as a favor for that, they let me shoot the runaway, or whoever he was. They *let* me shoot him." Indie shook his head. "I puked my guts out afterwards. Looking back on it, I'm not sure he was a runaway. So, I quit the human hunting business."

"I remember that day well," Sheriff Brick said. His mouth quivered. He clenched his fists. "I was that young man you pistol-whipped."

Indie and Mattie gasped.

"That man was our pastor." Sheriff Brick swore. His eyes flared. His breath quickened. He gathered like a rattle snake and punched Indie quicker than he could dodge. Sheriff Brick's strong fist smashed into Indie's eye and forehead. The blow knocked him backwards and into the dirt.

A constable shouted. He rushed to Indie. Other men ran to Mattie and Sheriff Brick, too.

"No!" Indie shouted as the helpers reached him. "I'm fine."

"Is this man bothering you?" the constable said to Indie.

The saving witnesses ventured help.

"He's a suspicious character."

"What's he doing with her?"

"What's he done to you?"

"Are you in good straights, miss?"

"That dress is very becoming, miss."

"Leave us!" Indie said again. "I've offended him. He had a right to hit me."

The would-be-helpful men melted away, a few offering compliments again to Mattie. She thanked them with grace.

The constable brushed Indie off and turned to Sheriff Brick with a scowl. "You may come from some place that doesn't have as much care for the law as here in Denver. You may be accustomed to sorting disputes with fists. You may enjoy the responsibility of minding yourself and others. But don't think you can do that in Denver. Consider this a warning. And I think it'd be better if you left town."

"I intend to," Sheriff Brick said.

Indie dusted himself off. He felt his swelling face, which bled a little at the bony edge of his brow.

"Are you satisfied with yourself?" Mattie said to Sheriff Brick. She turned to Indie. "You were right in the jail in Cannonball Springs; I can see it now. I thought you were a man against society, that the west had brought out your survival instincts, and outlawing was surviving. I didn't know that, before you came west and before the war, that you hunted men. You've always been an outlaw!

"I'm grateful for the incredible things you showed me about our home, and for engaging me and challenging me to learn." She shook her head, tears in her eyes. "But I can't stand you. I hope that you can find peace. I want you to live in harmony. Goodbye, Indie."

Mattie told Sheriff Brick that she would get their tickets. Sheriff Brick said he would join her soon at the station.

"Are you still going to let me go, Sheriff, and Fog, too?" Indie said when they were alone.

"For my sake, yes," Sheriff Brick said. "I said what I meant before."

Sheriff Brick paused and surveyed Indie. The surrounding hustle pervaded the scene. All was chaos. All was calm.

"For your sake—that man that you captured back in Mississippi when we were both young, he was a free man," Sheriff Brick said. "He was our preacher. He had a family. You wouldn't have been right to kill him even if he'd been a slave. Yet the law at least would've justified you. Oh, the law," Sheriff Brick shook his head. "I vowed once to kill the man who killed him. How is it you're here? And I could kill you easily. And yet, what would vengeance make me? It won't bring back the dead."

Sheriff Brick began to walk away from Indie. He turned back. "For his sake and yours, no, I shouldn't let you go, Indie Caloo. But we can always choose; we can choose to rise above." He turned back and was gone.

What just happened? Did he forgive me? Indie watched Sheriff Brick crest the hill and disappear into the station. *Mattie is married, and to a black man. Who would've thought; certainly not her father.* Every night and adventure Indie could remember with her flashed in his mind. He remembered Racida and Stanchion and Cannonball Springs and their people. *All those people. And who was I? Would they forgive me like Sheriff Brick has?*

After an "all aboard," the train to Kansas City began puffing and spitting. Indie boarded. He found Fog. He had pushed himself into his seat, crossed his arms and legs, and fallen asleep with his head held high and open mouth facing the ceiling. Indie ducked into the seat across from Fog. He watched the yard as the train groaned and hissed and rolled forward.

Indie saw the Cheyenne cars—red, black, and green—pass, partially obscured as his Kansas City-bound train passed belching mist and smoke. Mattie and Sheriff Brick would embark on that Cheyenne train. Indie would never see them again. *At least they'll be able to start off together rich. That could count for something. Maybe I could've made her happy. I guess now I'll never know. But at least she's happy. And that's a type of resolution.*

The sun shone through a knotty mess of clouds. Flat land stretched to the horizon, the mountains beyond. Green was sinking again into the prairie.

Indie took out his notebook. He pulled out his gold pocket watch, too, and noticed the time. *Always the same.* He returned the watch. He turned to look at the passing land again, the Front Range far in the distance. He sighed and pulled out a pencil. He began to write.

THE END.

www.ingramcontent.com/pod-product-compliance
Lightning Source LLC
Chambersburg PA
CBHW071838020726
47502CB00004B/1419